MW01611215

QUEST FOR THE SPACE GODS

THE CHRONICLES OF CONRAD VON HONIG

Edited by Jim Beard & John C. Bruening

A Flinch Books Production

QUEST FOR THE SPACE GODS:
THE CHRONICLES OF CONRAD VON HONIG
Copyright © 2018 by Jim Beard and John C. Bruening

"The Throne of the Heavens" © 2018 by Jim Beard
"In the Court of the Pale King" © 2018 by Desmond Reddick
"Blood of the Hummingbird" © 2018 by Frank Schildiner
"Unwelcome Back" © 2018 by Brian K. Morris
"The Iron Door" © 2018 by Terry Alexander
"Utnapishtim's Children" © 2018 by Fred Adams, Jr.

Cover illustration © 2018 Mark Maddox
Cover design and interior page formatting: Maggie Ryel

Editors: Jim Beard and John C. Bruening

All stories and characters in this publication are fictional. Any resemblance to actual persons, living or dead, is entirely coincidental. No part of this publication may be reproduced or transmitted in any manner whatsoever without the express permission in writing of the publisher, except for a brief passage as used in a review.

ISBN: 978-0-9977903-2-0

Flinch Books and the Flinch Books logo
© Jim Beard and John C. Bruening

Contact us at www.facebook.com/flinchbooks
and at flinchbooks@yahoo.com

TABLE OF CONTENTS

INTRODUCTION

It's hard to say exactly when and how the idea for this book came about. The most obvious answer would be Pulpfest 2016, when Jim Beard and I were sitting at the Flinch Books table in the dealer room, brainstorming ideas for our next anthology. In a moment of creative spit-balling, I said, "ancient astronauts." The conversation suddenly stopped, our eyes went wide, and we spent the remainder of the weekend attacking the idea like a couple of pit bulls.

That's the easy answer. The more accurate one might go back as far as the 1970s, when a Swiss writer named Erich von Däniken turned his 1969 book, *Chariots of the Gods?*, into a cottage industry that included more than a dozen sequels and several big-screen documentaries. All of it revolved around the writer's simple premise: What if extraterrestrials had visited earth in ancient times and influenced humanity's cultural and technological evolution?

Jim and I didn't know each other in the '70s. We grew up in opposite corners of Ohio, at least a generation before social media connected everyone everywhere. But when the topic of ancient astronauts came up in that conversation in the summer of 2016, we agreed that we'd found von Däniken's theories both creepy and intriguing as kids back in the day. Back then – and maybe even now – the only idea more fascinating than space aliens was the idea of space aliens who pulled certain evolutionary levers thousands of years ago to make us who and what we are today.

We're well aware that much of von Däniken's theories and research have been debunked over the years by reputable archaeologists, astronomers and historians. But that didn't matter to two impressionable young boys from Ohio. And those same two young boys – who are now middle aged men, by the way – never let the facts get in the way of a good collection of adventure stories.

And thus was the genesis of Conrad von Honig, a globetrotting adventurer in search of definitive proof that intergalactic visitors had engaged with humans in ancient times and left their permanent mark on our history. If that proof was out there, von Honig would find it. Or he'd die trying. Think Karl Kolchak, *Altered States* and *The X-Files* all rolled into one. (And kids, if any of these references sound unfamiliar to you, go do your homework.)

Jim wrote "The Throne of the Heavens," the lead-off story that sets the tone and lays the groundwork for the five other fine writers who follow him: Desmond Reddick, Frank Schildiner, Brian K. Morris and Fred Adams, Jr. Collectively, they take von Honig on a journey that spans the globe – from civil war-torn Eastern Europe to the Mayan temples of Mexico to the Australian Outback and beyond. No matter the locale, no matter who is telling the tale, von Honig inevitably gets more than he bargains for. Along with the research and exploration come adventure, intrigue and danger – and even a bit of romance for good measure.

In every great story, as in life itself, the journey is just as important as the destination. Does Conrad von Honig's search for definitive proof of ancient astronauts come to an end by the last page of the last story, or does it just begin? We'll let you decide. As far as he's concerned, the answers to mankind's greatest mysteries are in neither the future nor the past. They're somewhere in the stars.

Enjoy the quest.

John C. Bruening
December 2017

THE THRONE OF THE HEAVENS

by Jim Beard

1.

Three figures walked along a stone ledge through a narrow pass between two mountains, hugging the flat face of one of the dual giants and stepping over and around instances of scrubby plant life. They seemed to disappear and materialize again from the dust and debris thrown up by the strong wind that battered them with every step they took, but they moved along, determined to reach their destination despite the opposition. The lead figure was wrapped from head to foot in multi-colored bands of thick material, much of it worn and repaired. The second figure was stooped over even more than the first, but the third held itself differently from the other two. This third figure clutched a knapsack and tried to stand straight in the face of the tempest while reaching out to tap the second figure on the shoulder.

"How much more?" the third traveler yelled in English over the singing of the gale. The second figure turned to reveal a male face with ruddy, round cheeks and squinting blue eyes. The man's mouth twitched below his immense mustache. His shoulders rose then fell once, but not again. He did not speak, but simply cocked a thumb at the lead figure, as if to say he was at the leader's mercy when it came to getting an answer to that question.

The third figure was also a man, but younger and with several days' beard growth on his tanned face. He frowned, but kept walking as he scrutinized each of his own footfalls.

The leader stopped abruptly, reaching out to the older man next in line and pointing with the opposite hand. It was a silent command to the other travelers to look ahead on the path and to one side, away from the mountain they hugged.

Both men looked. Both sets of eyes widened.

The wind subsided just enough for the party to look out and over a large space between the peaks that surrounded them. In the waning light of the day they could see that the area had recently been disturbed in violent fashion. So explosive was the disturbance that it had thrown rock and stone around like children's playthings along with copious amounts of soil and flora. The sides of the mountain across from their vantage point had sloughed off stone epidermis and the remains of it rested in small valleys and other natural catchalls. In all, it appeared as if the very gods had reached down into the mortal world to wage a mud battle.

The older man turned to the lead figure and spoke in deep tones, his voice straining to cut through the returned gale. The other man cocked an ear to the words, but it was clear he did not understand them. He tapped his companion's shoulder.

"What?" he asked.

"Shelling," came the reply. Both men nodded at each other.

The lead figure's hand shot out to grab at the older man, turning him back to the scene before them. The hand released him just as quickly and pointed downward with a single, insistent finger. The man craned his head to follow the finger, but remained wary of his position on the ledge.

The younger man, due to his own position on the rock, could not see what his companion saw, and so waited for the man to fill him in on the new development.

After gazing downward for nearly a minute, the older man turned to look back at the lead figure with cold, narrowed eyes. He spat out a few words, their meaning unclear to the younger man, but laced with a clearly rising ire.

"What is it?" he called out. "What do you see?"

His companion ignored him, but held his stony gaze on the figure who had brought them to this place. More words flowed from his mouth, still with a hint of anger. In response, the object of his ire whipped off its hood to reveal a female face, beautiful and proud under grime, with dark brows, a Roman nose, and full lips. The woman's eyes flamed at the older man, then darted to the younger man.

"I'm saying 'what of it?' to her," grunted the older man. "Dragged here to this godforsaken spot…" His voice trailed off into his own language, and what seemed to be curses to his companion. The woman spoke again, or rather spat out words, her manner terse and insistent. The older man sighed heavily and despite the wind in his face and its mighty roar in his ears, looked downward again at the spot the woman indicated. After a silent moment, he grunted and ruffled through his pockets. Producing a large, round coin, he did a most incredible thing with it.

Holding it up before his face, several inches from the end of his round nose, he closed one eye and widened the other. To the younger man, it appeared as if he was sighting down a gun barrel, perhaps using the coin to gauge something far below the ledge they all clung to. After another silent moment, he lowered the coin and stared off to the horizon. His lips trembled and he muttered a single word under his breath.

"At the risk of repeating myself," said the younger man, clearly annoyed at being at the fringes of a discovery, "what the hell do you see?"

His companion shook himself from his reverie, glanced once at the woman, nodded curtly, then turned to the younger man. His eyes looked odd, as if filled with disbelief. Before anybody could say anything else, he reached out, took hold of his younger companion, and shifted his own bulk past him along the ledge. Seconds later, the younger man occupied the vantage point overlooking the mystery of what lay below them. He craned his neck, looking downward as the wind tore at their garments and the brush and bramble around them.

"Okay," he said after several seconds of observation, but without turning to look at the others. "How can we get down there?"

As if in response to his question, a young boy appeared, seemingly deposited onto the ledge by the wind. He stepped out of the cloud of dust and debris, moon-faced and wrapped in rags, his eyes serious despite his less-than-a-decade of years.

The boy danced past the two men, and the younger of them sucked in his breath at how nimbly the child side-stepped them to gain the lead position next to the woman. Landing by her side, he turned to jabber at her, not excitedly but with purpose. The younger man strained to listen over the gale.

"Can't get it," he muttered. "Dialect's too thick." He slapped his companion's arm. "What does he say?"

The older man turned his head, but just barely. Instead he watched as the woman looked up from the boy's report, her eyes darting around them. Her lips parted finally, and she loosed a few words to him.

"Turn around, turn around," the older man said to his younger companion, waving him back the way they'd come. "The child's found a way…he's found something."

It was fully dark by the time they descended from the mountain and regained level ground. There was no rest ahead of them, though, for the boy led the party into a small valley and behind a clutch of boulders, some of which looked like they'd been set there recently.

"The shelling," said the older man, matter-of-factly.

They picked their way over some rocks and soon found themselves staring at the entrance to a cave, its rough opening no more than five feet tall and barely as wide. The younger man produced a large flashlight from his pack, and tried to pierce the darkness beyond the cave opening. Sighing, he led the charge into the shadows, the boy by his side, clinging to his coat and pointing ahead of them.

The party delved deeper, and to the astonishment of them all, the floor of the cave leveled out and soon became nearly smooth. The younger man trained his light on it and discovered it to be worked by human hands, yet as ancient-looking as anything he'd ever seen. The boy urged them on, and within a few short minutes they stood in a larger area.

It was most definitely a room of sorts. Above them, they could hear the howling of the wind. The younger man swung his flashlight beam up to find the source of the sound, and in doing so illuminated the walls of the area.

"Christ…"

The older man pulled out a cigarette lighter, and flicked it open to produce a small, dancing flame. He began to walk around the chamber, holding the lighter up to cast its weak light onto the surfaces around him. The younger man did the same with his flashlight, but the woman remained frozen in the spot in which she'd entered the area, her eyes wide and uncomprehending.

The two men eventually met after making a circuit of the room. They looked at each other, both clearly confused. The older man tried to speak, but found words difficult. Finally, he managed to croak out a feeble inquiry as to what they were seeing.

"I don't know," the other man replied, shrugging. He walked back to a particular spot on the wall and cast his flashlight beam upon it. His hand reached out and he caressed the wall with nervous fingers. After a moment, he turned to his companion.

"But…I know someone who might."

As he exited the airplane onto the cracked and worn tarmac, he glanced up at the mountains in the distance, and the cold, blue sky their peaks touched. The cold blue of his eyes lingered on them for only a moment until resting upon the low, one-story building before him. He walked toward it, clutching a small handbag in one hand and a European style hat in the other.

As he passed under the large letters on the top of the building that read "AERODROM," he was stopped by a small, uniformed man who verified his identity in a thick Western Balkans accent. Nodding, the man ushered him off to one side of the airport toward a plain, nondescript door and walked him through it.

The space beyond the door looked to be an office of some sort, with a counter running down the middle of it, a few old chairs placed haphazardly about, and a desk overflowing with clutter. Ancient, tattered travel posters adorned the walls of the room, but directly behind the desk a newer poster was taped to the wall, showing a seated blonde woman in a red bathing suit, smiling with her head thrown back and her large, white teeth gleaming. He glanced at the image and shook his head in disdain.

"Even here," he said.

A thick man with a large mustache and a uniform similar to his guide stood up, his brow knitted in confusion. He sidestepped over to a closed door near the desk and rapped on it once with his knuckles. The door opened immediately and a young man stepped into the room, tall and disheveled. His face and hands were tanned brown, but his hair was nearly as blonde as the woman in the poster.

"Mr. von Honig?" he asked. "Welcome to Tirania. I'm Brad Bikkelman."

Conrad von Honig frowned slightly and accepted the man's proffered hand. He glanced around the room again before focusing on Bikkelman once more.

"You're a reporter?"

The young man nodded. "Yes, been here, oh, three years now. A little more." He smiled sheepishly. "Well, not here, of course. Over there." He waved a hand to something off to one side. "In Majavaca."

Von Honig did not nod nor smile back. "Can you tell me what it is, then, Mr. Bikkelman?" He glanced quickly at the man behind the desk. "What you've found?"

The reporter gestured for von Honig to step over to one corner of the room and threw himself down into one of the dilapidated chairs. Looking up at him, Bikkelman chuckled quietly.

"You find something about this amusing?" von Honig asked with serious intent.

"Most people would ask, oh, I dunno, about what they'd be getting into over there." The reporter waved his hand again at that same nebulous something off in the distance. "Maybe *how* they'd get there. You cut right to the chase."

Von Honig cocked his head and narrowed his eyes. "I'm an author and researcher, Mr. Bikkelman. I've been around the world a few times. I don't waste time on details that don't really matter to what I do–that don't matter to my *work*."

The reporter frowned and looked over at the man behind the desk. Getting up from the chair, he pointed to the door. "Okay. Let's, uh, start walking. I can fill you in on the way."

Together they exited the room. As they walked, Bikkelman assessed the man next to him. He took in his slight build, his dark, wavy hair above mildly handsome features, his simple yet expensive clothes, and the prominent scar running along the left side of his neck. The reporter's eyes left his guest and settled on the tiled floor of the airport.

"There are very few people here," von Honig observed. "For an airport," he added.

Bikkelman nodded. "Yeah, but that shouldn't come as any surprise. Very few Tiranians want to fly so close to a war zone." He stuck his hands into the pockets of his leather jacket as they neared the double glass doors to the outside. "So, I've seen you speak before, not long before I took the assignment here. In Brussels. We even spoke briefly after the talk, but I doubt if you'd remember that."

The author said nothing, gave no acknowledgment, but simply continued to walk.

"It was an…interesting talk," the reporter continued. "Not everyone in the room believed you; I could tell. But I never forgot that, what you talked about. *How* you talked about it. That's why I contacted you about…this."

Von Honig stopped abruptly and wheeled around to face the man.

"Have you read my books, Mr. Bikkelman?" he asked.

"Well," the reporter replied, not meeting his gaze, "I read one of them, the second one, I believe. Most of it, at least."

Von Honig continued to stare intently at his host. "Forget that. I don't require everyone to be a believer, just to keep an open mind. The world's in the state it's in because of too many closed minds. I find this nearly everywhere I go, in nearly everyone I have to deal with. The human race is better than that. We just need to wake up and realize it."

Bikkelman snorted and shook his head. "Well, I might be a believer now," he said. "After what I saw. What you'll see."

The author stepped closer to him. "Again I ask: what is it, exactly?"

Bikkelman indicated that they should keep walking. Von Honig seemed to resist the notion for a moment, but followed the young man through the exit doors and to the curb outside the front of the airport. The day had become cloudy and off in the distance it looked as if rain was sweeping in to drench the mountains.

'Be easier to tell you about the war first."

Von Honig sighed. Placing his small homburg on his head, he shifted his bag to the other hand. "Okay, I will indulge you then. What of it?"

The reporter scanned their surroundings for a taxi. "Twelve years now, one of the most brutal civil wars in Eastern Europe—maybe one of the most brutal anywhere. Back and forth fighting, back and forth land-grabs." He looked over to von Honig. "Back and forth atrocities. On *both* sides."

The author nodded slightly, frowning. "Something about religion?"

"Well, sort of," Bikkelman said with a shrug. "After the war–World War Two–half of Majavaca adopted communism, while the other half clung to their religious roots. Clung? No, *bolted* themselves to them, so strongly that they wouldn't even hear of anything red. Things got pretty dicey after a few years and by 1964, outright hostilities."

"So, now the religious right is fighting to win back their country?" von Honig asked.

The reporter looked at him with an odd expression, confusion that melted into pity.

"No, Mr. von Honig–you say that as if they're the rebels. The *communists* are the rebel force. Probably backed by the Soviets. No one's really sure, though I've been trying to ferret out that connection almost the entire time I've been here. Regardless, it's a mess, and it–"

"Doesn't matter."

Bikkelman's eyes narrowed. "Say again?"

"It doesn't matter to me," von Honig insisted with a curt slice of one hand through the air in front of him. "Religion, politics; it's very much all the same. It's squabbling and posturing when there are bigger, more *immense* things beyond it all. It doesn't matter a whit to me."

The reporter crossed his arms over his chest and turned to look out over the front of the airport.

"Maybe it should if you're going to step into the middle of it."

A strained silence descended upon the two men. After a moment, Bikkelman managed to hail a taxi, and as the dingy grey vehicle pulled up and stopped at the curb in front of them, he turned to look at his guest.

"Do *they...did* they have wars?" he asked quietly, almost hesitantly.

Von Honig whipped open the rear door of the taxi and ducked to insert himself into the cramped back seat.

"Mr. Bikkelman," he said, settling himself for the drive, "it's hard for me to imagine...very, very *difficult* for me to imagine that one could harness incredible energies to conquer the problem of interstellar flight and *not* have risen above the concept and the execution of war."

The reporter got into the taxi and shut door with slam and a half-smile. "Forget I even asked that question." He looked over at his guest. "But here's a different one for you: some call you 'Con Man' von Honig because of, well, you know what. Care to comment on it?"

"It's difficult," said the author, "to comment on matters about which many have seemingly made up their minds. Suffice to say, as my lawyer might opine, that I was cleared of those charges. I had nothing to do with them. Now, you have photographs for me to look at?"

Bikkelman sighed and dug into his pack.

"Yeah, but they're not too good…"

2.

"Noel? Noel, listen to me…I'm in a situation."

Brad Bikkelman peered out from around a corner of an old brick building and down the narrow, cobblestoned street. His eyes scanned the scene as he dug the thumb of one hand into its palm.

"Who are you talking to?" he asked his companion.

Conrad von Honig lowered the phone receiver from his ear and placed a hand over the mouth piece. "My publisher," he said. "Keep looking, please."

Raising the receiver to his face again, he spoke into it.

"What? Very funny. No. I'm in Majavaca. Say again? I'm not certain." He looked over at the reporter again. "What town is this?"

"Ulcanj," said Bikkelman without turning his head.

"Ulcanj," repeated von Honig into the receiver. "I have no idea. Listen, I can't believe I found a telephone here, let alone one that actually *works*. If you can call this working. What? No, just *listen* to me. They're coming for us."

Bikkelman turned his head at the phrase, his face blanched. He clutched his pack a bit tighter to him and leaned out farther past the corner of the building. "Hurry it up!"

Ignoring him, the author continued.

"Noel, if I disappear…yes, I understand that. Of course. No. No, that's insulting. Never mind that now. I think I'm on to something. The photos were poor–" he glanced at the reporter "–but I saw enough to convince me that there's something there."

"Here they come," Bikkelman hissed. "We have to go *now*."

Von Honig nodded curtly. "Noel, I'm going. I'll contact you again as soon as possible."

He slammed the receiver down into its cradle and stepped out of the booth while peering down the street. At its far end, he saw a small group of dark figures heading toward them. Bikkelman turned away from the scene and slapped the author on the back, pointing in the opposite direction.

"Let's go."

The two men walked swiftly down the street and made a sharp turn around a corner, the reporter leading the way. Overhead, the clouded sky provided only feeble illumination.

"Is this normal here?" asked von Honig.

Bikkelman shook his head. "No. I'm a little dumbfounded. Never with guns drawn. Never ready to *arrest* me." He looked over at the author as they moved along. "It must be you."

Von Honig almost smiled. "Possibly. It wouldn't be the first time."

"Here. In here."

The reporter indicated a doorway and a short, wide oaken door. The sign over it was weatherbeaten and barely legible. Von Honig gripped the door's handle and threw it open. The smell of food and alcohol drifted out from the open portal.

Once inside the small tavern, they took a table at the back, one dimly lit and not visible from the doorway. The establishment held few patrons, not quite a dozen. No one looked at the two men.

Barely settled in his seat, von Honig leaned over the table. "What else can you say about the site? How far is it from here?"

Bikkelman sat on the edge of his chair and stared back at his charge. "Incredible."

"What?"

"We were very nearly arrested and they're still coming for us and you sit there and ask me about a goddamned *hole in the ground*."

Von Honig dismissively waved one hand in the air between

them. Never mind that. I want to know–"

"Listen," the reporter interjected. "Do you hear that?"

The author stopped, turning his head ever so slightly back and forth. "Can you tell me what am I listening for, please?"

Bikkelman stared at him. "Shelling."

Von Honig stared back. "Yes?"

"Shelling. Cannons." The reporter made explosive motions with both hands. "Boom-boom."

The author's face turned cross. "Thank you. I am aware of what shelling is. You might be surprised at how aware of it I am. It's in the distance." He listened for a beat. "I would say…fifty or so kilometers away? These people here–" he spread his hands to indicate the patrons "–seem to take no notice of it. Why should I?"

Bikkelman slumped slightly and lowered his eyes to look down at the table. Threading the fingers of both hands together in front of him, he spoke without looking at the author.

"Man, you are one real piece of work." He slowly shook his head from side to side, then looked up again. "The Majavacans? They live with this every day. Hate to say it but they're used to it. Fact of life. They probably figure they're gonna get it sooner or later."

He unthreaded his fingers to point directly at von Honig.

"You? You run around and dig stuff up and you write your books and have no idea what the people around you might be going through, what they're living with. No, you? You're more concerned with goddamn space aliens–"

The author held up a hand. "Stop, please. There's no need for this…er, Brad, is it? I apologize if I came off a bit…ah, cold. It's simply my nature. I have a lot on my mind."

Bikkelman's eyes softened and he nodded. "Okay. Okay. I called you in, I invited you here. I brought you into a war zone. I get it. No harm done."

"You can get me to the site?" von Honig asked.

The reporter nodded again. "Yeah. I can get you there, sure. Not sure what the hell you can possibly do with it, but if you still want to go, yeah."

He stood up, pushing back his chair.

"If truth be told and I have to admit it, I'm pretty curious. I want to know what the hell it is myself."

Von Honig lifted himself from his chair. "I'm afraid that may prove to be difficult." He began to slowly raise both hands.

Bikkelman's brow creased as he stared at him. "Well, yeah, I guess so…why are you doing that with your hands?"

The author shook his head and frowned.

"I believe it's customary when a gun is being pointed at you."

The reporter turned slowly to look behind him. Three men in ragged uniforms stood there, pointing pistols at him.

"These gentlemen," said von Honig, "will most likely be making it even more difficult…"

They were brought outside, down the street and to an awaiting, nondescript flatbed truck with its motor running. Bikkelman saw a driver sitting in the cab, smoking. The man turned his head to glance at their arrival before the reporter and von Honig were taken to the back of the truck by the soldiers who'd arrested them in the tavern.

Through a series of pantomime gestures and a few words in Serbo-Croatian, they made their intent known: come with us, do not try to leave, or we will shoot you.

As they came around to the rear of the truck, the two prisoners saw a man sitting on the flatbed with his back to the cab. He was dressed all in black with heavy trousers and boots, a kind of high-collared peacoat, and what appeared to be a white apron or smock hanging out from the bottom of the coat. On the garment were blood stains, reddish-brown and smeared as if by fingers.

The man looked up from his reverie as von Honig and Bikkelman approached. His face was thick and European with coarse features below dark, thick hair streaked with grey, especially at the temples. His dark eyes were cold and reptilian.

The soldiers motioned for the prisoners to get up into the truck. Trying to stay as far away from the man as possible, they positioned themselves midway down the flatbed, one to each side and up against the bed's slatted wooden sides. Two of the soldiers got up into the truck themselves, taking spots at the edge of the bed, while the third got into the passenger side of the cab.

The strange man in the truck looked them over without expression, first von Honig and then Bikkelman. He settled his gaze on the reporter, and his eyes never seemed to leave him throughout the drive away from the town of Ulcanj.

As they rode in the truck, Bikkelman indicated the mountains off to the northwest to von Honig. The author nodded, seemingly comprehending what he was being told.

"I will see it," he said calmly. "despite this…detour."

"Yeah," Bikkelman replied. "I've been through this before. Maybe not this bad–" he side-glanced at the soldiers and their weapons "–but it may be nothing. Check our credentials, that sort of thing."

"Good," said von Honig, wincing at a sudden bump in the road. "That's very good. There are much larger things."

The reporter rolled his eyes, but said nothing.

The truck stopped abruptly with a squeal of brakes outside a small clutch of buildings on the outskirts of the town. Hustled off the flatbed, Bikkelman and von Honig were directed to enter the nearest structure, an old brick affair with the look of a jail about it. The man from the truck did not get out, but remained where he was seated–exactly where they'd found him.

Once inside the building, the prisoners looked around and then at each other.

"This has been co-opted, obviously, and recently," said the author. "The rebels are taking over this town?"

Bikkelman snorted. "This isn't the rebels. These guys are the legal governing body."

"Whoever they are," von Honig retorted, "they'd better be brief about it."

One of the soldiers pointed to a door on the far side of the room they'd stepped into and barked something. The reporter nodded and motioned for von Honig to follow.

"Must be the commander in there. How's your Serbo-Croatian?"

The author frowned deeply. "Not particularly good."

"Be careful of *everything* you say here," Bikkelman cautioned, eyeballing the soldiers, who had not put down their weapons. "Maybe even let me take the lead on this one, huh? I kind of know these people."

Before von Honig could answer, they found themselves in a large office with heavy, dark curtains drawn over towering windows along one wall, massive oak furniture, and a ticking clock of antique vintage. All of it danced with small tongues of light cast by flickering candles placed about a huge desk that squatted in the middle of the room. Over the desk, high up on the wall, was a crucifix covered with dust.

Behind the desk sat a toad of a man.

Corpulent and smelling of exotic spices, the specimen sported a gigantic beard and a bald head. Immense, horn-rimmed glasses with thick lenses sat high up on his bulbous nose, making him appear as an overweight owl in a worn olive uniform and dress gloves. The insignia on his shoulders and breast announced him as a general.

The man looked up and looked back down again just as quickly, focusing once more on a sheaf of papers before him and waggling the fingers of one hand to bid the prisoners to step forward.

Two soldiers took positions next to Bikkelman and von Honig, flanking them, their guns still raised.

"Sir, I don't know who you are, but–" the author began.

"Jesus Christ!" swore Bikkelman.

Von Honig swung around on him. "I have a right to speak, and I–"

"*I* told you I–"

The general flicked one hand at the soldiers, who immediately drove the butts of their weapons into the stomachs of the prisoners.

Bikkelman blew out air and grunted. Von Honig crumpled to the floor moaning. The soldiers began to beat them.

They used their guns and their fists, as well as their booted feet.

Neither the reporter nor the author received more blows than the other, but neither did they take on less than the other. The soldiers covered their bodies with punches and kicks, aiming at pressure points along their arms and legs, their midsections and their backs. For some reason they avoided striking either in the face or head. The beating was savage and without mercy, but also controlled and well-executed.

It continued for many minutes until the general looked up from his papers and motioned for the punishment to stop.

The two men lay on the floor, their breaths coming out in short bleats of pain. After another several minutes, the sounds of wordless outrage fell off into low moans.

"You are spying," said the man behind the desk in monotonous, heavily accented English. It was not presented as a question.

Von Honig raised his head. Tears streamed down his white face. A lock of hair fell over one eye.

"What?"

The general's brow creased in the middle, then smoothed over. "Spying," he repeated. "Do not deny."

The author tried to raise his torso from the floor, but only managed to get one arm underneath his chest and push one side of his body up. He glared at the general.

"I...do," he said through gritted teeth, his lips curled back from his colorless face.

The general snapped his fingers at one of the soldiers, who produced the author's bag, unzipped it, and dumped its contents onto the desk. Clothes tumbled out; a shirt, pair of pants, two pairs of socks. A small shaving kit followed along with a set of three paperback books bound together with a large rubber band.

The general picked up the books, snapped the rubber band off them, and tossed them aside one by one after he'd scanned each cover for a second, maybe two. "This?" he said to von Honig. "What?"

"I'm...an author."

The man pointed at the name on one of the book's covers. "This you?"

Von Honig nodded as he tried to pull himself up. His entire body shook from the strain. The general glanced once at him, then said something to one of his men in his language. The soldier departed through the door and returned seconds later with a book in his hands, which he gave to his commanding officer.

The author managed to get himself to his knees, his upper body wavering as he tried to right himself by reaching out to grip the front edge of the desk. He saw that the book was a paperback, but did not recognize the cover design. The general turned the front to him, and he was able to see the title was set in Cyrillic.

"Your book," indicated the general. "Russian." He then said another word in Serbo-Croatian and threw the book down on the desk.

"I take that," said von Honig through his pain, "to mean you didn't...think much of it."

The man gazed at him with his cold eyes. "Why you here? For this?" He stabbed one plump finger down on the book in staccato fashion. "Is nothing."

Von Honig shook his head. "It may be...something."

"Is not important," said the officer, still staring at him icily. He waved at the ceiling and the walls. "*This* is important."

Von Honig's face reddened. Drawing himself up as much as he could, he hissed through his teeth from his pain. "It's *more than important*, sir!"

The man drew back a bit in his chair, his face betraying his mild shock at the author's tone and fire. "Can not fight," he replied, "can not *kill* with this." He stabbed at the book again, yet more violently than before. "I need things to fight with."

"That's...*bullshit*," von Honig screeched. He waved at the room, just as the officer had done a moment ago. "All of *this* is bullshit."

Something made him look down suddenly, and he saw that Bikkelman had raised his head and moved his hand to lay it on von Honig's ankle, his finger curling to grip it.

The soldiers pointed their weapons at the author.

Ignoring everything, von Honig continued.

"You fight and you...*squabble* and you kill each other in these...

disputes, but you never look at the bigger image of the world. Everything I've found...everything I've...*learned* to this point–" he paused, as if searching for the words, "–*shows* me that we're nearly nothing...in the larger scheme of the universe. And we *should* be."

The general stared at him, his eyes unreadable.

"You may dismiss me," said the author, "and you may dismiss my work, but I dismiss *you*. And I dismiss your stupid little war."

He looked at each of the soldiers, and back to their superior, meeting the man's gaze with equal force.

"We are bound for bigger things as a species." He looked down at the reporter before returning his eyes to the general. "But some of us are holding us back."

Silence fell over the room as the two combatants stared at each other. Finally, the general reached over and pressed a button on a small console at the side of his desk. No sound issued from it, but seconds later there came a creak of metal and a movement in the air as a door at the back of the office opened and swung forward into the room.

The moment the door opened, the sound of human misery issued out from behind it.

A dark figure stepped into the room and shut the door behind it. The sounds of pain and terror ceased the second the door met the doorframe once again. A carnal smell accompanied the figure, who stepped into the flickering candlelight.

Von Honig saw that it was the man from the truck. He no longer wore his heavy coat, but was still dressed in his blood-smeared white apron or smock. His eyes were the same–dark and cold, like a reptile's.

The general did not turn to look at the man, but simply raised one hand to indicate him languidly.

"Need something," he said to the author, "to end all fighting, to send him home from the fighting. He likes his work, but...still..." He pointed at von Honig. "You? Worthless in this. More so, even."

The author vibrated with fury. A small dab of spittle dripped over

his bottom lip and onto his sleeve as he opened his mouth to speak.
"*None* of this *matters*."

The general tilted his head to one side and without preamble the soldiers dragged the prisoners out of the room.

3.

The prisoners were left without ceremony in a small, dark cell on the back end of the building. There was only one cot, but neither of them possessed the strength to pull themselves into it.

The day became night, and the night passed without incident. Both men simply lay on the cold floor of the cell, drifting in and out of sleep until a rumble of thunder awoke them sometime in the morning. Rain began to fall and the wind lashed the small building. In the distance, the mountains stood in mute testimony to the inclement weather.

Bikkelman stirred and looked up to see von Honig had pulled himself to his feet and positioned his beaten body in front of the cell's one small, barred window.

"This isn't what I imagined this day'd be like," said Bikkelman

The author said nothing, but continued to stare out the window. Bikkelman shifted himself gingerly to begin the process of rising to a sitting position. His face twisted into grotesque expressions of pain.

"We're not going anywhere," the reporter said, breathing heavily from his exertions. "Whatever's going down. We're... What in the hell...? Are you...? Is that...? Are you into that TM stuff?"

Von Honig opened his eyes and ceased silently mouthing a pattern of words over and over. "It's called transcendental meditation. It's practiced by nearly a million people worldwide and is thought to have many health benefits. You should try it."

Bikkelman shook his head, which brought a look of pain to his face. "No, thank you. Some yogi or somebody the Beatles used to go to says it's good, so a million people jump off a bridge with him.

Can't believe you're into it. Aren't you an atheist?"

"God has nothing to do with it."

"Whoopee."

"You're scared."

The reporter glared up at his companion. "Damn right I am," he hissed. "*Nothing* like this has *ever* happened to me here. Did you see that guy? That–that *butcher*? Christ…that's where we're headed. Goddammit, I don't see any way out of this…"

"We have to get out of here," said von Honig as if he hadn't heard anything Bikkelman had said. "I'd go myself, but I need you to lead me to the site."

The reporter leaned against the cot, his face pale and drawn. "Nice to be needed," he murmured. "You got your crap for your books and I got…" He began to chuckle to himself.

Von Honig turned away from the window and looked at him with narrowed eyes. "What do you find amusing?"

Bikkelman continued his mirth for a moment, but finally fell silent. "I just remembered: it's my birthday today."

The author turned back to the window and the mountains, but found a face peering into the cell through the bars.

It was a woman.

Von Honig gazed silently at the lovely face for a moment, then turned to the reporter with a questioning look.

"Susac," said Bikkelman, trying to lift himself up off the floor. Von Honig continued to question him with his eyes. "Her name. That's her name. Susac. She owns a farm not far from here."

"Why is she here?" the author asked, looking back at the woman's face framed by the small window. "You know her?"

Bikkelman stood finally, wavering in the dark of the cell. "Obviously. She's the one who led me to the site–me and the mayor of her town, who she trusts for some reason. Susac, it's me. Brad Bikkelman." Then he uttered a few words in Serbo-Croatian, which caused the woman's brow to crease in confusion.

"Dammit," the reporter complained. "She speaks a weird…some

24

kind of crazy offshoot. Her dialect is so thick I can barely understand her."

"Tell her we need to get out of this cell."

Bikkelman shot the author a dirty look as he passed by him to step over to the window. "Do you ever listen to anybody?" He said a few more words to Susac, who replied in what sounded like the same tongue. Bikkelman hung his head upon hearing it, shaking it from side to side.

"Huh. I *think* she's telling me that we're stuck here."

"Please move out of the way," von Honig commanded. "Maybe I can–"

Susac frowned and held up a long key for the two men to see.

"Or maybe I'm wrong," said Bikkelman.

Von Honig surged forward and reached for the key, his arm scraping past the reporter to the window. Bikkelman whipped around to face him, his white cheeks flooding with color.

"*What the hell are you doing?*"

Von Honig paused. "We're being offered a way out of here. I'm taking it. I have to get up to that site."

The reporter clutched at his arm. "Are you *insane?* We can't, can't *escape* from here! My Christ–do you know what they'll do when they catch us? Do you have a death wish?"

Von Honig composed his face. He stared back at his cellmate, meeting his angry eyes with his own calm gaze. "You brought me here, Bikkelman. You told me you had something to show me, showed me blurry photos of what appears to be a promising discovery. You gave me hope of expanding my knowledge of what I chase. This woman here–" he indicated Susac with a pointing finger "–has our means of escape, yes, from this place. Nothing will stand in my way of reaching what I seek. I've already wasted too much time here."

The reporter released von Honig's arm and curled his fingers into a quavering fist. It hung in the air only inches from the author's face until Bikkelman unclenched it and let his arms drop down to his side.

"Alright," he said simply. "You do what you feel is right. You'll be dead soon, so it won't matter. I'll probably be dead soon, too, when they see you gone."

He hung his head, his chin dropping to his chest.

"I hope it'll be worth it."

Conrad von Honig took the key through the bars from the woman outside and moved to the cell door gritting his teeth in pain. He slipped his hand between the door's bars and inserted the key in its lock. With a turn of his wrist he unlocked the door and swung it open.

Without hesitation, the author walked through the open door and down the passageway outside, leaving the door ajar behind him.

He passed two soldiers in the larger room at the end of the passage, both of whom sat slumped in chairs, their mouths open but their eyes closed. Walking past them, he barely gave them a glance.

Outside the building, the rain seemed to have let up and there was no sign of other soldiers, the general, or even the flatbed truck that had brought him there. He looked around for the woman and saw her slip around the corner of the building from the back. She trotted up to him, her upper torso wrapped in intertwining layers of cloth, her legs covered by a long skirt, and her face sporting an expressionless countenance.

"Susac?" said von Honig. "Your name is Susac?"

The woman nodded. Her dark eyes swept over the author and one corner of her mouth quirked up slightly, not quite a smile. Suddenly, she whipped her head around from side to side and pulled at von Honig's arm.

Together, they swept away from the building and into a nearby stand of trees, the rain returning to pelt their heels as they ran. Once among the tree trunks and under branches that provided an umbrella to the rain, Susac motioned for the author to stop.

A soldier exited the building, lurching in his steps and wagging his head as if to clear it of something. He leaned off to one side of the doorway and vomited into the gravel there. After a short series of dry heaves, he straightened and looked around. Susac drew von

Honig further back into the blind of the trees and they watched as the man called back into the building, apparently to his comrade. No response came. He turned away from the door, withdrew a side-arm from a holster on his belt and walked into the rain.

His path would take him several yards from where Susac and von Honig stood. "Can't we leave now?" asked the author, his voice vibrating with annoyance.

Susac looked at him, obviously confused at the foreign language directed at her. What might have been realization spread over her features then, and she shook her head in the negative. She reached out a hand to touch him on his arm as if to emphasize her point.

A twig or a branch snapped somewhere behind them and off to their left. The author opened his mouth, but the woman spread her hand to cover it in an instant. Von Honig did not speak, but reached up to move her hand away.

The two stood silently and listened. More sounds reached their ears, apparently moving away from the direction from which the first originated and moving to their right and still behind them. The noises, which also sounded like twigs being snapped and fallen leaves crushed underfoot, did not seem to come from the direction of the searching soldier.

Then, almost as soon as they began, the sounds died away.

Susac held von Honig at the spot for nearly five minutes as she listened for the sounds to return. Nodding to him, she pulled him through the trees and together they exited them some twenty feet or so from the place where they'd entered them. The author saw the mountains through the rain and stepped in front of the woman to see them better. A pull on his arm swung his attention to first Susac and then to the still-open door of the jail.

Bikkelman had appeared there, moving slowly, but looking all around him at his surroundings.

Susac beat her fist on Honig's shoulder anxiously. The author took two steps forward and gestured with his hands and arms to silently warn Bikkelman about the soldier patrolling the area. Bikkelman paused and nodded an acknowledgement, then disappeared back into the building.

The author and the woman darted from where they stood toward another line of trees and the mountains beyond them.

4.

Stooping low to pass under a particularly large rock outcropping, Conrad von Honig stepped into the chamber.

He waved at the woman to hand him her flashlight. Its beam was weak, but it sufficed to illuminate his surroundings and allow him to explore it. His eyes focused to the poor lighting and he swung the beam over the room's walls, sweeping them from floor to ceiling as he walked the circumference of the area.

Yes," he intoned quietly. "Yes…indeed."

He stopped at one spot, gazing up at what his light showed. There were markings on the wall before him, huge figures clearly delineated on its surface.

"This isn't Roman. It isn't Illyrian, either. Older, much older. Oh, I know they were both here in this region, but the Balkans can lay claim to far older peoples."

Susac, standing several feet away from the author, quirked an eyebrow, but remained silent and tracked his every moment while she clutched at her wet garments to keep them in place.

"If only I could get more *light* in here," von Honig whispered, shaking his head. "Look here–this figure?" He pointed at the wall. "This is significant."

The woman stepped closer to him and looked up at the wall. The flashlight's beam illuminated the painted image of what appeared to be a man, but with a bulbous head, rounded like a melon. Susac gazed at it for a moment, then turned her head to look at the author with uncomprehending eyes. She shrugged and uttered a few words in her language.

"No, I understand," von Honig told her and trained the beam on something painted on the wall beside the figure. Susac's eyes widened when she saw it and she nodded slowly in comprehension.

"Now you see?"

Next to the first figure stood another, man-shaped, but far smaller and bowing to the first, which was much larger and taller.

"Then look here," said von Honig as he trained the light on more pictograms further down the curving wall. "And here…and here…"

He walked the chamber's circumference until he returned to Susac after completing the circle, all the while pointing the flashlight at its walls.

The chamber was filled with human figures, interspersed at regular intervals with giants.

In the faint light, the author's eyes took on a strange cast. They passed over the images, back and forth, taking them in with a look of satisfaction.

"The size, nearly three heads taller than the humans around them…the rounded craniums, like helmets…see here the delineating line that suggests a separate piece from their actual heads? There, what appears to be a single eye…not uncommon, but significant. The long arms, but stocky torsos. And this. This right here. What might be a representation of the sexual organ to some, but what I believe shows a possible extra limb of some kind…"

Susac stepped nearer to von Honig, gazing up at the images, too. She reached out one hand to stretch her fingers toward the giant, not fully touching the painted surface of the wall, but lightly grazing it with her fingertips.

"All the figures," continued the author, "are static, not in motion or performing tasks. They are…frozen, in a way. More so than simply being captured in these renderings, but rather…I'm not sure. Waiting? Biding their time?"

He took a step backward, then two, still viewing the images. "The humans around them are not–"

The author stopped suddenly with a short burst of exhaled air through his lips. Turning slowly in place, he swung the beam of light away from the walls, throwing the woman into total darkness and spotlighting what he'd backed into.

"What's this…?"

29

At the center of the large, circular chamber sat a pedestal of sorts, fully stone and standing roughly four feet high at its highest side. Von Honig began to walk around it, training the flashlight over its top and sides.

"Somewhat concave and higher on one side than the other." He reached out a hand to run it over the surface of the thing. "Smooth. Worn down from…some water collected in it. From…"

He looked up suddenly, the flashlight's beam following his stare. The light illuminated the chamber's ceiling and the large, round hole in it.

Von Honig stood mute for several seconds, looking up.

"*Mon monde, ma vie*…is it?"

He reached into his shirt to pull out a small cellophane packet. From inside of that he took out a folded piece of tissue. His hands trembled a bit as he unfolded it.

"Can you…can you hold this, like this?" He motioned to Susac to come and take the flashlight from him, and in a wink she was at his side reaching out for it. Once she'd trained the beam on the ceiling, von Honig clutched the sheet of tissue and held it up over his head. He looked from the sheet to the hole and back again, over and over. On the surface of the tissue were dark pencil marks showing a circle with marks all around its circumference at various intervals.

Susac uttered a few words, her own eyes flickering back and forth between the author, his drawing, and the hole above them. Von Honig smiled slightly.

"I wish I knew what you were asking me," he said. "But if I were to guess, I'd say you're wondering what it means." He looked back to the ceiling. "I wish I knew. I've carried this with me for, well, years now, ever since I traced it from a painting in, of all places, a museum in Brussels of a…well, it doesn't matter. Suffice it to say it stuck out like the proverbial sore thumb."

He pointed at the hole. "You see there? That these markings on the drawing match nearly perfectly with the notches around the edges of the hole?" He lowered the tissue. "And that hole is positioned directly above this–" he paused, looking at the stone dais and struggling for the proper word to describe it "–this seat? It would be more suited to a very large, tall being than a human. A very large *king*, perhaps…and a…throne…"

The woman was very near him. His nostrils flared and his eyes narrowed. He took a very deep breath and held it, closing his eyes for a moment and opening them to stare at Susac. She returned his stare, her full lips parting as if to say something.

Instead, she leaned toward him and pressed her mouth to his, at first gently and then hungrily.

Von Honig reared back somewhat, but maintained the intimate connection. His entire body stiffened and then relaxed as the woman ran her hands over his arms and shoulders in the semi-dark, the flashlight now lying on the dais, pointing in their general direction. They broke their kiss and Susac whispered something, her words incomprehensible to the author, but her intentions clear.

He shook his head, dipping his chin to his chest, and watched his own hand creep underneath Susac's wrappings along her warm belly and to her breast.

She inhaled sharply and pressed his hand tightly against her, her body flexing as if hearing music, her other hand roaming his body before reaching down to her waist and undoing a leather cord there to allow her skirt to slip over her hips and legs and pool around her ankles on the stone floor.

The author's eyes widened as he leaned her back against the dais and fumbled at the buttons of his trousers.

"What the *hell*…?"

They turned their heads from their sudden passion to see Brad Bikkelman standing at the entrance to the chamber, shining a light nearly in their eyes. In fact, the beam of illumination was focused more on their bodies and their hasty state of undress.

The reporter started toward them, his light bobbing over their equally hasty attempt to collect their clothing. Susac dropped down to gather up her skirt, which complicated von Honig extricating his hand from beneath her wrappings. In the process, winding fabric caught on his fingers, exposing even more flesh to Bikkelman's probing light.

"I mean—what's going on?" he asked, clearly confused.

"It doesn't matter," retorted the author as he stepped back and rebuttoned his pants. Susac turned away, trying to rebind her wrappings. She spat out words with heated rapidity and stumbled over them.

Bikkelman neared the two. "She says...I think she says she doesn't *know* what happened?" He looked at von Honig.

"*I* don't know what happened! But it *doesn't matter*!" the author insisted angrily. "*She* doesn't matter!" He lifted both his hands and swept them apart to indicate the chamber. "*This* does!"

The reporter tore his eyes from the woman as she melted into the darkness, her back to both men. He managed to look around and back to von Honig.

"I tried to get here sooner. I slipped away in the dark, but I had to move slowly and watch my step to avoid drawing any attention." He paused, scanning the space. "I–I'd hoped to have been here when you first saw it, man."

"It's like nothing I've ever encountered before, Bikkelman. The pictograms...they remind me somewhat of such that I found in Turkey, near Ankaras. They may be related." The author swept up his flashlight and trained it upward. "And *this*. This is..."

Bikkelman snorted a small, brief laugh. "Yeah, I thought that would interest you. It's perfectly round. Saw it from the outside first and tested it by sighting down a coin at it. I'd swear it's perfectly round."

"It's not natural," von Honig said with utter conviction. "How it could have retained its roundness—and the notches around it—for a millennium or two, I just don't know."

"Notches?" the reporter asked, craning his neck to see.

Von Honig nodded, looking down at his tissue drawing. "Never mind that now. I have to figure out how I can document this. I'll need a camera, a good one, and a recorder to make notes. And–"

"What is it?"

The author looked up at Bikkelman's simple question with a blank stare. "Well, I can only surmise at this point...but it may have something to do with astronomy."

Bikkelman snorted again. "You're kiddin' me, right? We're not up in the mountains—we're down in the valley, or whatever. How the hell could it be something about looking at the stars?"

Von Honig swung his light to a portion of the curving wall, throwing illumination on one of the giant figures there.

"It's not for *us*," he said. "It's for *them*."

The reporter stared. "H-how?"

Von Honig took up the tissue and began to refold it. "Everything you see is to accommodate them. The size of this chamber, the height of the ceiling, the distance between the wall and…this." He indicated the dais. "This is proportioned for them. Not us. When they sat here…" He shook his head again. "…and looked upward. I don't know, Bikkelman. I can only guess."

"It hurts my head, von Honig. It makes me cra—"

The reporter stopped talking abruptly enough for von Honig to look over at him. In the beam of his flashlight he saw a hand appear at Bikkelman's throat, a thin, silvery, glinting object protruding from it, set horizontally in mid-air, neatly bisecting the man's Adam's apple.

"Go on," said the butcher. "I'm listening."

Bikkelman held his breath, the blade less than an inch from his throat. Von Honig cocked his head, staring intently at the new arrival in the scant light. It was the man from the truck, the general's torture-master, and quite possibly his executioner.

"Yes, I speak English. And better than the general."

The man's accent was heavy, but his words infinitely clearer than those of his superior. He held fast to the reporter, his reptilian eyes glinting in the beam of the flashlight.

"Go on, Mr. von Honig. It is fascinating."

"What do you want?" asked the author, his voice even and controlled, despite the situation.

The butcher nodded. "You are a cold one. Your friend here, he has a knife at his throat, and you remain calm."

"Leave him be. He only helped to lead me here. Please, just let him go on his way."

Bikkelman shifted, but stilled himself when the butcher brought his blade up against the skin of his neck.

"Hmm, a glimmer of compassion? But still, like I said, you are a cold one," said the man. "And you are not unlike myself. I too am not a believer. I do not believe what the general believes."

Von Honig looked confused. "What do you mean?"

The butcher's lips stretched into a taut, thin line across his face. "I am an atheist. I only believe in what's best for me. Like you." He turned his head to one side to peer into the darkness.

"Woman!" he bellowed, then spat out words in Susac's language. "I have told her to make herself clear to me," he said to von Honig. "Ah, here she is."

Susac appeared out of the shadows, from behind the dais on the opposite side of it from the author, her dark eyes wide and laced with fear.

"Now," said the butcher, "go on. What is this place?"

Von Honig spread one hand and waved it through the air. "I don't know. Not yet. I need to study it."

"Do you? And then you will write it into one of your books?"

"Perhaps."

The butcher almost smiled. "And me...will I appear in one of your books, too?"

"You're merely a man," replied the author. "I write about larger things."

"Well, then, I will give you something to write about."

And with that he drew his knife across and into Brad Bikkelman's throat.

5.

He talked while he cut.

Using implements he took from a leather case he'd unrolled on top of the dais, the butcher sliced away at the reporter's body with methodical precision, laying open muscle and bone and organs, all the while putting voice to his thoughts.

"The general had been watching him–" he indicated Bikkelman with a blasé gesture "–for a while. Something about him made the general suspicious of his actions, and so he had him followed."

The butcher paused, studying his handiwork.

"For myself, I only saw the kind of man who steals women from other men. A professional, a worldly man who flies here and there with the wind. The kind of man I loathe."

He returned to his cutting, separating limbs from torso. The blood from his work flowed down the sides of the dais from its lowest edge.

"See here, Mr. von Honig?" the butcher indicated the blood flow. "It does not pool on the floor of this chamber. Some sort of drainage system? Something for you to discover, to add to your books."

The author stood against a wall, his face ashen, his chin smeared with vomitus, and his eyes fixed on the blood. Susac sat crumpled on the floor some several feet from him, her eyes cast downward, her face pale in the weak light. She had curled up within herself the moment she saw what was happening to the reporter's corpse.

"This…throne, as you may call it," said the butcher, slicing through a muscle mass with a small grunt, "is not…conducive? Yes, *conducive* to my work, but it will do. Uneven surfaces are always a challenge, but I appreciate the history in it."

Von Honig stirred from his seeming lethargy. "You shouldn't do that."

The butcher paused again, looking up from his labors.

"Say again, please?"

"You shouldn't be doing that," hissed the author, low and sibilant. "I…it's…"

"See?" said the butcher, shaking his head as he looked back to the vivisected corpse. "You *are* a cold one. More concerned with *where* I do what I do, not *what* I do. Yes, we're very much alike, you and I."

"Do not *presume* to know me, sir!" screeched von Honig, pushing himself away from the wall and clenching his fists in fury before him. "You make me sick with what you do and who you are!"

A silvery knife whipped away from cutting through an artery to hang in the air between the two men, the pointed tip of it directed at von Honig's heart.

"That will be enough," the butcher told him with a frown. "That will be quite enough of that, Mr. von Honig of the Space Gods. I'm almost done here, and–"

A growl of thunder rumbled above the cavern and through the hole in its ceiling. A moment later, the rain began to fall through the opening to splatter the remains of Brad Bikkelman.

"Look there, look there." The butcher motioned toward the dais. "See? The rain's come again to wash away my sin. To clear the throne of usurpers."

He wiped his hands and instrument on his pants and coat and turned away from his work. "And beyond the thunder? Listen–more shelling. The rebels attempting to retake the town would be my guess."

He stifled a small yawn. "I have grown fatigued. I'll nap now." He looked at the author and then at the woman.

"We shall all rest now. We won't be going anywhere tonight." He glanced up at the incoming rain as he settled himself against one section of the curved wall, cradling a flashlight.

"Sit down, Mr. von Honig. And don't get any wild ideas. I'm a very light sleeper."

He awoke with a start to the sound of shelling in the distance and the tap-tap of dripping water onto the stone dais. He could make out the still form of the woman a few feet from him, sleeping perhaps, and with a turn of the head in the opposite direction, the sitting shape of the butcher holding a knife in one hand. It was not immediately obvious whether the man was sleeping or not.

Slowly, he unfolded his legs from underneath himself and stretched them to revive circulation. Then, still slowly, he stood up, glanced at his jailer, and walked toward the dais. Once he'd reached it, he stepped to the other side of it and turned his back to it.

Somewhere in the darkness of the chamber lay the remains of Brad Bikkelman, washed clean by the rain, and he wanted to avoid looking at them at all costs

Conrad von Honig slid his back down along the dais until he reached a sitting position on the stone floor. He crossed his legs and leaned his head back until it too touched cool, almost smooth stone. Bringing one hand up before his face, he looked at the quaver in it for a moment and then set it in his lap to join his other.

Then he looked at the stars.

The author sat like that, looking up, for several minutes before he finally closed his eyes and stilled his breathing to a nearly imperceptible level. His mouth began to move slightly as his lips formed words. The words, repeated over and over again, went unheard amid the rumble of distant explosions.

More minutes passed. His eyelids fluttered once, twice, and he opened them to peer up at the stars once more.

Framed by the round hole in the chamber's ceiling, the pinpoints of light in the Balkan skies began to reach toward him.

At first the light appeared consistent down the shaft from star to the nearest end, but it grew in intensity as it neared him. Each shaft also began as white, warm, light, but soon they shifted beyond white and into color, each beam settling on a different hue: blue, pink, yellow, green.

The lights grew closer and as they did their outer edges touched one another, creating a snowflake-like pattern of intersecting points and swirls among them. Where they touched and crossed, new colors arose from the unions, some indescribable. This effect expanded, eating away at the dark of the night sky until finally it consumed it whole and filled the chamber with pulsing, living light.

He did not blink at this, but continued to drink in the colors and the light that fed them.

Somewhere beyond the light, he could still hear the tap-tap of rain water.

Warmth flooded over him as the light touched him on his outermost extremities, and then followed those touchpoints to blanket him at all parts on his body. The criss-cross of colors became one color and that hue was unnamable.

Then he heard sounds, but not the detonation of explosives. This was not unlike a hum. It seemed to pulse with the light at first, but then grew into its own, separate thing that then opposed the light and threatened to disrupt the all-pervading illumination. Finally, that too died away and the light was all.

Shadows appeared around the edges of the white, hot radiance, moving gray areas that seemed to push into the sphere of light and then periodically fall back. They would gain ground and then nearly disappear, only to appear again to vie for attention. They were amorphous things, unrecognizable, intangible shapes that slid across the surface of the light and never touched each other. The shadows moved about and then stopped, settling down around the fringes again, taking up stationary posts.

He heard more sounds.

The light parted down the middle. The two edges that formed there swiveled to lie down horizontally and then curved to create a vision of the edge of an immense ball or sphere. The two halves of light, one below and one above, changed colors to distinguish themselves from each other.

More bodies entered the picture, huge, gigantic spheroids hanging in a void of immeasurable distance. These remained motionless until a new hum appeared on the horizon and they followed it and danced and swirled around each other. Their paths created contrails of still even more colors.

He heard…talking. Words were forming somewhere in the dance, but remained elusive, washed out by the movement of the spheres. Then they died away, pulled out by tendrils of light that were seemingly unconnected to anything else that existed in the scene.

He closed his eyes. When he opened them again, Brad Bikkelman stood before him, whole and unharmed, looking down upon him. The image rippled like water, then faded away.

He tried to scream, but the light and the colors and the spheres and the shadows merged to form impediments and he choked on them, sobbing into the void.

A new voice came to him, grounded in reality.

"Wh…what…what have you *done?*"

The butcher staggered at him in the darkness. Von Honig reared back, bumping into the dais, throwing his hands up in front of him to ward off his attacker.

"What did you do?" bellowed the butcher. In one hand he still clutched his cutting blade. The other was formed into a claw.

The author's eyes widened in horror when he saw the man's own orbs were ghostly white like coddled eggs, dead and unseeing.

The butcher crashed into him. "I can still do it!" he seethed. "I can still *smell* you!"

Von Honig caught the wrist of the hand that held the blade and exerted every iota of strength in himself to stop it in its path.

"You son of bitch!" he screamed.

Then he fought. Instead of grabbing the butcher's other hand or trying to block it, he balled his fingers into a fist and sent it smashing into the man's face. He pulled back and punched him a second time.

"You goddamn son of a bitch!"

The butcher's left eye blinked from the spittle thrown in it by von Honig's oath and he yowled in pain, but did not retreat. He tried to break the author's grip on his wrist while fending off more blows, his blind eyes swiveling in their sockets, bulging and white.

"Kill you!"

Von Honig continued to curse, his voice ringing like a bell in the chamber. He kicked out with one foot, but it seemed to have no effect on the butcher. Then, in a wink, he was being bent over the top of the dais, the silvery blade inches from his face.

He blinked and his attacker was on top of him, many pounds of dead weight.

Von Honig pushed the man away and the inert form crumpled to the stone floor. Behind him stood Susac, a flashlight clutched in both hands and a smear of blood on its glowing head.

The blood matched that on the back of the butcher's head.

The woman began to sob and her knees buckled. The author leapt to her and took her up in his arms as the sound of shelling grew suddenly louder from all around them

"We've got to go–*now!*"

The first rays of morning light came up over the mountain tops to cast strange shadows through the trees where they'd been hiding. From their vantage point, von Honig and Susac watched in silence as the rebel forces swept down into the area and marched in the general direction of the cave opening they'd exited only a few minutes before.

Susac made him follow her pointing finger as she indicated a tank that was cresting a small ridge at the back of the line of ragged troops.

Von Honig frowned and patted her hand.

"Let them blow it all away," he said somberly. "I've taken everything I needed from it already. It's…it's a *tomb* now. Whatever it was–an observatory, a…a place of worship…a throne–it's just a burial place for the dead now. I–I don't know if what I saw in there was real or just my mind playing tricks on me, but Fate as usual is showing me no favoritism. These people will do what they will do, the larger universe be damned."

They also watched as the butcher stumbled from the entrance to the cave and into the path of the front of the line of rebel soldiers. He seemed to hear them–maybe even smell them–but he was still blind and staggering from the blow to his head.

The rebels listened to him for a minute, their eyes tracking every gesture he made toward the cave and the mountains and most likely to Conrad von Honig, wherever he and the bitch with him were no doubt hiding, damn them.

Then they shot him where he stood.

A few minutes later they sent a shell down the mouth of the cave opening.

Susac turned to the author, her face a stew of mixed emotions.

"You have a farm, yes?" von Honig asked her. She nodded after a moment, as if understanding his strange language. "Well, we'd better get to it, then," he said, standing up and dusting off his shirt and trousers.

"You're an innocent in all this," he told Susac. "If any of us truly may claim such a status. I'm…sorry about what you've witnessed."

They started to leave the spot, but he hesitated. Turning his head, he looked back at where the cave entrance had been and started to turn his body, too. One step, two, in the direction of the cave, but he made a full stop and hung his head, chuckling softly, quietly to himself. When he finally returned to Susac's side, he spoke to her.

"Your farm?" He motioned for them to continue walking through the Majavacan woods. "We'd better make sure everyone's okay there…"

IN THE COURT
OF THE PALE KING

by Desmond Reddick

onrad von Honig sipped wearily from his espresso, sneering at the bitterness. He preferred tea, but the selection at this cafe on Rue de Maupassant was wretched. The cafe a few floors below his flat, a ten-minute walk away, was a little more expensive and a little slower of service, but they were the only Frenchmen he'd come across who could actually make a decent cup of tea. However, one didn't invite a dead man to a cafe near one's home.

Dr. Charlie Bolinger had been von Honig's most influential anthropology professor at the University of Sydney. He wasn't dismissive of von Honig's theories, though he didn't necessarily buy into them. His knowledge of the aboriginal people of Australia and their mythology was very helpful to von Honig's studies. They'd kept in touch for years via letters, but the last time von Honig saw him, Charlie was in a box being lowered into the ground.

So he considered himself justified in his suspicions when Noel telegrammed him to say a Charlie Bolinger wanted to meet him. Von Honig sat facing the door of the cafe waiting for the impossible to happen, or waiting to be extremely disappointed. His career had prepared him for both.

"Conrad?"

It startled him. The dark-haired woman who spoke his name had escaped his notice when she walked into the café, seeing as she wasn't a hefty, mustachioed man in his sixties. Now, as she stood before him, he was surprised he had failed to notice her.

Her full cheeks protruded in a smile, clearly in response to what must have been a puzzled look on his face. She appeared bookish and wore a conservative sweater and knee-length skirt, with her arms crossed over a thin attaché case across her hips.

Conrad allowed the small shock to pass as he reminded himself to stand and shake her hand.

"I'm Charlie Bolinger," she said, obviously enjoying the delighted confusion she had stirred in von Honig.

"I'm sorry," the writer said, blushing. "You clearly take after your mother."

Now she blushed.

"As my father was fond of saying."

"Excuse me. The last time I saw you, you must have been nine or ten."

"I was twelve at dad's funeral."

Thirteen years ago, von Honig noted to himself.

"I recognized you from your photo in *To Seek the Space Gods*. Dad had copies of all of your books. When he passed, his library became mine."

"You read it?" von Honig asked.

"Aye, all of them," she said. Her eyes told the truth and the tone in her voice was one of admiration.

Von Honig was used to being commended for his first book, but many of the rabid fans of that book never bought his subsequent works. Or if they did, never finished them.

"Dad was very fond of you."

Von Honig stopped grinning like a lovesick dummy. "And I him," he said. He took a breath, thought about how she was more than ten years younger than him and began to think more about the circumstances of their meeting.

"As I understand, you didn't necessarily take up the family business," he said. "What drove you to come see me all the way from Australia?"

"I live in London mostly," she said. "And yeah, I make my rent writing for *NME, Melody Maker, Sounds* and a couple others that aren't shy about paying their freelancers."

She must have seen puzzlement in his face.

"They're music magazines," she said flatly. "I write about punk and new wave, mostly. Some heavy metal, too."

"You don't look like a punk rocker," von Honig said before mentally reminding himself to stop flirting.

"Yeah, well, you don't need to wear a Mohawk to be a fan."

"I must apologize that I haven't read your work. I don't make a lot of time for new music these days."

"Have you heard of James Floyd?" she asked.

"I will apologize again."

"Well, you might want to make some time for him," she said, lifting her attaché case.

Von Honig realized they had been standing the entire time and motioned for her to sit in the chair opposite his. Once she was in her seat, he turned and took his. By the time he was facing her, she was pulling LP records out onto the table. The waiter delivered an espresso to her as Charlie laid the records out in front of him.

"Floyd was the bass player in The Earthworms a while back," she began.

"I've heard of them," von Honig offered, a little too enthusiastically.

"Yeah, typical mediocre second-wave British Invasion nonsense. They charted at 17 once and that's about it," she sipped her espresso. "So, a few years back, The Earthworms implode. The guitar player and drummer left to do a jazz thing, the singer went the pop crooner route. That has served him pretty well. "

Von Honig was pleased she'd stopped naming band names and artists, as he feared he was beginning to look ignorant.

"And Floyd?"

"That's the thing," she said, excitement building in her voice and a smile lighting up her face. "He disappeared for a few years. I mean, gone. The record label couldn't find him to deliver royalty checks, even."

"But…?" von Honig prompted.

"But when he reappeared five years ago, he was different."

"Different how?"

"Now he's larger than life. A real glam rocker. Make-up, platform boots, glittery bodysuits, the works."

"This all feels like something up your alley, or one of your colleagues?" Von Honig tried not to be rude, considering how lovely she was and how excited she seemed to be about the topic on his behalf, but his patience was wearing thin.

"Look at the records, Conrad."

He looked down at the four LP covers on the table in front of him. Had he been prepared, he would have stopped himself from audibly gasping. He would have immediately engaged his analytical mind. Instead, he allowed himself a moment of incredulity. And what a moment it was.

Displayed before him from left to right: a cover with a lush jungle growing around a crystal skull, a cover depicting Egyptian pyramids mirroring a strange light pattern in the sky above them, a cover of green rolling hillsides with what could have been Stonehenge on a hill in the far background, and a cover showing a carved throne illuminated by torches and positioned in the center of a cave.

Von Honig inhaled sharply, and the confusion must have been more than evident on his face.

"Now," Charlie said, "I don't know you, but having read your books, this might be of interest."

"How…?"

Von Honig was trying to express the thought that no one would know how these images would appeal to him without the proper context. But before he could find the words, Charlie reached into her attaché case again and pulled out a magazine.

"This is the last interview with James Floyd," she said, thumbing through the publication before finding the article and folding back the flipped pages. She passed it to von Honig. "A colleague did it with him via correspondence."

Underlined in blue ink somewhere in the middle of the interview was a quote from Floyd: "Yes, I believe that aliens once visited Earth to seed our civilization. I've seen the proof."

Von Honig noted that he too had seen the proof, and much of the proof that he had seen was displayed in rather accurate portrayals on the man's album covers.

"Perhaps I should be talking to the man who painted these," von Honig offered.

"They're painted by four different artists. All from Floyd's descriptions."

Von Honig's skepticism must have been obvious during his moment of contemplation.

"He does everything on his albums by himself," Charlie explained. "Guitar, bass, drums, vocals, keyboards. Everything. He creates concept albums and tells the artist exactly what to paint on the covers. His rebirth is kind of a concept career. Everything has been very single-minded. He even produces his own stuff. The guy is like Zappa or something."

Von Honig actually recognized the name as a fringe modern classical music composer, though the derision in the young woman's voice as she spoke it told him she would not be impressed with his musical knowledge. Instead of speaking, he took another moment to consider.

"You said the writer did this interview by correspondence?" he said.

"Yeah. Floyd's never done an in-person interview since his…rebirth."

"How do you expect me to find him, then?"

"From your book, I understand you're a man who can get into some tough places."

"Where is he?" von Honig asked.

"Germany," Charlie answered.

"West Germany?"

"West Berlin."

~ ~ ~

The train shook for the entire journey, bumping and rattling from below rather than from side to side. The rough ride made it difficult for the travelers to sleep, which suited von Honig just fine, as he only ever slept on intercontinental flights as a matter of convenience.

The long ride afforded him time to think without distraction, a rare luxury in the modern world. The beautiful countryside could have been anywhere in Central Europe, if not for the East German soldiers visible along the fenced corridor if one paid attention. They were young men, gaunt and miserable, the spark of life pulled from their faces already, most of them barely out of grammar school. Von Honig thought it must have been torturous for a young man with young man's dreams living behind fences and walls, forced to guard those same fences and walls, to see a train full of free people.

He supposed they weren't entirely free, since it was difficult for him to get a ticket on such short notice. But Noel de Sapin, his publisher, had his charms. After a few greased palms and blushing ladies, von Honig was sure Noel had made it happen relatively easily. Easier than it would have been for von Honig, anyway. He had little time for such chicanery. His energy was better spent on getting access to hard-to-reach places rather than arranging travel plans, however difficult. He was much more capable of finding someone to take him up a mountain in a Jeep during a civil war than he was trying to line up airplane flights and connecting train fares. It was all so mundane to him. Even the notoriously tricky Stadtbahn train through Soviet-controlled East Germany.

So Noel would take the cost of such logistics and arrangements out of his next advance. As long as it made it easier for von Honig to further his research and develop the next book, Noel would always be willing to do a little bit of tricky work, even if it meant getting von Honig on a hard-to-get train ride through East Germany to West Berlin. Not an easy feat in today's climate. In what was surely an incredibly tense few moments for most German travelers on the train, von Honig merely saw the stops in Potsdam and Leipzig—complete with drug dogs and brusque East German soldiers with machine guns demanding to see passports—as inconveniences.

Though he did find it amusing that his Australian passport made it easier for him to travel in his home country than his German documents. That probably had more to do with the British military control of the railway than anything else. For one so heavily involved in geopolitics, it was enough to make the head spin.

Not so with von Honig. The political dynamics and schisms of the day meant very little to him, considering that the mysteries of the universe and the very beginnings of human existence were always just out of his reach. Just barely out of his reach, it seemed.

He had listened to all four of James Floyd's records front to back upon returning to his flat after his meeting with Charlie. He wouldn't pretend that it was necessarily his kind of music, but he enjoyed the chance to dust off his record player.

The first record, *Return to Earth*, had only six tracks, but they were long, sweeping arrangements with organic, swirling effects added to many of the instruments. Von Honig wasn't sure if the effects were added during the performance or if they were the result of some kind of studio wizardry. It didn't matter. The music was both sloppy and calculated at the same time. It felt like a live performance, which was quite impressive, considering that Floyd played every instrument. The body of work evolved from that first, joyful, album to the fourth, *Initiation*, which was cold, removed, paranoid. The arrangements became increasingly electronic as well. *Initiation* was, for the most part, all synthesizers with jagged guitar work layered over the top. Droning, nihilistic loops filled in the quieter spaces that the earlier organic records would have used as opportunities to build something louder and grander.

The music tracked an artistic evolution. Indeed, had von Honig merely listened to the first and fourth albums and nothing in between, he would have assumed they were the work of two different and very distinct artists. On the other hand, the evolution seemed natural across the span of all four records.

It was the lyrical content that he paid most attention to. It, too, showed evidence of an evolving psyche. The first record was joyful, reminiscent of the peace and love of the 1960s. It wasn't necessarily

The Age of Aquarius, but it was close. What was telling were the specific references to aliens throughout all of the recordings. On the first album, Floyd referred to them as benevolent gods. In the song "Building Pyramids," he sang:

> *"The Creators built us a world*
> *A place of finite love*
> *A mirror to the endlessness*
> *Of their cosmos beyond and above..."*

Calling them "creators" was positively Native American. It invoked mankind as caretakers of someone else's world. And perhaps, von Honig thought, he was right.

The third record is where the lyrics turned colder. Some were even paranoid, painting the aliens in a completely different light. On "Back from Exile (No Such Thing as Squatter's Rights)," Floyd's vocals were a sort of monotonous talk-singing:

> *"Architects*
> *Leave the void behind*
> *When they return,*
> *What will they find?"*

The song went on to posit that a returning civilization would find much to dislike with what man has done to this world. And again, von Honig noted that he himself had pondered such ideas.

The sense of paranoia ramped up considerably on the last record. A refrain howled over shrieking guitar in one song and muttered over a thudding beat in another was *"They can end us when they want..."* Apocalyptic musings were all over that one.

Von Honig couldn't help but think of colleagues in the fringes of archaeology and theoretical psychology or astronomy who bought into their own nonsense and took it overboard. They were the people who were inevitably dismissed as conspiracy theorists and "wackos." They were the ones with whom von Honig was often lumped together in some circles. While he maintained his commitment to scientific theory and a healthy dose of skepticism, he was certainly troubled by someone heading that way based on his own research. And it seemed that's what was happening with James Floyd.

~ ~ ~

After a tediously long wait while his passport was scrutinized when he got off the train, von Honig checked into his hotel and went walking through the neighborhood with his notepad in the brown leather satchel slung over his shoulder.

Despite being born there, he had only ever returned to Germany for his father's funeral. That was back in Stuttgart, of course, and was rather unpleasant for many reasons. Enough to strike it off the list of travel hotspots for him. He had never been to Berlin before, but that had more to do with global politics than a lack of desire. Having a research subject, though, afforded him the ability to check out the city, albeit on a shortened schedule. Glass reflected neon light right beside aged brick on street after street. It was a vibrant mix of old-world Europe and modern society, in an almost city-wide state of reconstruction. He imagined it would be in that state for a long time.

He arrived at Metropolis, the club where Floyd was scheduled to perform that night. There was no marquee, and the box office window was shuttered. It did not look like a venue that was set to open to a large concert in a few hours, but von Honig was anything but an expert in the protocols of the modern rock scene, so he supposed that the staff was milling around inside, stocking the bar and preparing to open the doors shortly before the show was set to start. There was no rush to these kind of things. Von Honig knew his fair share of touring musicians, and was at least aware that they tended to go on late.

He walked around the outer perimeter of the venue, noting an attractive young woman standing on the corner looking furtively back and forth down the sidewalk on either axis of the building's corner. She wore tight jeans and a long flowing top with hair flattened and falling straight down past her breasts.

As he approached her, von Honig noticed her eyes darting back and forth, even when she wasn't moving her head. He smiled quickly as he caught her eye and walked past her to look down the sidewalk.

"He's not here yet," she said with all the faux-authority a young person can muster when they believed they had knowledge another did not.

"Excuse me?"

"James Floyd," she said. "He only ever shows up right before his shows."

Von Honig nodded.

"You're a fan," he said to her. It was an observation more than a question.

"No," she said, her face turning deathly serious and her eyes still darting from side to side. "I'm his girlfriend. We're getting married, and when we do, we're going to take our place amongst the stars."

The almost angry look on her face turned to a serene smile as she looked to the sky. It was at that moment that von Honig clued in to the fact that her accent was American. How much trouble must this young woman have gone through to get to this place?

"What do you want with him?" she asked, her face again twisting into a righteous—even jealous—form of anger. She leaned forward, her long, lean body hunching down and looking as if she might spring forward like a jungle cat. Her teeth were bared.

This woman was clearly troubled, and von Honig didn't want to do anything to jeopardize the possibility of his meeting Floyd. Creating a scene in the streets was enough for police on edge from heightened security to take them both into custody. That would make a small interview with what could simply be a celebrity fan of von Honig's a whole lot of trouble for nothing.

"I only want to talk with him for a few minutes."

"Well," she stopped baring her teeth and scrunched up her face like she was smelling something unpleasant. "Beat it! Because he doesn't talk to losers like you."

At that, she turned and walked away, toward the front doors of the venue. As the wind picked up and billowed her long shirt, von Honig could see a black nub protruding from her closed fist: a knife handle.

He exhaled and turned to walk away. He occasionally lamented the diminishing popularity of his later books, worried he wouldn't have a large enough base to continue supporting his research. Still, he was very glad that he had yet to run into a fan of his as crazy as that young lady. But the night was young.

~ ~ ~

Though he generally liked to keep his head as clear as possible, von Honig needed a beer. As he sat sipping a crisp Pilsner on the sunny patio, his mind mulled over the events of the past few days: the grown daughter of his old mentor; Floyd and all his art implied; the crazy fan. It all pointed to something deep-seated in darkness.

While the fan had looked like a Summer of Love beauty, she turned out to be more like a member of the Manson family. Floyd went on a journey with von Honig's research that took him some place very cold and dark. Hell, even meeting Charlie Bolinger as a grown woman—whom he had last seen in pigtails and a child's funeral dress—made him suddenly feel very old.

After another beer and a belly full of sausages and fried potatoes, he felt a little better. It was already approaching eight o'clock. He paid the check and added a modest gratuity, then made his way back to the Metropolis. The doors would be opening soon, and he still didn't have a ticket.

When he was a block away, he could already hear the shouting. He knew enough German to know the issue was another crazed fan. As Conrad neared Metropolis, he could see the cause of the commotion. Heavy set with wild, stringy hair, the man lurched about in the middle of the street, apparently trying to make a beeline for the front door.

The titan of a security guard was making any forward momentum impossible for the fan by merely standing on the sidewalk with his arms crossed. The guard was tall and built like an upside down pyramid. The width of his shoulders and the narrow nature of his hips almost seemed to von Honig to be evidence of extraterrestrial life. His legs were planted on the cobblestone sidewalk like marble columns.

"I have a message for him! I need to see him!" The fan shouted in German.

"He is not taking visitors. You must leave."

"I bought a ticket! I have just as much right to be here as anybody else."

"The box office will refund you."

While the fan was clearly on edge and not in his right mind, he still had enough of his wits about him to know that pushing further with the security guard would not have ended well.

The fan stood in the street watching as the security guard turned and walked back to the club's entrance. The lineup to get inside began moving again. That was when von Honig approached the fan.

Only seconds ago, he had been raving loudly, but the man standing before von Honig now seemed broken. Tears welled in the corners of his eyes as he stared at the building's facade.

"I bought a ticket," he repeated quietly.

Von Honig wasn't sure whether the man was talking to him or to himself, but he saw it as an opportunity. He took a moment to conjure up the proper German words and spoke.

"My friend," he said, "I understand you need to talk to James Floyd."

Mentioning the name broke the man's concentration.

"I do."

"I do as well," von Honig continued. "Perhaps I can convince him to come and talk to you outside after the show."

A smile cracked the man's sad face, then quickly faded.

"Why would you do that for me?"

"Because you have a ticket that you cannot use, and I am without one."

Von Honig smiled and the man quickly dug the ticket from his pocket and held it out to him.

"You swear?"

"Yes, my friend. If I can talk with him, then I will ask him to give you a moment of his time."

The man nodded and thrust the ticket into the writer's open palm.

Von Honig felt a little bad as he smiled at the man reassuringly, but he had lied, cheated and stolen to further his research before. He had knocked people out, broken out of prison, seduced women and even set fire to a car to get closer to the truth. That was almost all to gain entry to secluded sites or protected areas to get glimpses of the planet's ancient–and possibly alien–origins. He had never done anything so drastic in order to meet a musician he didn't care for. Still, if Floyd turned out to be the flake that von Honig worried he might be, perhaps he would throw the fan a bone and sneak him in.

The club was unimpressive. Maybe it had been more luxurious in the cabaret era, but it had since fallen into disrepair. Dull brass railing shook loosely on the walls they were barely attached to and the once vibrant red carpet had faded to an almost neutral brown with well-worn runs exposing the even older granite floor beneath. Von Honig supposed old nightclubs and theatres made for good rock and roll venues, especially when the real estate is a steal.

An old concession stand in the lobby was now a bar, but von Honig walked right by. He had already had a few beers, after all. The doors opened into the venue itself and a ring of chairs surrounded a scuffed, wooden dance floor. At its center was a surprisingly small stage. People filed in and milled about, all of them talking with each other in animated fashion. Some were clearly excited enough to slosh and spill a few drops of their beer and spirits. Others who were less social quietly found places to watch the show. These people sat in solitude, not even looking around. If von Honig had believed in such things, he would certainly have said these people gave off negative auras–uninviting energy that kept others away. He respected that.

Though the triviality of attending these concerts religiously bothered him, Conrad understood why people whiled away their lives, living for these events. He just had a hard time rationalizing it on his own. To each their own, he supposed.

And with that, the lights dimmed and a hush fell over the crowd. In the dark, one could see men walk out from side stage: a drummer, a guitarist, a keyboard player, a bassist. The crowd cheered as they took the stage, then roared when the last man appeared: James Floyd.

The spotlight hit him the moment he stepped up to the microphone, and in that moment, von Honig was taken in. The stage looked much bigger in the dark, and, at its center was the giant, gaunt Floyd. A lanky enigma in a tight-fitting black suit who grabbed the microphone like it was the only thing he knew how to do.

"Welcome," he said as the crowd fell silent, "to the rite of return."

A wave of noise swept over the room. It was a mixture of the crowd clearly reacting to the thrum of a keyboard and bass at the beginning of a well-known, favorite song. Then, guitar and drums kicked in, and von Honig immediately recognized "Back from Exile," the song he had researched more than others, though he couldn't remember the parenthetical title. Cones of colored smoke appeared above the band as the lights came to full power.

"Coming," "New Religion," "Only the End Is Guaranteed," and "Tightened Collar" were some of the other songs he recognized. They were all heavily pulled from the later, darker material. And the music had that same abrasive, sharp edge that he'd found on the records, though live drums had replaced the electronic beats of those cold symphonies. Floyd and his band added a few songs from earlier albums here and there as well, but they were delivered with the newer, edgier sound. Most notably among these were "Building Pyramids," which Floyd sang with a cynical sneer. Impressively, half of the stage lights during that song shut off and the remaining three became brighter, turning the cones of colored smoke into what looked like pyramids on some distant mystical horizon.

Von Honig tore his eyes away from the stage to observe the crowd. The revelers, sloppy with their drinks, danced and screamed their appreciation. More amusingly, the anti-social ones bounced up and down, shouting along to the lyrics of the songs–quite accurately, von Honig noted.

Along with the music came a dizziness. He could feel the drumbeat in his chest, and the thrum of the bass guitar and low end of the keyboard in his knees, as if the sound was burrowing its way under the floor and coming back up to attack them all from below.

With that, von Honig decided to leave the show and plan his next move. He returned to the lobby and asked the young man behind the bar for water. The bartender lifted up a bottle of bubbly water and asked: "*Mit gas?*" Von Honig realized that the man was going to give him bottled water at an exorbitant price–something he wasn't accustomed to, thanks to his Australian upbringing–and waved it off.

"*Nein, danke,*" he said before pausing to think of the right words in German. Then he settled for English. "Just tap water, *bitte*." He got his water with a complimentary eye roll.

Ignoring the bartender, von Honig surveyed the lobby. It was remarkably empty, considering how many people were packed into the club, but he assumed no one wanted to miss their hero's performance. He strolled about, noting the two bathrooms off of a hallway on one side of the lobby, and on the other, a door that must have been a cleaning supply closet and a dark stairway leading upward. On a chain stretched across the banisters hung a sign that read "No Admittance" in German, English and French.

Von Honig recalled the alley on the back of the building having a double-steel door at street level and a metal staircase coming from a single steel door above. The double-steel door must have been for deliveries and moving equipment in and out of the club, while the upstairs *had* to be the dressing room.

Seeing that the bartender had turned his back to stock a cooler, von Honig decided to do some reconnaissance. He gingerly stepped over the chain that blocked the stairway and made his ascent. The hallway at the top was darker than the stairwell, and it felt even more ominous with the throbbing music in the theater below. It was still loud, humming through the floor, and the crowd sounded like they were still enjoying it. In fact, shouting and applause was now drowning out the music. It took a second for von Honig to realize the show was over as the music was no longer playing but the cheering continued.

With all the noise, he wouldn't have heard footsteps coming up behind him even if the flooring wasn't carpeted. Since it was, combined with the darkness, it was almost too perfect for being surprised from behind. Something sharp hit his lower back as an angry, albeit high-pitched voice shouted in his ear.

"I thought I told you to beat it!"

Von Honig spun around on his left leg quickly enough to see the Manson girl's thrust coming. It was aimed squarely at his belly, so he threw his hips back and the butcher's knife punched through and tore his shirt. He thought about attacking in that moment, but she was too quick.

Her arm arced toward him, threatening to plunge the tip of the blade into his neck. It was all he could do to get his forearm up in time. The blade cut into his shirt and sliced across his arm. It stung, but the alternative would have been far worse.

She was fast, but von Honig was much stronger. With his forearm still impeding her thrust, he pushed her backward into the wall of the hallway hard enough to bounce her head against the wall, but not hard enough to knock the knife from her hand.

She was tenacious, he had to give her that.

The girl kicked at him and stomped at his feet. It must have seemed an odd dance as he stepped and moved his legs and knees trying to dodge deflect and block her lower-body assault.

"He's...mine!" she shrieked.

"Men prefer women to be a...little...less...possessive!" von Honig countered, punctuating his words with another hard slam into the wall. However, it didn't have the momentum and strength of his earlier thrust, so she continued to hold onto the knife and began unintelligibly screaming in rage.

"*Halt!*"

The voice was heavy, bellowing from von Honig's right. Instinctively, both combatants slackened their holds on each other and turned to see a massive security guard. Von Honig had thought he looked large outside, but in this cramped hallway, he seemed gargantuan, cutting an imposing profile as the faint light from behind him silhouetted him to an almost pitch black.

Von Honig felt the girl's wrist tighten. In response, he renewed the pressure against her while the security guard ran toward them.

Realizing what was happening, the guard grabbed her wrist and twisted while squeezing. The knife fell, thudding against the carpet floor. She shook against him, and in the scuffle, managed to kick the knife down the stairway. The guard pulled her arm around her back and pushed her toward the stairs. The girl stumbled on the top two stairs, but grabbed a shaky railing and quickly steadied herself before descending into the lobby and out into the night.

"What the hell are you doing here?!" the security guard demanded of von Honig in heavily accented English.

Von Honig opened his mouth and paused. He had become quite good at lying in the course of his many years of research site subterfuge, but he was out of his element here. The wheels were turning, but the pregnant seconds of hesitation gave him away. Whatever he was about to say—if, indeed, he would ever be able to come up with something—would be a bold-faced lie.

The giant guard moved toward von Honig, who balled his fists and prepared to fight his way out. But he could tell that the guard was not only a massive meathead but also former military and clearly in top fighting shape.

"That will be all, Werner. Thank you."

The voice came from down the hall behind von Honig. He didn't want to turn away from the guard because the only thing worse than being punched is being sucker-punched. But Werner's face betrayed a desire to continue his attack, though he'd been politely but firmly ordered to stand down.

Von Honig spun to see James Floyd. Rather, he saw part of James Floyd. The rock star who only moments ago had strutted on stage like the consummate showman was now cutting a very different profile. He leaned against the door frame of the dressing room like it was the only thing keeping him from sliding to the floor.

"Thank you, Werner," he repeated.

Werner spun on his feet and walked down the stairs.

Von Honig held out his hand to introduce himself, but Floyd had other ideas. "Mr. von Honig," he said. "I was wondering when you might come find me. Come." With that, he disappeared into the dressing room.

The sweet, pungent smell of marijuana greeted von Honig at the threshold as he saw Floyd lighting a joint with one of many candles on the coffee table before collapsing into a large cushioned chair. He held the joint at his lips with one hand and gestured toward the loveseat to his right with the other.

Floyd toked off the joint and held it out, offering it to von Honig as he sat.

"No, thank you," the writer said, trying not to sound as disgusted as he actually was.

It was funny, von Honig thought, that he had witnessed primitive tribespeople in the Amazon partaking of their own leaf-derived mind-altering substances, and von Honig had looked on in fascination. Yet, here he was, judging Floyd for doing essentially the same thing. His own hypocrisy on the matter didn't escape him.

Von Honig's refusal of the joint made Floyd shrug, take another long drag and then stub it out on a shabby wooden side table.

"Wine!" Floyd barked shortly after groaning back in his chair. He swiveled quickly, grabbing a bottle off of the side table. He scanned quickly back and forth over the table longer than he should have, considering there was only a partially smoked joint, a lighter, some candles and a handful of change on it. Von Honig assumed the musician was looking for a glass. He also knew that there were a few glasses sitting on the counter of the kitchenette beside the steel door that must have led out onto the staircase to the alley. Not wanting to confuse things, von Honig politely stopped him before he looked elsewhere.

"It's fine, thank you. I don't drink," he said, "much."

Floyd swigged heavily from the bottle and put it back on the table beside him, nodding. He smiled, looking back at his guest and pointing.

"You're a smart man," he said, slurring the words at first. There was a calculated way about how he did it, though. Von Honig didn't think it was an act. It was almost as if it was a combination of the altered state and his mouth catching up to his rapidly firing brain. Von Honig could understand that, more or less. "It's why I like you."

Von Honig smiled his thanks.

"I'm enamored with your work," said Floyd. "But I suppose you know that already."

"That's why I'm here."

Von Honig watched Floyd. He knew only the two of them were in this room, but he was beginning to think that Floyd didn't know that. His eyes darted back and forth, constantly, barely resting on anything other than a shadowed corner for a moment. In those tiny pauses, von Honig thought he could see a micro-expression of fear in Floyd's face before he continued his skittish expressions.

"Is it?" Floyd asked.

"Beg your pardon?"

"They didn't…send you, did they?"

Von Honig saw the fear in his eyes again.

"They?" He knew that he couldn't push hard. As daunting a character Floyd was on the stage and on his records, it was clear that he maintained only a thin veneer of sanity. Pushing him for information could make him crack, or worse. "The government, James? Is that who you mean?"

He laughed, the fear escaping his face in a guffaw.

"Governments! What a concept. Let me ask you, Mr. von Honig–"

"Please, Conrad."

"Let me ask you, Conrad: has your government ever done anything for you?"

Von Honig thought for a second. He no longer resided in Australia, nor his country of birth. He barely lived in his flat in Paris. In many ways, he was a man without a country. He couldn't recall the last time he'd voted in an election. However, he certainly had gained the help of governments in his day through research grants and access to nationally recognized historic sites, for example. But von Honig knew he didn't want this conversation to turn into some sort of political argument.

"I suppose not, James."

"Tea!" He leapt from his chair and made his way over to the kitchenette. "Tea?" he offered.

"Tea would be lovely, thank you. Just black is fine."

"Coming up. They don't have milk in this dump, anyway."

Floyd filled a teapot in the sink and set it on the small stovetop. He collected cups from the counter and set about rinsing them out and pulling tea accessories out of drawers and a cabinet above.

"We vote for the person we hate the least—or who lies to us the best—to go to Parliament to represent us, but really all they do is try to rig the rules in their favor so that the coffers open up to them and their friends more than the voters who put them in that position in the first place."

The teapot shrieked at about the same moment von Honig realized he pretty much agreed with everything the stoned philosopher in the kitchenette was saying. The rattle of a spoon on the inside of the tea cup was accompanied by Floyd continuing his apolitical rant.

"Then we expect them to govern over us benevolently. Imagine that! Someone like that having *our* best interests in mind?"

He closed the distance between himself and von Honig in a few long steps, handing the writer his tea before sitting back down in his chair.

"We're gnats to them, Mr. von Honig. Gnats."

The two men sat in silence for a moment, sipping tea.

Von Honig looked expectantly across the coffee table. "Are you still talking about the government, James?"

Floyd chuckled and looked away.

"You think I'm a madman," Floyd said. "You think I'm some

sort of junkie fan who went off the deep end reading your books too many times."

"I would be lying if I said at least part of me didn't think that," von Honig offered.

"But you're here."

"Yes, I'm here."

"You're here because of the album covers? Is that it?"

"They're awfully close to the pictures in my books."

"Those detailed paintings on the covers of my albums are something other than 'awfully close' to the grainy black and white photos in a 70p paperback! What about the colors? What about the site that isn't in one of your books yet?"

"That's why I'm here," von Honig conceded. He thought of the covers and, more specifically, the large carved throne in the middle of a war-torn Majavacan cave. It was a chamber for giants from beyond the stars, now buried inside a mountain. To add to all that, as far as von Honig was concerned, the only two people alive who had seen it were him and an exotic beauty who spoke a language he couldn't understand. James Floyd may have been a well-traveled and curious fellow, but von Honig was certain that Floyd had never been to the places he himself had been.

"I saw them," said Floyd, finishing the last of his tea.

Von Honig was halfway through a long gulp of his own tea, finally cooled to the point where he could drink it without burning himself. He noted the odd aftertaste and put the cup down on the coffee table. The good thing about very hot tea, he supposed, was that it was not as easy to taste the intricacies of the flavor. That tea was awful. Then again, the man who made it was clearly in some sort of drug-induced psychosis, so he shouldn't have been surprised.

"What did you see, James?"

"The sites. I saw them all. And more!"

"More?"

"Yes," Floyd said with a smile. He licked his teeth and laid back in his chair. "I've seen things you've never seen. Maybe things you'll never see."

Von Honig noted fresh beads of sweat on his upper lip and forehead. He was puzzled for a moment, as the room was not hot. It was stuffy, as there were no windows, but the temperature was not a problem. He cleared his throat and sat forward, with his elbows on his knees.

"James, you asked earlier if 'they' sent me. Who were you referring to?" Von Honig opened his heavy-lidded eyes wide and blinked a few times. He was suddenly feeling very tired.

"The Architects, Conrad. You better than anyone else should know who I was referring to. The star men. You'll excuse my earlier paranoia. It comes and goes, especially if I am not properly medicated. And I prefer to hold the sole responsibility for my own medication. Again, the paranoia."

The sweat turned cold on von Honig's face as his vision blurred and stomach drew into a tightened knot. He groaned.

"What...what was in the tea, James?"

"It's cool, Conrad. It was just mushroom tea. Psilocybin mushrooms. A blend of several types, actually. My own powerful concoction."

"You...poisoned me?"

"Oh, don't be so dramatic, Conrad. You are so cool and analytical. You visit exotic locales the world over, meeting with people of all cultures, but I'm willing to bet you never once took part in any kind of cultural communion with those people to help you really see. Not much of a social animal, are you? Well, man is a social animal, and have been experiencing all kinds of trips–inner and outer–as a tribe, together, since we started walking on two feet. If I went to China, Egypt, Mexico, the Amazon–hell, even North Dakota–I would be damn sure to sit down with the native people there and partake in any ritual they provided that would help me experience the visions they had to offer in a little more heightened manner. Peyote, mushrooms, ayahuasca–these are all things given to us by the same beings who created us, and I think that they were given to us so that we could experience reality the way that they do."

Von Honig struggled to his feet.

"Conrad, you came to see," said Floyd. "So, open your eyes."

For von Honig, Floyd's voice deepened and disappeared down a long wind tunnel. His stomach tightened further and the few lights in the room arced across his vision as he turned his head. He tried to blink his sight back to normal again and made his way toward Floyd, who lounged in his chair like he was just settling in to watch a movie.

Conrad, Floyd's voice boomed to him from somewhere down the tunnel, though the man who it belonged to sat right in front of him. *I apologize, but you have to understand. You came for answers, and I didn't want to disappoint you. Relax. Let it all happen.*

Von Honig wasn't sure why, but he decided to take a deep breath and do as Floyd said. While he didn't appreciate being dosed with hallucinogens in the slightest, he had enough wits about him to know that it was far too late to do anything about it. Perhaps he would find answers. Curiosity got the better of Conrad von Honig once again.

He wasn't sure if his body was swaying, but it certainly felt that way. Or perhaps the room was moving. He didn't know. He laughed about it, wondering how solid his answers could be during this trip if he couldn't verify the simple answer to that.

For our safety, we won't leave the room, Floyd continued. *But our consciousness, our higher mind, can go anywhere. Everywhere.*

The shadows dancing on the walls of the room seemed out of sync with the candles that threw them. As von Honig drew long, deep breaths, he slowed his increasing heart rate. Still, he was able to see that Floyd's face, when he spoke, contorted unnaturally. It was as if awkward facial movements were a sort of strange vocal projection, rather than simply pushing air through vocal cords and moving one's mouth and tongue–although that was essentially the same thing. Every thought came to him as a revelation, and every sight something fear or marvel at.

We are intrepid travelers, Conrad. Regular people, like sheep, flee what they do not understand. You and I, we run toward it to gain that understanding. In this case, we seek the stars.

Von Honig's body temperature was escalating. He was sweating profusely and panting. Tracers swam in his vision as he felt a rapid vibration behind his eyes.

Though he could barely focus his vision, he took off in the direction of the back wall of the dressing room and ran into the door. Fumbling with the handle and finding it locked, he turned the deadlock and threw the door open. The cool night air blasted his face as he tumbled out onto the steel landing of the staircase.

Lying on his back, von Honig peered up at the clear sky, the stars a billion pinpricks, glowing sharply and clearly. He heard a drone, like the synthesizer music from Floyd's last record, menacing and grating. Some of the stars were eclipsed by dark shapes that came into view.

Something was falling.

Von Honig pushed himself to his elbows as he looked up and saw hundreds of bodies plummet to the earth. He couldn't tell at first, but, as they fell past him, time slowed down to the point where he could see they were human. Their faces did not show terror. Instead, their expressions evoked...boredom. The bodies crashed onto the cobblestone road below, making only dull, wet thuds.

Backing into the dressing room, von Honig screamed as another crashed into the steel landing. A dull ringing clang broke the synthesized drone and the room fell into silence.

I told you not to go outside, Floyd said. This time his voice was so deep and clear it felt to von Honig as though it was inside his head. *I thought you might not be able to handle it. I was right.*

"But–"

One need not see the stars to travel there.

"Those people. Falling from the sky."

Afraid of what the stars held for them, Conrad. Cowards whose brains are simply not ready for the true majesty of this universe and all its unknown history. Content in their politics and their wars and their sports and their sexual conquests, never seeking truth, only distraction.

Von Honig's stomach roiled.

The door to the stairwell slammed shut, plunging the room into candlelight once again.

Von Honig looked at the walls. He saw pyramids shadowed there–Egyptian, Mayan, Aztec, Cambodian and even Mesopotamian. Others he didn't recognize. His perception of the pyramids swung outward and he could see tiny dots of light, like stars in the sky poking through the darkness on the wall. It took him only a fraction of a second–or maybe it was much longer, for time had become elastic and immeasurable to him in this state–to realize he was looking down on those points of light that represented the pyramids. If it was indeed a flattened representation of the earth, the unrecognizable ones would be placed in Arctic Canada and Antarctica. Or if it was meant to represent the globe and he could see through it, then one of the points would be in Siberia or the Northern Atlantic. Or maybe it was both. He was in a strange psychic place, not in a state between enlightenment and ignorance but a place where the two were equal.

They're coming back, Conrad. I don't know what the map on the wall means, but I can tell you that they do. The grand experiment has reached its conclusion. They will return to us as men to an anthill.

Von Honig looked at Floyd, but he still couldn't make out his face, the twitching blur making it difficult to even keep his eyes on him.

"Why?" It was all von Honig could muster, having much of his thought process devoted to trying to take in all of the stimuli being presented to him.

Look at us, Conrad. Petty squabbles based on political ideologies. Inventions of man and nothing more. We use them to eradicate each other by the millions. It's all we have ever done since we crawled out of the primordial ooze. The only certain change is that we have gotten so much better at it. We've used it to destroy each other and this world they left us.

No one can say for certain why they are returning, but it is safe to say that they will not be impressed when they get here.

Von Honig turned away to look at the wall again, the candlelight flickering where the star map coordinates once projected. His head swam and his stomach roiled again.

Dropping to his knees, he held steady to one of the arms of the loveseat and squeezed his eyes shut to stop the room from spinning. With darkness bringing peace to his eyes and Floyd's deepened voice no longer ringing in his ears, sleep finally took him.

~ ~ ~

Von Honig awoke groggily with a heavy groan. He ran his tongue along the back of his teeth, tasting the putrid remnants of vomit just before putting his hand down into a puddle of it on the floor. He was sitting up against the couch on the floor, his bottom sore from being there so long.

He looked around but saw no sign of Floyd. The room was still lit by candles, though they were burned down to tiny nubs and would soon snuff themselves out.

Like the men falling from the sky, von Honig thought.

Then the flood of memories came at him mercilessly. A night of unintended misdeeds forgotten in the haze of the waking brain. The implications of what he'd seen–or rather, what he'd experienced–the night before ran through his mind as he pushed himself to his feet. He opened the dressing room door and found the hallway outside empty, but lit both by overhead lights and early morning sunlight from the large windowed facade at the bottom of the stairs.

Fearing setting off an alarm in an empty nightclub or running into someone with dried vomitus on his chin, von Honig went to the sink in the dressing room and splashed water on his face. He wiped his face on a hand towel and opened the steel door to the landing.

Every rational atom in his body knew he wouldn't see the corpse of one of the fallen men on the landing, or the street littered with the bodies of the dead, but a part of him, however small or irrational, still expected it. Instead, all that greeted him was the gentle morning light. He sighed in relief and made his way down to the street.

Once his circulation improved, he felt a short but sharp headache coming on. It did not surprise von Honig in the slightest. Other than the occasional beer or after-dinner liqueur, he generally kept his temple clean. After a copious dose of poisonous mushrooms, a headache was a small price to pay.

As he turned around on the middle landing of the staircase, he saw the security guard at the bottom, lighting a cigarette.

"Werner?" von Honig asked, unsure of whether he was getting the name right.

"*Ja?*"

"Have you seen Floyd?"

"He left a while ago," he said in the same heavily-accented English as before. "To continue the tour. Paris and then United Kingdom, I believe."

Von Honig chuckled. Werner looked at him, dragging on his cigarette, clearly puzzled by his laugh.

"I came here from Paris," he said. "To see him."

"Ah, *ja*," he said, exhaling. "Is difficult to get here."

Von Honig nodded his agreement and surveyed the empty street. It was still very early. Five a.m., maybe earlier.

"Well, good day."

Von Honig waved as he made his way right, around the corner toward his hotel. He saw, at first, what he thought was a vagrant of some kind sitting up against the wall in the street. It was an uncommon sight. While the West German government had its issues to deal with, their treatment of the poor was certainly better than in France.

The man rasped as he breathed. The closer von Honig got, the easier it was to see that the huddled figure was the fan who had given him his ticket the night before. He immediately felt bad, but he felt worse when he noticed that the fan was clutching a bloody spot on the front of his shirt, near the bottom of his rib cage.

"Are you alright?" von Honig asked, scrambling to his knees beside the wounded man. His face was ghostly pale and sweat streamed down his face.

"Was it good?" asked the destitute man.

"I beg your pardon?"

"The performance. Was it good?"

"Uh…yes," von Honig replied. He didn't particularly care for the music, but decided that it wasn't important at the moment.

"And did you get to talk to him?"

"I did," von Honig said after a moment of hesitation. He felt even worse now than when he'd first seen him, but he decided that no man should be lied to just before he dies. "I'm sorry," he added.

"It is okay," the fan said before gasping for a small harrowed breath. "This happened to me moments before I watched him leave. Regardless of whether or not he would have spoken to me, she already decided I was unworthy of his presence."

"She?" von Honig asked. The fan looked up at him—and ultimately beyond him. His body lost all rigidity as he breathed his last.

"I must apologize," the girl's voice was close.

When the fan had looked past von Honig, he thought the destitute figure was simply shuffling off this mortal coil. The girl's voice startled him, but the accent told him it was the crazy American girl with the knife. He spun around on his squatting legs to look at her. He did so with his hands up.

"Apologize to me for trying to kill me or to him for succeeding?" von Honig asked as he slowly rose to his feet.

"To you," she said flatly, seemingly not disturbed by the victim at von Honig's feet or by the fact that she still held the bloodied murder weapon, albeit loosely and non-threateningly. As non-threateningly as one can hold a bloodied knife, that is.

"Make it quick, then," von Honig said gruffly, "I have a long train ride ahead of me and only a headache to keep me company."

"I didn't know who you were at first," she said reaching behind her.

Von Honig dropped into a defensive stance, but rather than pulling a more dangerous weapon than the one she held in her hand, the girl produced what one of von Honig's old history professors would refer to as the most dangerous weapon of all: a book. This specific book was a dog-eared and yellowed copy of *The Space Gods Revealed*.

"You're one of James Floyd's acolytes," she said, pointing to von Honig's name on the cover.

Though his pride itched at him, von Honig decided not to disagree with the crazy lady holding the bloody knife. He simply kept a straight face and did not answer her.

"He would only ever give so much time to someone in his inner circle," she said. "I see that you are one of us now."

Von Honig had to refrain from laughing in the deluded woman's face. *One of us?* he thought. *Lady, you know James Floyd about as well as I did yesterday afternoon.*

"Will you sign it for me?" she asked, a pleading in her voice.

Just when von Honig thought the last twenty-four hours couldn't get any more surreal, this happened.

"You'll excuse me if I refuse," von Honig said, nodding down at the hand holding the book.

The girl turned the book over in her hand and realized that the bloodied hand holding the bloodied knife was holding the book out toward him.

"Oh, right..." she said, embarrassed. "Another time, then?"

"Another time," von Honig lied.

When it seemed as if she had run out of reasons to speak, von Honig spun on his heels and walked briskly away. He had a train to catch, but first a shower and a two-hour nap back at his hotel to try to rid himself of his headache.

As he walked, he thought about this unique experience in his career. He replayed the images he'd witnessed the night before and the man with whom he'd witnessed them. While many fantastical things had occurred, they were all within the framework of being under the influence of strong hallucinogens.

The fact that Floyd seemed to have witnessed von Honig's visions without von Honig actually expressing them was somewhat troubling. But von Honig's skepticism borne of years of research and critical thinking told him that, while Floyd appeared to be in the room with him, it was clear that he never saw or heard Floyd's speak the words. And given the amount of hallucinogenic compound rushing through his system, he very well could have imagined the words in his head. He couldn't even be sure that Floyd was in the room with him for most of his experience. He was aware that there was some discrepancy in his ability to perceive the passage of time as well.

While intriguing, there was very little basis of reality he could definitively ascribe to the whole experience other than an interesting experiment in psychonautics.

Von Honig sighed as he approached the hotel, but he was not disheartened. If there was one constant in his life that made this experience like all the others, it was that he would be walking away with more questions than answers.

BLOOD OF THE HUMMINGBIRD

by Frank Schildiner

Conrad von Honig ducked the clumsy punch aimed for his head. He fired a quick left-right combo into his attacker's gut. The adversary, an emaciated, hairy, foul-smelling college drop-out named Dean Butters, collapsed to the ground, gasping and wheezing. He was the closest this group had to a guard, which didn't say much about this so-called terrorist cell.

The effect of Butters' presence was two-fold. Von Honig was momentarily halted, and those climbing the steps were nearing the top. Three figures—a tall rangy youth, a large heavy-set man, and a slightly built woman in a green outfit—were barely visible at the summit of the legendary pyramid. This was bad. If his theory was correct, Dr. Oscar Harms was up to no good. Blood would spill, unless von Honig could interrupt their terrible rites.

Breathing deeply, he stepped over Butters' fallen, groaning form and made his way onto the steep stone stairs that lead up to the sky. One step down, ninety more to go. A life, possibly many, were in the balance. He had to hurry, which was never a good plan when striding up the side of a pyramid.

Why was he, Conrad von Honig, striding as fast as he dared up the side of the legendary Temple of Kukulcan in Chichen Itza,

Mexico? The story was long, but could be summed up with one name: Lana Tan.

Everyone who even glanced at the society page knew the name of Lana Tan. She was the daughter of Gus Tan, the banker who had bought out a flagging film studio years earlier and brought it back to the top. Since then, Gus Tan reinvested and expanded his billion-dollar fortune into television stations, radio networks, and dozens of other businesses.

Lana, a large-eyed, waif-like figure, lived the life of a modern American princess. Anything she wanted was hers. She drove the newest sports cars, wore the softest mink and sable furs, appeared at the hottest nightspots around the world. Lana Tan's world was the stuff of dreams, a bacchanalian delight where even the greatest wishes were granted with the simple stroke of the pen on a check.

Which was why the kidnapping was such a surprise. Girls like Lana Tan did not just get grabbed and ransomed in the United States of America. That just wasn't done, not when said heiress' father was golfing partners with J. Edgar Hoover and regularly appeared as a consultant to the President. Yet this event not only happened, but it tied into the mysterious package von Honig had found on his doorstep days earlier.

"Forty-five steps complete," von Honig thought. "Forty-six remaining." He spotted the heavy frame of Oscar Harms, seated on a stair, leaning forward. They were taking a break up above. This was good. It gave the young archaeologist a small chance to make up lost time.

Conrad kept an eye on his climb, the harsh angle which made Chichen Itza so legendary. This step pyramid, built by the Mayans in honor of Kukulcan, the feathered serpent god, was one of the legendary location of pre-Columbian civilization. Incredibly advanced, even by modern engineering standards, this structure was a towering monument in a complex of uncanny structures. Also found in the surrounding complex were the Temple of Chac Mool, the Temple of the Thousand Warriors, and the Playing Field of the Prisoners. All made using stone age technology.

Normally, von Honig would spend hours marveling at the incredible sites in this holy site. There were places in the world that were special, just walking the grounds made one feel as if one were in the presence of power. He had experienced this feeling several times, having traveled extensively throughout the world in search of such locations. He'd felt similar power inside the Great Pyramid of Cheops, Stonehenge, the Great Serpent Mound of Ohio, Angkor Wat, and dozens of other locations. Chichen Itza possessed that same majesty, forcing visitors to behave with reverence despite themselves.

Sadly, von Honig was unable to take in the sights. He needed to prevent Oscar Harms from the madness which appeared to have taken root in his mind and heart. For the man was truly insane. His academic mind was now lost in a convoluted labyrinth of crazed beliefs based upon his personal views of the true origins of Mesoamerican religion.

Von Honig was about to lift his leg and step up when a hand encircled his ankle. Dean Butters, his bloodshot eyes shining in the twilight, giggled and yanked. He was weak, a bony scarecrow of a man. But von Honig's precarious position upon the huge stone steps rendered that unimportant.

"Going to toss you down the stairs, pig," Butters said, his voice a high-pitched screech. "Watch your head break open and all the pork fall out." He tugged and cackled, resembling a dark creature of folk tales instead of a son of a wealthy supermarket chain owner.

"Let me go!" von Honig snarled, grabbing for the step above. Another jerk upon his leg caused him to tip slightly. Leaning forward, he managed to right himself for the moment. The insistent pull was keeping the upper step out of reach, putting von Honig's in a position as dangerous as that of a tightrope walker.

"No way, man. Time for all white pig oppressors to die!" Butters reached both hands up, his crazed mind adding strength to his mission.

Von Honig shook left, right and backwards. Then all balance was lost and he began to fall. And it was a long way down...

How did Lana Tan and her kidnapping lead Conrad von Honig, researcher and writer of ancient mysteries, to this precarious spot? As he tilted towards the edge, that moment between life and death, he remembered the first part. He recalled it in less than a heartbeat's time, yet the clarity of the image was startling.

It was a mere two weeks ago when the knock on the door shook him from a doze. Von Honig, seated in the study behind a mound of books, nearly fell from his chair in shock. The thrum-thrum-thrum of a heavy hand upon the distant wooden portal was a surprise, to say the least.

Rising, von Honig shook off the drowsiness which afflicted him since coming to stay at this house. This place was not his home, not even close. No, this was the Hollywood Hills home of a good friend who had bought it from Alan Swann, the deceased actor who had succumbed to alcoholism in his later years. According to von Honig's friend, the current owner of the house, the place had required heavy fumigation to mitigate the effects of alcohol fumes and soiled cheap cotton panties. Apparently, the late film swashbuckler was a notorious ladies' man—on a par with such hedonistic wild men as Errol Flynn, Jonathan Lord, and Neville Sinclair. If a tenth of the tales were true, the house probably could have used an exorcist too.

More importantly, the Hollywood Hills home was secluded and hidden behind a wall of thick, high hedges. Add to that neighbors who only spoke to people through their agents or lawyers, and this was the perfect location for von Honig to reside. He needed contemplate his next investigation, his next work about the hidden history of the world. His books, though controversial, were well-researched. He studiously avoided the errors in history, linguistic interpretations, or scientific details. Such failures on the part of other writers tested the credibility of the theories, allowing the skeptics to dismiss the larger implications.

Therefore, the knock was a surprise, probably not a welcome one. As a guest, one who spent most of his time reading and swimming in the backyard pool, von Honig was not prepared for a prolonged conversation with a crazed resident's representative. According to tales from his friend, the lawyers tended to behave like gangsters out of the Capone era. The agents were worse—fast-talking hucksters burying listeners under a spit-storm of barely comprehensible words.

"Who is it?" von Honig asked, hoping he could keep a layer of wood between himself and the barrage of words. If the scene became unbearable, he could always simply walk away and call the police. They might respond…or not…

His question was met with silence, which forced him to sigh and repeat it more loudly. Sadly, no sound returned through the door. Von Honig closed his eyes and counted to ten, steeling himself for the possible nastiness to follow. He really didn't need this distraction. The search for a new direction for his research had proven elusive over the past month.

Opening the door, von Honig blinked as the bright sunshine momentarily blinded his vision. Oddly enough, the doorstep was vacant. Nor was anyone visible in the distant walk heading to the street. Even the driveway was empty of all cars, von Honig's own vehicle was entombed in the massive four-car garage.

He was about to close the door when a brown parcel on the edge of the second step leading to the door caught his eye. Stepping out, he picked up the rectangular box, surprised to see "Conrad von Honig" written on a large white packing label. While the box had some heft, he didn't consider it heavy.

Intrigued in spite of himself, von Honig returned to the study. Clearing the desk of his books and many sheaths of notes, he opened the box with a letter opener. Not surprisingly, the contents appeared to be papers. Fortunately, none appeared from his cursory review to be a writ or legal notice. Even a writer of esoterica such as von Honig suffered through such occasional indignities.

The first page was an article cut from the *The Los Angeles Tribune*, a familiar headline he'd read weeks earlier. The infamous kidnapping of Lana Tan by a group calling themselves the Peasants' Freedom

Revolutionary Alliance for a Free Future. Lana Tan, heiress and party girl, was last seen in the company of her occasional boyfriend, Jocko McGee, an Australian lifeguard and rumored drug dealer who was also missing and considered a suspect in the kidnapping.

The next article was the follow-up that had run in the paper a week later. Gus Tan had received the ransom demands in the form of a tape recording. The garbled mass of ambient sounds and voices in the background of the recording rendered Lana's shakily read statement unclear. After a long diatribe about inequality and the alleged evils of the capitalist establishment, little of which made any actual sense, the demands were simple: the delivery of two tractor trailers filled with food and clothing to the worst neighborhood in Los Angeles, along with fifty-thousand dollars in unmarked twenty-dollar bills.

Gus Tan—a businessman famous for paying near-starvation wages to writers, actors and directors—paid up immediately. In fact, he sent two trucks to every poor district in the L.A. County area. The funds were, according to rumor, delivered by a professional go-between named St. Ives.

Yet Lana Tan remained missing. She had not been returned to the loving arms of her father and her fifth stepmother, who was also her former classmate in school. Jocko McGee also remained at large, and no trace could be discovered of the Peasants' Freedom Revolutionary Alliance for a Free Future. The only article about this group questioned whether it even existed at all.

Skimming the articles over his morning coffee, von Honig remembered reading them as they had been published over the course of the previous weeks. Odd, but such situations did occur. In his opinion, the only reason this crime was noteworthy was because Lana Tan was famous for her vapid lifestyle. Had she been the daughter of a butcher, her name would likely have never seen print.

Reaching into a box within the package, von Honig discovered a thick treatise with a copy of the first article attached. The sender underlined the statements about the recording, mentioning the odd garbled sounds making Lana Tan's statements difficult to hear. A large question mark had been scrawled across the article, along with an arrow pointing towards the title of the thesis.

"Some Considerations of Nahuatl, the Aztec Language" was the title of the work. A second essay was attached to that with a similar title, "Some Considerations of Quechua, the Incan Language." Both were written by a man named Oscar Harms, Ph.D., a graduate of Barnett College.

The garbled words, von Honig mused and reached for the telephone. *Could it be?* He knew a nice woman, a writer who worked for a local television station. Possibly she could supply him with a copy of the audio feed. With these treatises, perhaps there was a clue about where Lana Tan was located and why she had been kidnapped.

Not to mention why this was sent to me, von Honig thought as he dialed Emily Cowles, the TV news writer. *I'm not exactly a detective. Still, there does appear to be a reason behind this package. The Aztec and Incan information is intriguing.* He waited for a connection on the line and hoped his friend could be helpful.

~ ~ ~

Von Honig was about to plummet downward, when he suddenly turned and leaned his body back towards the pyramid's steps. Tucking his chin, he crashed on his rear end on the edge of the stair. He fell backward, almost slamming his skull on the hard rock wall. He knew he would be very bruised in the morning, but at least he was alive, for the moment. Dean Butters was still yanking upon his leg, trying to drag his fallen body down again.

"Going to kill you, piggie!" Butters howled, still giggling like a maniac. "Time to die, establishment man!"

Angered because of his brush with death at the hands of this drug-crazed fool, von Honig lashed out. Lifting his free leg, he kicked Butters in the face with his heavy hiking boot, smashing the thin lips. Butters moaned and collapsed, crumpling on the stone stairs and whimpering with pain. He sounded as if he was about to start weeping.

Breathing deeply, von Honig backed up and stood, keeping an eye on his fallen foe. It was only when he rose three more steps that he dared to look towards the top. Oscar Harms, Jocko McGee, and Lana Tan arrived at the top. They were heading into the small temple on the summit. There wouldn't be much time.

Von Honig picked up his speed slightly, still wary of falling. He didn't want to tempt fate a second time, but lives were at stake. He had a feeling the rites about to take place above would be short but lethal. There was no time to waste.

As he ascended, he heard a *basso profundo* intonation mingling with a softer, more tentative sound. The voices were speaking an odd-sounding guttural tone, one von Honig recognized as a form of Nahuatl. The sounds were very different from any other language, a stream of syllables that were unique to the ears and quite unmistakable. The voices grew louder as von Honig approached, but he was unable to comprehend the words.

Von Honig stepped onto the summit of the pyramid, spotting the three figures in the enclosed stone temple of the ancient, almost forgotten deity known as Kukulkan.

It was then that von Honig realized a true oddity he'd missed earlier. Lana, Harms and McGee were all praying in Nahuatl, the language of the Aztec. But this pyramid was built by the Maya, a different people who spoke their own language. He found it all very odd. What was going on here?

Stepping toward the chamber, von Honig watched as McGee lay upon the stone altar and exhaled loudly. Harms, dressed in a shining white robe with a feathered headdress, pulled a long obsidian blade from his sleeve. The blade was half-moon in shape and looked both ancient and wickedly deadly. He lifted it above his head and waved it in a swift circle.

"*Huitzilopochtli ticana naxca tlamictizque,*" Harms intoned. "*Nitlanahuati ne naxca monemac.*" His voice grew deeper and more resonant with each word.

Then he plunged the polished obsidian into McGee's chest. The Australian lifeguard and drug dealer moaned softly, going limp as a crimson shroud of blood spilled across his tanned chest. The sparse golden hairs across his torso were instantly bathed in the viscous red fluid.

Lana Tan stood by McGee's side, her eyes staring down at his prone form. She was almost unmoving, save for her plump lips moving slowly as she continued to pray in Nahuatl. She was dressed in an odd costume, a jade skirt with a loose green top and a headdress covered in jade stones.

"No, stop!" von Honig shouted, rushing forward. He pushed Harms aside and reached for McGee. The young man was barely breathing, his eyes closing and his body quivering slightly with pain. Von Honig was about to reach for the knife, when a hard arm encircled his throat. McGee exhaled again and fell limp as the arm around von Honig's neck squeezed hard and cut off his air…

~ ~ ~

Emily Cowles had delivered the tape personally, having decided that her career as a writer for television was coming to an end soon. It didn't matter that she was earning decent money producing copy for the anchors. Her interests were elsewhere.

"Conrad, dear, I find the daily toil of crime and silly garden party stories to be a strain," she lamented, already sounding older than her years. "A cousin of mine is about to retire from writing advice columns and crossword puzzles. I will take her place and move to Chicago to work for a small wire service. In the meantime, good luck with your next book, dear." If she sounded older, she also sounded very content with the idea of a quieter life. Von Honig wished her good luck on her future course, hoping her co-workers would appreciate the kind woman.

The tape, a third-generation copy, was cleaned up by one of the TV station's audio experts. The background noise wasn't easy to decipher, not having been the focus of the efforts of the newspaper employee. Fortunately, the friend at whose house von Honig was staying possessed an advanced sound system, complete with a tape machine and earphones.

The examination was slow, but thanks to painstaking care and the use of the two works by Oscar Harms, words in Nahuatl and the Incan language of Quechua emerged in the background. Each one was disjointed, but he could comprehend the actual meaning.

The first word was "Quetzalcoatl," which roughly translated to "feathered serpent." This name was that of a god of the Aztecs—a creator god, to be specific. He was also known as Kukulkan to the Mayans, and was one of the most important religious figures in Central America.

The second word was "Huitzilopochtli," another Aztec god. Huitzilopochtli was one of the most important figures in Aztec mythology. His name translated to "hummingbird," and the Aztecs sacrificed humans in his name. A greedy god who held back the infinite night of chaos, Huitzilopochtli was revered by the warlike tribe as the driving force that would defeat all enemies that would stand in the way of the Aztecs' rise to power.

The third word was in Quechua, and it required several hours of listening and researching to understand. The word was "Siwar Q'enti," which also meant "hummingbird." Von Honig found it odd to hear the word in two different languages, but there it was on the tape. This development confused him. Yes, the hummingbird was a symbol in multiple cultures in Central and South America, but that didn't explain why someone was muttering the word in two nearly lost languages on a tape ransoming a kidnapped heiress. There were a great many confusing aspects to this situation, and von Honig was getting ready to give up, wondering if it was a prank of some type.

That was until he heard the final ancient word. This one was easy to understand by any archaeologist. The word was "Nazca," and von Honig knew that South American word as one of the great mysteries of the world. Now the archaeologist knew he was on the edge of a fascinating story, one that might save a life and give him a new book to write.

Nazca was a town and a desert in southern Peru. It had been the site of a now-extinct tribe of the same name. The desert itself is a low-lying territory of plateaus and valleys, a unique location in the world. However, the topography itself was not especially fascinating to those around the globe. The feature that attracted flocks of academics to this corner of South America were the legendary Nazca Lines.

The Nazca Lines are a series of enormous ancient geoglyphs etched into the land. Created between tfifteen-hundred and two-thousand years ago, they were marvels of the stone-age world. The engravings were an impressive sight to view, between fifty and twelve-hundred feet in length and only viewable from a great height. The etchings consisted of hundreds of straight lines and geometric patterns, but those were largely ignored by archaeologists and historians. The lines that received far more attention consisted of more than sixty engravings of animals and plants.

Pulling out a book by one of his teachers—noted archaeologist Jean Kariven—von Honig carefully searched for the section on the Nazca Lines. The chapter was extensively researched, with multiple theories presented in the French scientist's legendary sardonic style. Von Honig read the work multiple times and wasn't looking for a refresher course on the many reasons these ancient objects existed. He sought the pictures, taken from a plane with a powerful camera.

Finding the photographs, he took a moment to marvel at the impressive work by these unknown prehistoric people. The hicroglyphs had been etched in the shapes reflecting much of what the early artists observed in the natural world: a condor, a monkey, a tree, a pelican, a whale, a dog. When he reached the last page, von Honig exhaled deeply. The etching was that of a hummingbird in flight.

"This is so uncanny," he said to himself as he stood. Then he noticed the box was not empty...

~ ~ ~

Von Honig fell backwards, yanked off his feet for the second time in the last fifteen minutes. The heavy arm squeezing his neck belonged to Oscar Harms, the discredited archaeologist and mastermind behind these bizarre events. Von Honig caught the tangy scent of perspiration mixed with Old Spice cologne. The blinding white robe that covered his bloated body covered part of von Honig's face, a satiny muffler that added to his difficulty in breathing.

An odd thought crossed his mind as he struggled to free his windpipe: *This robe was made from a bedsheet. One was listed as missing when Lana Tan vanished.*

The kidnapping victim in question stepped forward, her movements slow and similar to those of a sleepwalker. She appeared disinterested, or possibly even unaware of the struggling pair at the other end of the tiny temple. Her eyes barely blinked, her breath was slow and her moist lips continued to whisper words in Nahuatl. That alone was as odd as the rest of the situation. Lana Tan, while wealthy and attractive, was believed to be close to illiterate.

Yet there she was, speaking Nahuatl as if she were a native of the ruined city of Tenochtitlan. It was well known among linguistic experts that Nahuatl was one of the most difficult languages to learn and speak, yet somehow Lana was now a better speaker than modern descendants of the scattered Aztec tribes.

She repeated the ominous phrases in an urgent whisper: "*Huitzilopochtli ticana naxca tlamictizque. Nitlanahuati ne naxca monemac. Huitzilopochtli ticana naxca tlamictizque. Nitlanahuati ne naxca monemac.*" Lana slowly approached the corpse of her sometime lover, Jocko McGee.

Seeing darkness on the edge of his vision, von Honig knew he didn't have much time before Harms would strangle him to death. Lifting both arms up, he slammed his elbows backward into Harms' bloated belly. The former academic wheezed and loosened his grip, allowing von Honig a chance to gulp in some much-needed air. Harms still hung on, his grip looser but still rendering von Honig unable to get free.

Across the room, Lana reached the remains of McGee, her recitation becoming longer and involving words von Honig could not fully make out. She moved her hands in a slow and complex pattern across McGee's body, her fingers moving in time with the cadence of the Nahuatl phrases. She dipped her fingers in McGee's blood, etching out a series of pictures across stone altar.

"Lana, stop!" von Honig called out, trying to free himself from Harms' grip while at the same time wake the woman from her apparent trance.

"Speak not to her, unbeliever!" Harms commanded. He spoke with a voice that was deep and resonant, sounding more like a radio announcer than a crazed cult leader. "Never speak to Chalchiuhtlicue! She of the jade garb shall usher in the new world!"

"You're insane!" von Honig snapped back, fending off Harms' arm as it sought to encircle his neck again.

"The gods, they return!" Harms screamed. "And they shall cleanse the land of all invaders!" His grip on von Honig's body grew stronger.

Across the chamber, Lana Tan, her fingers glistening with viscous crimson fluid, reached out one tiny hand to the obsidian blade protruding from her boyfriend's chest. "*Huitzilopochtli ticana naxca tlamictizque...Nitlanahuati ne naxca monemac*," she whispered as she pulled the knife from the corpse.

Still whispering, she placed the black blade's tip into a protrusion on the altar and stepped back. She dropped to her knees, head bowed and bloodstained hands extended above her head in supplication.

Von Honig, no longer willing to suffer Harms' hands on his body, realized a means of escape. Instead of pulling forward, he pushed back hard, slamming the obese man's back into the stone wall. Harms moaned, releasing his grip on von Honig's body as he crumpled to the hard, unyielding floor.

Then the altar began to glow with a golden light...

~ ~ ~

Looking down into the box again, von Honig spotted another stack of papers and other loose items. Reaching in, he pulled out a stiff square of paper, a cheaply developed photograph. It was a picture of four people seated under a gnarled old tree on a thick patch of grass. The woman in the picture was easy to identify: Lana Tan, dressed in a peasant gown with her hair loose and in disarray. She was attempting to look like a free spirit, a child of the Earth. This unpretentious style looked good on many women, but the attempt came off as artificial and ostentatious on the young socialite. She resembled what she was, a child of privilege attempting to mingle with the underclass.

The effect reminded von Honig of the tales of Marie Antoinette, the murdered queen of France. While children were starving in her country, the infamous monarch commissioned the building of a special farm called Hameau de la Reine. This "farm" allowed her to behave like a peasant–or at least a version of peasantry she held in her fantasies. She would dress an idealized version of a shepherdess, pretending to tend to her flock of sheep. The real employees of the farm managed to keep said animals clean and perform the actual work while the queen acted out a utopian version of the harsh life of the farmer. This became fodder for the revolutionaries, who pointed to her porcelain buckets and royal comforts as mockery of the true life of the peasantry of France.

The second figure was labeled in black ink as none other than Oscar Harms. Harms was seated with his back to the tree, gesticulating while unaware of the photographer. He was a large man, heavyset with some visible muscle beneath the blubber. His head was nearly bald and he possessed a thick beard streaked with gray. Harms was dressed similar to the others, his look that of the downtrodden farmers of the world.

For the second time in as many minutes, von Honig felt an immediate negative reaction at the sight of another human being. Harms was the type of academic he knew all too well–the variety he considered the lowest form of life in that world. Harms was the professor who wished to be friends with his students. He would tell them to call him by his first name and would assure the students that the lessons were an exchange of ideas. Tests were merely a method of having the academic's theories written back to him, a method of boosting his flagging ego. These teachers were often popular with students, though the universities rarely offered them tenure. Von Honig had known several of this kind, and he knew those who favored such mentors rarely achieved anything beyond open hero worship and parroting the pet theories of the moment. That was Oscar Harms, and von Honig had a strong suspicion that the work he'd read earlier was from decades ago, when his pursuit of knowledge was still more important than his ego.

The third figure in the picture was as familiar to von Honig as Lana Tan. Jocko McGee was seated next to the slumming heiress, a long, golden-tanned hand resting on the young woman's thigh. McGee resembled the Hollywood depiction of a surfer. Tall with loose blonde hair, deeply tanned skin and a wide, white smile. In every picture published since his sometime girlfriend's kidnapping, McGee presented an unflagging allegiance to his beach lifestyle. He always wore cutoff jeans that presented his muscular legs to full advantage. In this picture, Jocko was wearing a sleeveless t-shirt, though most pictures depicted him as naked from neck to waist and smiling in a roguish manner. He was smiling this time, though the look appeared slightly forced.

The final figure, listed as Dean Butters, was another familiar type in the academic world von Honig knew all too well. Thin to the point of emaciation, with a patchy beard and ill-fitting clothes, Butters stared at Harms with rapt attention. His open admiration for the older academic appeared almost worshipful, that of an acolyte absorbing the lessons of a priest king. Von Honig knew such men and women over the years and felt sorry for them. They were the fervent followers of the popular academic, ego boosters who often acted as factotum and dogsbody, unpaid servants when they weren't telling the "great man" how they were the wisest beings on the planet. The results were sad and von Honig always felt empathy for such individuals, knowing they would suffer when they discovered their hero's proverbial feet of clay.

Placing the photo aside, von Honig began reading the remaining documents. The information was startling and surprising. Harms' theories became wilder, his papers more like rambling manifestos.

His most recent work, unpublished but heavily distributed, declared that the Aztec, Mayan, and Incan myths were all true and all answers were hidden in the holy complex of Chichen Itza. The work was clearly that of an unhinged mind, a barely comprehensible treatise that combined mythological beliefs with conspiracy theories of the oddest and most unbelievable rumors.

Despite the bizarre nature of Oscar Harms' work, von Honig was able to discern his true intentions. The former academic turned cult leader wished to usher in a new age, one he believed came from beings who once came to Earth from the stars. In Harms' crazed mind, all gods were merely advanced visitors from other worlds. This nugget might have been the one truth in the ravings that made up his work. Happily, von Honig also knew the location of Harms' attempted contact with the visitors from beyond.

Reaching for the telephone, von Honig's hand stopped midway. *The police won't believe a word I say,* he thought. *They'll think I'm a lunatic or a publicity seeker. I doubt Gus Tan would even take my call.* He dropped his arm back to the desk.

Standing, he pushed back the chair and headed for the bedroom, his mind still weighing the circumstances. *Harms and the others have to be moving carefully. If they'd been spotted crossing the border, the FBI would receive a report immediately. No, I can beat them, or at least meet them before they do anything insane.*

Von Honig grabbed a suitcase and began packing. As he did so, he carefully plotted his route. Plane to Mérida Airport in Mexico, then buy a car and drive the remaining distance. Hopefully, he would be on time and beat Harms and company to the legendary site—the temple complex known as Chichen Itza.

~ ~ ~

The golden light pulsed in a slow and steady rhythm, a heartbeat in the gloom of the tiny temple. The energy spread across the altar, the illumination chasing across the heavy stones, revealing hidden symbols and characters etched beneath the surface. The shadows vanished within seconds, and von Honig stood in wonder as the golden light moved across the ceiling with the same pulsing intensity.

A large symbol, one whose complexity rendered it impossible to completely discern, appeared on the roof above the head of Lana Tan. The light appeared to slide across the images, pulsating over specific glyphs in a pattern that von Honig's mind could not follow.

He stood frozen amid the dancing luminosities within the temple of Kukulkan on top of the great pyramid. The sheer uncanny magnificence, hidden away for centuries, shimmered before his eyes. But the cost of conjuring such magnificence was the blood and life of a human. The cost was too great, a terrible price to pay for the secret history of the world.

A moment later, the glowing etchings above Lana Tan's head grew brighter, their pulsating luminosity increasing with each passing second. The images appeared to swirl, a kaleidoscope of ancient symbols whose strobing light forced von Honig to wince and shield his eyes.

Then it stopped, and a golden tablet fell from the ceiling. The plaque was round, about a foot wide, and glowing with the same intensity as the now fading energy in the chamber. Von Honig stepped forward to examine the tile, catching only a glimpse before pain exploded in his head. In his fascination with the display, he'd forgot about Oscar Harms. The crazed cult leader used the extra seconds created by the distraction to recover and attack him from behind. Just as the black curtain of unconsciousness covered his vision, von Honig observed Lana Tan rising with the low, deliberate movements of a sleepwalker.

~ ~ ~

Daylight awakened von Honig on a hard stone floor. It took him several minutes to remember why he was laying on this, unforgiving surface in semi-darkness. Had he worked so hard he fell asleep on the floor of his study? No, his home didn't possess stone floors—only hardwood covered by rugs in some places. Nor did the Hollywood

Hills home where he'd been staying. The only stones on that property were outside in the garden. This was different, not the type of rock one would find in a home in the States or Europe.

Then he remembered, his fuzzy brain and throbbing skull reminding him of recent events. Lana Tan. He'd been attempting to follow the missing heiress and rescue her from a crazed former academic turned cultist. The cultist...what was his name...? Harmons? No, Harms. The man somehow stumbled into an area of research that von Honig himself had made his life's work, the possibility of life from beyond the stars influencing humanity. The difficulty was the man's beliefs, no matter how firmly held, were couched in the crazed narrative of a drug-influenced psychotic.

This much von Honig remembered in a rush as he slowly sat up and felt as though his head were about to explode. That was when he remembered, despite the splitting headache, the rest of it. The temple of Kukulkan in Mexico. The jade-clad Lana Tan reciting the Aztec incantations with the fluency of an ancient priestess. The death of Jocko McGee. The light and the plaque...

So many terrible events.

Using the wall to pull himself to his feet, von Honig felt for his belt. Locating the military flashlight he always carried, he took a deep breath and switched it on. Designed for severe combat positions, the device still worked. Scanning the room, he opened his mouth in shock, unconsciously expelling all the air from his lungs.

The body and blood of the dead Jocko McGee were gone. The bloody eldritch tracery upon the ancient stone structure no longer dried in the tropical heat of the Yucatan jungles. Instead, von Honig found a flat rock, worn down by the hand of man as well as the winds of time. Running a hand over several spots where McGee's blood flowed, he felt nothing more than the smooth, cool surface of the stone.

Testing the strength of the altar, von Honig stepped up and stood mere inches from where the glowing symbols had appeared above Lana Tan's head. He closed his eyes and ran his fingers carefully and gently over the places where he remembered glyphs appearing.

He continued to run his hands across the stone surface for a full fifteen minutes before sagging in defeat. Nothing—not even a tiny, infinitesimal indentation—was visible or detectable upon the ceiling. The only proof would be his testimony, and that of the hypnotized or drugged Lana Tan and the maniacal Oscar Harms. Dean Butters he discounted. The man was unconscious when the uncanny events had occurred atop the pyramid.

Jocko McGee is dead, but I can't prove it, von Honig thought as he began a slow climb out of the pyramid and down the steep ninety-one steps. *Something strange happened because of the blood sacrifice, but I have no proof. To tell anyone might result in the death of other people. This has to remain a secret. But I need to find Harms and stop him from whatever he has planned.*

As he descended, he spotted a bus in the distance. A tour group was coming to the legendary ruins, completely unaware of the terrible rites that had taken place there the evening before.

Hours later, von Honig reflected upon the events. He'd achieved a possible milestone in his search for the truth, but nothing could come of his observations. He was unwilling to repeat the events of the night before, knowing some would actually take lives to validate their theories. There was no means of discovering what energy had illuminated the temple. Nor was there was an easily explainable means of discovering the etching within the stone. He wondered if there might be a device for digging into the rocks and unearthing the glyphs, but it didn't matter. To do so would destroy priceless antiquities, transforming him from a seeker of the truth into a mere treasure hunter.

There were men and women in this world, under the guise of discovering history, who were little more than grave robbers. Take that American archaeologist in the 1930s. He'd found a pre-Columbian temple which was supposedly a myth only mentioned by a few records. The details of how such a structure was built, not to mention the items found within would have been as great a find as the tomb of Tutankhamen by Howard Carter. Instead, the American was more interested in one gold idol, which he lost to another grave robber. The statue was eventually found in the collection of a Nazi art collector, and it has sat in the Smithsonian museum to this day. Only those in the world of archaeology mourned the destruction of the temple, knowing that secrets of the past had been irrevocably lost.

Von Honig vowed to never be that type of man. His search was a fringe science. Few could credit the theory of alien visitors interacting with ancient man. Few reputable scientists were willing to accept the concept of life beyond the confines of the Earth. Even with that in mind, the concept that said visitors from other worlds possibly interacted, assisted, or even served as religious entities to early man was something out of a pulp magazine tale. Those who did hold to such theories rarely applied the empirical steps of scientific discovery in the quest for knowledge. To most of this sort, the search was more like that of a prophet seeking answers from a distant deity.

Not von Honig. To act in such a manner would bring further disrepute to his field of study. It was too easy to be ignored as a crank or a publicity seeker. The best means he had at his disposal was to act in manner that fit with conventional scientific investigation. This way, he would not fall into comparisons with those who wrote upon the subject with more fervor than academic comprehension.

His thoughts were cut short by the vigorous motions of the airport clerk, a man named Jorge Garcia, who agreed to help him get to Peru as soon as possible.

"You are in luck, Señor von Honig," said Garcia, his hand covering the mouthpiece on the heavy black telephone receiver. "I spoke to a friend of my brother in Mexico City," he said. "there is a cargo plane headed for Lima tomorrow morning. They agreed to let you travel with them, but you must bring your own food and water. Is that acceptable?"

Von Honig considered for a moment. He'd thought of a series of quick hops, possibly catching the last flight to an area near the Nazca desert. But a direct flight, even one with multiple stops, would be effective. Possibly he could induce the pilot to use his radio to secure a flight to his ultimate destination. Yes, this would be the best method, if slightly slower than he'd originally hoped.

Nodding, he paid Jorge Garcia and within an hour was flying on a commercial airline to Mexico City. This would be a long, arduous trip—almost three-thousand miles in a cargo plane. Not quite the comfortable ride one hoped for when traveling in search of a missing heiress, a crazed cultist, and the possible answers to a theory about ancient astronauts.

~ ~ ~

Conrad was in luck for the first time in his travels. The pilot, a Frenchman named Rene Artois with a severe case of wanderlust, knew of his books. As a fan, he made sure the journey was far more comfortable than von Honig would have otherwise expected. For one thing, he was granted a seat in the cockpit, the only heated area within the plane. The machine itself was an elderly Fairchild C-119, better known as the Flying Boxcar. Artois, a heavyset mustachioed son of a French resistance hero, was happy to tell of the many near disasters the plane underwent in its long, sordid history.

"…kicked the wheels and they popped into place seconds before we were about to crash. A woman with a good kick, she is dangerous but quite special, no?" Artois quipped, ending his story with a loud guffaw. Von Honig only listened to snatches of the man's stories throughout the flight, but did get the idea that he was flying in a death trap piloted by a madman.

Despite von Honig's fear of crashing, Artois proved to be an excellent pilot and travel companion. He appeared more interested in women than piloting, a characteristic inherited from his elderly war hero father.

Stories about Artois' love life did help make the flight less dull, and they were a better alternative to hearing tales of close calls in the plane in which he was currently a passenger. Von Honig was anxious to get to Peru, to rescue Lana Tan and discover the secrets unearthed by the maniacal Oscar Harms. That might also provide the answer to how an unimpressive, insane pseudo-academic was able to unearth the rituals required to receive a golden plaque. Also, why was a golden tablet of an Aztec god and a South American geoglyph discovered in a temple on top of a Mayan pyramid? There were just so many unanswered questions.

Who sent me all this information? he wondered. *They put everything together, but why did they point me in this direction? Nothing in this situation adds up. Yet I did see the temple of Kukulkan pulse with energy. And a plaque with the symbols of Huitzilopochtli and the Nazca Lines Humingbird visible. Which means I need to get to that location before Harms does. He was willing to sacrifice that Jocko McGee person to receive the object. Who knows what else he has planned?*

The questions swam in von Honig's mind as he closed his eyes and tried to get some sleep. They were over the water now and unlikely to land for some time. Artois was in the middle of one of his rare periods of silence. This would probably be the best time to sleep and let the hours and miles pass more quickly.

~ ~ ~

After numerous hops and stops, none of which lasted longer than the time it took to refuel the battered old cargo plane, von Honig and his pilot landed in Lima. The airport was a busy place, a major hub for shipping and traveling for this region of the world. Artois, after clapping von Honig on the back and accepting a signed copy of his latest book, vanished into the airport crowds. His destination was the home of a widow who owned five butcher shops and was rapidly on her way to becoming an important, wealthy woman.

"I stay until she mentions marriage again," said Artois. "If you need a flight back, look for me!" And they parted ways. Von Honig wasn't sure if he could classify the French pilot as a good man, but he could at least call him "unique."

Fortunately, the mad Frenchman was well-liked wherever he happened to travel. After speaking in repulsively accented Spanish to a contact at the Lima Airport tower, he was given the name of a man with a light aircraft who traveled to Nazca regularly.

The pilot, a neat, tall, handsome man named Joaquin Machaca, greeted him with a nod and accepted payment without a word. He flew a well-maintained Avro Lancastrian mail plane that he checked with painstaking care. His pre-flight check within the cockpit was as professional as any von Honig had witnessed in his travels–as cautious as the pilot he'd once met who had flown a member of the British royal family.

The only words Machaca said to von Honig were, "Do not unbuckle your seat belt. The turbulence can appear suddenly."

The flight itself was uneventful, though the scenery was impressive. Peru was a beautiful country, a unique world unto itself. Several times, von Honig spotted what he thought might be man-made designs in the rocky surfaces. He did not comment, knowing his pilot was disinterested in any conversation other than for the purposes of the flight.

This did, however, cause him to contemplate some of the legends he'd stumbled upon throughout his studies. The most interesting tale, one he read in the notes of a first edition copy of Tobin's *Spirit Guide*, was that Peru and Chile were connected to the legendary lands of Lemuria–the so-called lost continent which was said to be ruled by an ancient race known as the Dragon Kings. Along with Atlantis, Mu, Acheron, Stygia, Hyperborea, and Ultima Thule were all lands that appeared to exist only in legend. Or at least that was what most people believed. Von Honig and a few others believed otherwise, sensing this and the legends of wise men from the stars to be part of an underlying truth. In this situation, he was unable to deliver any of his findings to the world at large. Though possibly, if von Honig could stop Oscar Harms, some evidence would remain.

Thanking Machaca after they landed, von Honig headed into the medium-sized town of Nazca. It was a pleasant location with impressive aqueducts to mitigate the effects of the heat and desert heat. The town was only a little more than one hundred years old, established on the site of one of the Nazca tribal ruins. A pleasant place, though there were hints of mining operations coming in the future. This would increase the local population and spoil the quiet beauty of the region. Sad, but such was the way of the modern world.

Discovering a man who sold cars and Jeeps, von Honig purchased a bottle of tasty local wine called *pisco* to get him talking. The salesman, a thin young man named Felipe Martinez with swarthy skin and a neat mustache, smiled at von Honig with paternal benevolence.

"I can tell you that no *blancos* such as yourself came through Nazca," he said. "But there are some who come through the desert to visit the Lines. Foolish, but I expect nothing less. Now, you wish a Jeep? No, very bad idea, amigo. The Sechura Desert, which is the true name of this land, is not like that of other places. It is not mounds of soft sand hills and heat. No, that would be far easier to traverse in a motor vehicle—if you are wise enough to pack enough water in case of mechanical failures. No, no, no. Our land is rocks and hills and valleys. A Jeep or truck would fail, and you would be in danger." Martinez spoke as one lecturing a very slow-witted child, gesticulating broadly his dismay at the idea of an automobile attempting to traverse this territory.

Recognizing the man had something in mind, von Honig played his part. Sighing dramatically, he asked, "Can you suggest a better method of travel for me? I must get to the Lines in the desert."

Martinez pretended to think upon the subject as he sipped his wine. He then snapped his long fingers and smiled. "I have it. My wife's cousin's son owns three donkeys he uses to carry goods to *blancos* who work on the Lines. I will send for him and he will carry you to where you wish and back—if we can agree upon a price, of course."

There followed a lengthy negotiation. Von Honig was anxious to get to the Nazca Lines, but knew he could not appear too eager. That would appear suspicious, and Martinez was a wise enough man to know that he should avoid dangerous situations. After buying the man a second bottle, the price was finally arranged, and half was paid immediately.

The distant relative—a bedraggled youth known only as Simon, and who spoke only in grunts—arrived the following morning. The donkeys were three gray-brown creatures, all of them disinterested in von Honig and apparently quite used to their work. Simon waved von Honig to the second animal and led them off towards the desert, only pausing long enough to accept a small packet of cash from Martinez.

The journey out of the town of Nazca was slow, almost interminable, but the donkeys kept a steady pace. Within an hour, the town was out of sight and they were winding their way slowly through a series of hills and valleys. Von Honig doubted they'd traveled more than five miles, but realized Martinez hadn't been wrong. Any car or truck in this region would break a tire or even an axle in the difficult terrain.

They had traveled in silence for another full hour when Simon stopped the donkey train. They had just entered a small plain, a dusty patchy of rocky, flat land that stretched out for several kilometers. The young man raised a hand a pointed ahead, neither speaking nor advancing.

Von Honig climbed off his donkey, patting the creature's side gently. He walked to where the young man stood, posed like a statue of a great explorer waving on the advancement of his company. Von Honig scanned the landscape for a full minute before he understood what had caught the young guide's attention.

A body, at least half a kilometer away. The fallen figure was crumpled in the middle of the clearing, unmoving in the harsh, relentless glare of the sun. Von Honig was tempted to run to the other's side, but knew that would merely exhaust him as well. Nodding, he walked forward, Simon following with the mule train trailing. Several minutes later, he knelt over the fallen form and frowned.

The body was that of Dean Butters. His withered form dressed in stained khaki pants and a shirt. At first, von Honig assumed he'd died from the heat and sun. But then he spotted the livid, still-moist cut across Butters's throat. He'd been murdered, another victim of his cult leader's insane ambitions.

It was easy to guess what had happened. Oscar Harms, either no longer needing Butters or tiring of his faithful follower's lapdog loyalty, slashed the poor, deluded creature's throat. Butters had died a sad, pitiful death, abandoned by the man he viewed of as a prophet for the new world.

Von Honig stood and looked over at Simon. "How many hours away are the Nazca Lines? I mean by donkey, not foot."

Simon appeared to consider, cocking his head to the left and right several times. Finally, he held up two fingers and pointed the direction Butters was laying.

Von Honig knew it would be close to dark by then, but he wasn't concerned. He could survive for a time on his own, so long as he had enough water. Nodding to himself, he walked over to his donkey and checked his water jugs. There were three—one half-full, the others untouched. He'd be okay for the time being.

"Let's put this man on the other animal," von Honig said. "You take him back to town and then return for me. I'll pay you double for this help. I don't want to leave this man here to be eaten. Oh, and please don't be too long." He gave the donkey some food and water as he spoke. The animal was his lifeline to civilization.

Simon once again tilted his head left and right, eventually nodding in reply. A few minutes later, with the deceased Dean Butters strapped to the donkey's back, he was off, returning to the town of Nazca. Von Honig sent a brief thought or prayer to whoever might be listening that the taciturn Peruvian returned quickly.

Kicking his own donkey lightly, von Honig and the small, powerful animal were off. Fortunately, the creature knew his way, having traversed this distance upon multiple occasions. They only stopped twice, both times for food, water, and a short rest.

The sun was just beginning to dip into the horizon when he heard the cry. A high-pitched shriek suddenly filled the air and the little donkey's ears twitched. Dismounting, von Honig tied the reins to a rocky outcropping and climbed to the top of a nearby rise.

He spotted them in an instant, a pair of figures moving slowly towards the huge etching of the hummingbird upon the desert plain. One was the sweaty, bloated form of Oscar Harms, dressed once again in his bedsheet turned robe.

In one of his huge meaty hands was the wrist of Lana Tan. She was still dressed in the green skirt and top, but she no longer wore the jade-covered headdress. She was struggling in vain and screaming as she tried to wrench free of Harms' grasp.

"Let me go!" she shrieked. "Let me go, you disgusting pig!"

Harms's only response was to chant the Quechal words over and over again: "*Chay hinaqa apukuna noqapah rimanqaku. Chay hinaqa apukuna noqapah rimanqaku.*"

Von Honig didn't speak, but was already climbing down from the steep rise. Neither Harms nor Lana spotted him as the former dragged the latter into the enormous geoglyph of a hummingbird. Upon reaching the center of the etching, Harms placed the golden plaque on the ground. With a wrenching movement, he forced Lana to her knees and pulled out the same obsidian knife he'd used to kill Jocko McGee mere days earlier.

Slicing Lana's hand open, Harms ignored her painful scream and held the bleeding extremity over the golden tablet. The woman's blood dripped quickly across the metallic plate and immediately began to glow with a luminous golden light. The plaque pulsed, making the etchings across the face visible, even from von Honig's distance.

The energy then spread across the face of the geoglyph, the golden illumination covering the entire surface within seconds. The hummingbird pulsed, creating a heartbeat of soft light in the growing twilight. The beauty of the transformation momentarily stunned the injured Lana Tan into silence.

Von Honig, though also amazed by the vision, ran forward without pausing to stare. He knew what Harms had in mind, and he needed to stop the insanity.

Harms howled with laughter and stomped his feet. "I was right!" he shrieked. "I was right! They are coming! *Chay hinaqa apukuna noqapah rimanqaku!*"

Then he raised the blade, the black glassine face of the weapon seeming to shimmer in the light. Overhead, a golden light slowly grew and a small wind began kicking up dust. The pulsing light began to chase across the face of the plaque and the hummingbird, the speed intensifying with each second.

"*Chay hinaqa apukuna noqapah rimanqaku!*" Harms screamed, and he plunged the knife downward towards the cowering Lana Tan's chest.

"No!" von Honig shouted, and he caught Harms' thrusting arm. The blade stopped, mere inches from the fallen socialite's body, causing her to shriek with naked terror.

"No!" Harms yelled, straining against von Honig's grip. "I am so close! *No!*" His swollen form seemed to grow larger as he fought to stab his victim. Realizing von Honig wasn't giving in, he released Lana and delivered clumsy but powerful blows across the archaeologist's body and head.

Von Honig ducked and tried to avoid the punches, but he was taking too many to last. Looking at the figure of Lana Tan frozen in fear, he yelled, "Break it!"

"What?" The young woman looked confused.

"Break the plaque!" he yelled, seeing the fear filling Harms' eyes.

Lana didn't need to be told twice. She picked up the tablet and raised it over her head.

"*Noooooo!*" Harms screamed. He tried to push forward, but von Honig's restraining hands held him in place.

Lana slammed the golden plate to the hard earth, causing the metallic slab to snap into three pieces. The illumination across the surface of the tablet immediately vanished. The ancient geoglyph of the hummingbird went dark and the light in the sky winked out. Only stars were visible now, softly illuminating the desert floor.

Harms jerked himself free from von Honig's grasp, the obsidian blade dropping from his fingers. His face was wild with fury, his eyes enormous, his lips covered with white spittle. "No! I was so close! No! *No!*"

Von Honig stepped back and assumed a protective position in front of the cowering form of Lana Tan. In some odd part of his mind, he realized the golden plaque was no longer in sight. Very strange, but what in this situation wasn't bizarre?

Harms whirled and suddenly ran off into the desert, screaming and howling incoherently. He vanished into the darkness seconds later, his crazed voice echoing for a long time.

"Thank you, whoever you are," said Lana. She paused, then after a moment she said, "Can I ask you something? Where are we? Those doesn't look like Malibu." She stared about, her fear seeming to increase with each glance at the harsh, rocky desert.

Von Honig laughed weakly. "You're about four thousand miles off," he said. "Come on. We'll find my donkey and head back to the nearby town. Your father will be grateful to know you're alive..."

As he helped the girl mount the donkey, he resigned himself to the fact that he would never know the truth about what Oscar Harms had discovered. Possibly that was a good thing. The blood rites of the creature called the Hummingbird were too terrible for mankind.

But the search for the truth would continue...

UNWELCOME BACK

by Brian K. Morris

1.

If December 7, 1941, was Japan's day of infamy, Saigon's own dark day came more than three decades later, on April 30, 1975.

Inside the American Embassy compound, Rob Lewis pushed some cash into his son, Huy's, palm with a smile. "Go get me some of those local smokes, okay?" the older man said. "I want to take some with me to remember the 'Nam by." He smiled softly. "For *us* to remember, sorry."

Honoring one's father was important to Huy's people, a native Asian bloodline that stretched back for hundreds of years. The boy bowed and grinned, his blue eyes peering up from under his black bangs.

Lewis knew life would not be kind to his only son. With a mixture of Asian and Caucasian features, the *bui doi*, or "children of the dust," proved a painful visual reminder of Western interference in this ancient culture. Those children would know little more than contempt from both sides of their family trees.

And then there was the scarring around his left eye.

The six-year-old left the compound. His small frame enabled

him to slip between the bodies that struggled to access the embassy. With the local airport now overrun by the North Vietnamese Army, only American helicopters could carry anyone to safety beyond the country's borders.

Yesterday, forces swept down from the north to reclaim the southern half of the nation after four decades of conflict. Immediately, families gathered as much as they could carry to flee towards the west, trusting the frying pan of Cambodia over the fire spreading across South Viet Nam.

Many more took whatever they hoped would float and dove into the chilly waters of the South China Sea in the hopes of reaching international waters and potential freedom.

Once the gates of the American Embassy closed behind Huy, an unwelcome noise filled the air. The crowd parted for a moment, as if allowing Huy an opportunity to see a chopper rise into the air. Sitting in the back of the aircraft, his father scouted out the mob below until his eyes locked with Huy's.

The boy gasped. He'd never seen his father stare at him so coldly, as if being examined by a stranger's eyes. Then the helicopter rose rapidly into the air and towards the east, towards escape.

Huy screamed in Vietnamese for his father to return, then in English, followed by the broken French his mother once attempted to teach him. But no matter what language Huy was the most fluent in, he couldn't be heard above the din of the mob.

Long minutes later, Huy wandered away from the embassy. He sniffled repeatedly while wiping his eyes again and again. *Only babies cry*, he thought, over and over again, his mental voice hard and icy as tears flowed down his face without restraint.

Huy's sobbing continued for what seemed like too long a time until a sound demanded his attention. He slowly turned in a circle to see everyone staring at him blankly, every eye open wide. The boy's jaw dropped as the mob echoed his earlier thought at the top of their lungs, "ONLY BABIES CRY! ONLY BABIES CRY! ONLY BABIES CRY!"

~ ~ ~

Two years later, the streets of Saigon were quiet. Those who conformed to the teachings of Mao Tse-Tung were permitted to resume their normal lives while many of the dissidents who resisted the Chairman's wisdom were shot.

As for the others, a recently-erected prison camp rested at the foot of a short span of mountains just north of the Demilitarized Zone that once divided the northern and southern halves of the Republic of Viet Nam.

Two parallel walls of barbed wire restrained several barracks filled with possible dissidents undergoing "re-education." The guards and officers charged with maintaining the prison camp also lived inside the confines of the facility with little fraternization with the external world...with only one exception.

Colonel Bao Trahn left the prison camp at the same time each dawn. He marched upon a stone path that wound through the tall grasses outside the facility towards a small mountain range which cast its shadow upon the camp. The path curved upwards through the stones towards a special edifice.

A bullet-shaped building rested at the apex of the hills. Several huge oval windows provided light and breeze to whomever might be inside. As Trahn approached the building, he cast his eyes over the surface of the edifice, pitted and seemingly ancient, built from a substance that clearly wasn't from the surrounding stone, but obviously not metal.

Trahn entered the building via the 20-foot-tall opening that served as a doorway. The colonel ascended a stairway, one long ago hewn from the same strange substance that led to a floor one story up.

Inside, sitting cross-legged on a thin mattress pressed against one wall, sat Huy. The boy looked up, still not even a decade old, but with the serene expression of one much older. His left hand clutched a circlet made from the same odd material as the building around him, suspended from his neck by a leather string.

In Huy's other hand lay an open copy of *The Quotations of Chairman Mao*, from which Huy resumed reading in a whisper. Trahn smiled confidently, taking comfort from the familiar words and knowing what simultaneously occurred in the prison below.

Inside the camp, a half-dozen prisoners tended a small garden. An elderly man wrapped his gnarled hands around a hoe. "The force at the core leading our cause forward is the Chinese Communist Party," he muttered as his implement sank into the pale earth, creating a row of exposed soil where fresh wheat seeds would find a new home.

A teenage girl in the next plot whispered in unison with the guard who watched her, "The theoretical basis guiding our thinking is Marxism-Leninism," just as did the old woman who prepared the night's meal inside a nearby tent that housed the kitchen.

In the barracks where the soldiers spent their off-hours, a half-dozen voices spoke in chorus: "Without a revolutionary party, without a party built on the Marxist-Leninist revolutionary theory and in the Marxist-Leninist revolutionary style, it is impossible to lead the working class and the broad masses of the people in defeating imperialism and its running dogs."

Trahn mouthed those words in unison with the rest of the camp. The colonel smiled softly at the boy, just as he did a couple of years ago when he first laid eyes on a crying child who sat inside a deserted grocery, surrounded by useless American currency and several cartons of cigarettes.

As Trahn's men had closed in on the damp-eyed Huy, the boy's voice exploded inside their skulls: *LEAVE ME ALONE! FATHER! MOTHER!*

Once Trahn managed to get both of his eyes to point in the same direction again, he coaxed the young man to follow him to this encampment. Of course, Huy's mother was nowhere to be found. Whether she was arrested or escaped the city under her own power, she wasn't going to be found any time soon. And the father, no doubt, rejoined his fellow imperialists, gloating over his role in undermining the unity of Communist Asia.

After a few tests conducted with the cooperation of their Russian allies who specialized in the field of parapsychology, Huy's talents were explored, quantified, and then utilized for the benefit of the State. The young man received plenty of food, education, and security in exchange for re-educating any local dissidents. Huy lived alone with only Trahn for company, as was now the boy's whim.

As the new day dawned, Huy prepared to read another paragraph of the Chairman's wisdom to his–literally–captive audience.

2.

"And that brings this segment of *Sunrise L.A.* to an end. Thank you for joining us for our interview with noted science fiction author, Conrad van Henning."

Conrad von Honig had ceased to correct his young, blonde interviewer almost thirty seconds and four failed mispronunciations into their conversation. After removing the microphone from the lapel of his sports jacket, the writer muttered his insincere gratitude and made his way towards the studio exit.

Following a half hour's worth of deciphering a cabbie's version of small talk, von Honig entered his room at the Glendale Fiesta Inn. The motel's sparkle derived from neon and chrome from a decade before when hipness could be defined by the amount of plastic inside one's home.

Von Honig hung his jacket carefully on the back of a chair whose cushions had seen far too much use. He stretched out on the bed, trying not to roll into the rut running down the center of the mattress where dozens, no doubt, had lain there previously. *How the prominent have fallen from favor,* von Honig mused as his eyes ran along the numerous cracks in the ceiling's plaster.

The writer's years of historical and scientific study had yielded data that verified not only the existence of intelligent alien life, at least to Von Honig's satisfaction, but also their intervention in mankind's evolution.

However, after several successful blows to his credibility, von Honig found himself sharing his beliefs to any media outlet that would listen to him. At least the interviewer spoke English this time.

The telephone rang. A startled von Honig looked at the device on the nightstand. The numbers 1 and 9 were worn away to near-invisibility, while the O was cracked down the center. Cigarette burns marred the plastic housing.

The phone rang a second time, then a third before he picked up the receiver and pressed it to his ear. "Hello?"

"Conrad," the unfamiliar male voice stated with a peculiar confidence. "We need to talk."

"Then talk," von Honig commanded.

"I'd prefer a face-to-face meeting." The telephone died just as a rapping came from the motel door, startling von Honig once again. Without hesitation, he dropped the receiver onto its cradle and pushed himself from the bed and towards the door.

Standing outside was a dark-haired man whom the writer guessed to be at least four inches taller than himself. The man's clothing was casual, from the impenetrably dusky sunglasses to the freshly laundered polo shirt, khaki slacks, and tennis shoes.

A smirk teased the corner of this visitor's mouth. From one shoulder swung what appeared to be a handbag with a rainbow of wiring spilling from one end of the unzipped top. The visitor placed what looked to be a telephone receiver into the maw of the bag.

"Mr. von Honig," the stranger said as he removed his sunglasses and entered the room. "My name is not Rob Lewis, but that's what I enjoy being called." He closed the door behind him.

Von Honig studied the intruder as he might examine the bottom of his shoe after sprinting across a pasture. "Portable telephone, eh? Your toy earned two minutes, beginning now."

Lewis dropped his bag and sunglasses onto the bed without offering his hand. "I wish to hire you as a consultant in a visit to Viet Nam."

Von Honig shook his head. "Last I heard, America was not exactly on Viet Nam's Christmas card list."

"Well stated," said Lewis. "No wonder you got into the writing business." He sat down on the bed and rifled through the bag. He pulled out a photograph and offered it to von Honig. "I think you'll find this of interest."

With a short sigh, von Honig glanced at the picture. "A child," he observed. "Amerasian?"

Lewis nodded. "My son. I had to leave him behind two years ago when Saigon fell. I will assume you are familiar with the Central Intelligence Agency."

Von Honig handed the photo back to Lewis. "I know what CIA means. What do your poor parenting skills have to do with me?"

"Look at the picture carefully." Lewis returned the photograph to von Honig. "Particularly the left eye."

Von Honig scowled as if forced to study a particularly hideous form of mold. After a few seconds, his eyes went wide. His hand shook as he returned the photograph carefully to its owner. "So when do we leave?"

~ ~ ~

Rob Lewis had already planned their itinerary, even down to clothing suited to the jungles of Viet Nam. Two suitcases awaited von Honig as he entered the waiting rental car outside his room.

Lewis chauffeured von Honig to Los Angeles Airport for a flight to Hawaii. From there, a private plane took them to the Philippines for the next leg of their trip.

The following day, von Honig sat on his bed, looking beyond the balcony of his hotel room where vacationers outside frolicked on the white sands and in the Pacific Ocean.

Unlike the previous room that von Honig occupied in Los Angeles, this one was scrupulously maintained and clean at a level that might be suitable for a surgical procedure.

The sound of a key sliding into the deadbolt lock drew von Honig's attention, spurring him to his feet.

Lewis entered, that macabre smile on his lips again. "Contemplating your escape, Conrad?"

"I can always swim back to the States." Von Honig noticed that whatever emotion crossed Lewis' lips never found a home in his deep-set eyes.

Lewis sat down and crossed one leg over the other. "I have no doubt that you possess the determination to do so," he said with feigned joviality. Suddenly, his smile vanished and his eyes took on an almost polar chill. "I hope you're ready for dinner. I think the time has come to talk."

3.

"So tell me about Majavaca."

The restaurant proved every bit as upscale as the hotel above it. As one party of diners left, the wait staff moved with purpose to clear the setting and replace the linen as well as the candles, leaving the table ready for new clients in less than a minute.

Von Honig chewed his prime rib slowly, methodically, gathering his thoughts. "I hoped to restore my reputation there, but such was not to be." He took a sip of wine. "I would think the CIA would find extraterrestrial investigation beyond the scope of its authority."

Lewis came as close to a smile as the writer had seen in the last seventy-two hours. "And you'd be right," he said. "But let's discuss what's really on your mind, shall we?"

Von Honig nodded. "The boy in the picture. Yours?"

"Affirmative." Lewis afforded his guest the merest of glances. "Too much local hooch, a warm night, and opportunity wasn't the only thing that arose." He sipped his water. "She crafted jewelry, good with her hands."

Von Honig's gaze bored into his host's eyes. "*Very* good, I'd wager," he stated with a raised eyebrow.

Lewis chuckled, a throaty grunt sounding more practiced than sincere. "Quite. She wanted to call him 'Huy.' It means 'sending out light.' Not that I cared." He dabbed at his mouth with a silk napkin.

"Huy lived with his mother at her shop, but he came to visit me at... work frequently."

"Please make this relevant to me, Mr. Lewis."

The man stared into space for a couple of heartbeats. "For his third birthday, the boy's mother gave him a charm she found in the hills. It was a circle of, well, it's hard to describe. There was a hole in the center and she found a leather cord so he could wear it around his neck. Soon, things started happening."

Von Honig raised an eyebrow. "Huy's mother. What was her name?"

Lewis' face took on a blank look as he searched his mental filing system. "Lihn, I think. Anyway, it began as impressions at first. Hunger, thirst, soiled underwear..." His dark eyes met von Honig's. "The infant transmitted his feelings directly into my brain." He paused. "You don't look surprised."

Von Honig shrugged. "My capacity for considering the unimaginable is greater than you'd believe," he said. "Continue."

Lewis nodded. "Once the boy learned to speak, his commands became verbal. Before you ask, I had training that helped me mostly block him out."

The writer grimaced. "I believe dessert and a little bit of brandy would go well with dinner, followed by the rest of your tale."

~ ~ ~

After the sun moved below the horizon, tractors with powerful headlights traveled up and down the beach, dragging giant brushes which flattened the pale sands, leaving the surface in faux-pristine condition for tomorrow's vacationers.

But as interesting as Lewis found the activity from this vantage point atop the boardwalk, von Honig voiced more urgent concerns. "Tell me about the place where your lover found the object."

The agent *hrrmphed* at the mention of the mother of his child. "It appeared to be built into the side of a mountain, all from some odd material I couldn't identify."

"The markings on your boy's eye. I've seen them before. Was it the talisman?"

Lewis almost laughed out loud. "I suppose that's as good a name for it as any," he said. His expression returned to its grim default. "As the boy used the *thing* more often, those marks formed around his left eye."

Lewis stepped in front of von Honig and stated, "Listen, Conrad, we need to find my son and see if we can use it."

Von Honig's palms grew moist, anticipating the upcoming turn in their conversation. *The talisman, or the boy himself?* he wondered silently.

Lewis' right hand unconsciously formed a fist. "Big damn 'if here," he said, "but if we can utilize this whatever-it-is, can you imagine the advantage we'd have in Southeast Asia?"

Von Honig's expression was passive, but his eyes blazed with anger. "How very opportunistic of 'we,'" he said. "And what about your boy? Huy, is it?"

"Yes. Huy." Lewis sighed. "The mission must come first. But I do want to see the boy. I really started missing him a couple weeks ago. Don't ask me why."

The pair stared over the ocean listening to the power of the waves striking the shore again and again.

Lewis glanced at his wristwatch. "That's enough," he said. "Our plane leaves at dawn. I'll collect you a half-hour before. You'll get the rest of what you need to learn once we're in flight. However, you need to know one thing..." The agent paused and scanned their surroundings. When he was fairly certain they were alone, Lewis continued. "Your expertise is useful, but if you do anything to endanger the mission, or if you pocket something I can use just to save your damn reputation, they'll find your clothing all over the Mekong Delta, and you'll still be in most of them. Affirmative?"

Von Honig nodded.

Lewis allowed one corner of his mouth to rise slightly. "I hope you enjoyed dinner as much as I did," he said. "Thank you for your company, Conrad. Sleep well."

With that, Lewis turned on his heel and marched back to the hotel.

A cool breeze blew over the Pacific waters, feeling like the icy hand of death as it touched the sweat on von Honig's brow and neck. The writer walked towards what promised to be an uneasy night's sleep, if any was to be had at all.

~ ~ ~

That night, the dream returned.

Surrounded by shadows that stretched to infinity, Lewis could not move his feet to escape.

Looking upwards, he saw the entrance to the edifice. Inside the doorway stood a short figure dressed in black.

"I look forward to our reunion, Father," Huy said. His voice was as dead as his father's eyes.

Lewis awoke, his naked body covered in sweat but his mouth dry. He blinked once before falling back onto his pillow, the dream purged from his memory once again.

4.

Rob Lewis rapped on the hotel door an hour earlier than promised. Minutes later, he and von Honig were headed for a private airport beyond the city's limits. *I don't even know what the hell city we're in,* von Honig realized as he stifled another yawn.

After a few minutes, the car pulled up to a hangar where a small cargo plane awaited, its props whirling as if eager to get into the air. An Asian man, dressed in black from shirt to shoes, pulled the luggage from the automobile into the aircraft with silent efficiency.

"Strap yourself in, Conrad. Next stop, Viet Nam."

Lewis turned to the Asian and said something in a language von Honig didn't recognize. The man nodded curtly as he took his place in the cockpit while Lewis raised the ladder and secured the hatch.

Minutes later, the airplane made its way into the clouds with the full glory of the sunrise behind them.

Lewis pulled a metal lunch box from under the seat just as von Honig released his seat belt. The writer felt overwhelming relief to see Lewis produce a couple of sandwiches along with a thermos full of strong, black coffee.

"Enjoy it," Lewis said. "It's the last western food you'll get for some time."

"How long will we be in Viet Nam?"

Lewis' already humorless gaze, as well as his tone, turned dark. "We are there until we find Huy."

Von Honig nodded slowly. "No more Mr. Nice Guy?"

"There never was one." With a slight pursing of his lips, Lewis' hand snaked out toward von Honig's face. The writer felt a brief pressure on the temples, and then nothing.

When he awoke, Von Honig's tongue was numb and an antiseptic odor stung his sinuses. He pushed himself upwards in his seat to a more comfortable sitting position. His clothes felt odd as if they'd been moved...or searched.

Von Honig dropped a hand to his back pocket where his wallet should have been. A further search revealed the contents of his pockets were gone. Von Honig turned towards Lewis, who looked back at him and nodded slowly.

"Yes," Lewis confirmed, "your wallet and other personal effects are gone. My pilot will return to the Philippines and deliver them to your hotel room. I promise."

"Why?" Von Honig fought the urge to seize Lewis' shirtfront.

The agent spoke with barely controlled anger. "Use your brain, man. You live in a country that wronged both halves of the 'Nam. If you were caught with your identification, you'd be considered a spy and the American government would have to disavow your actions." The corner of his mouth lifted ever so slightly. "Wouldn't do much for your credibility, would it?"

Lewis waited for a reaction from von Honig that the writer was wise enough not to show. "Ah, Conrad. You notice how I engineered your 'nap' and how I communicated with the plane's crew? Perhaps you wonder if I'm…how might you say it…para-human? Perhaps tainted with alien DNA." He shrugged dramatically. "Mull this over: I don't know a single word of Vietnamese, and yet our pilot understood every word I said."

Holding out another sandwich to von Honig as a peace offering elicited a curt nod of gratitude from the writer.

"No, this food isn't an attempt to give you a case of Stockholm Syndrome, Conrad," Lewis said, furrowing his brow as if in thought. "But I promise you that if we complete my mission, you will return home safely with all the evidence you'll need to resuscitate your damaged reputation."

Then Lewis' eyes turned dark and intimidating again. "But if you screw up our quest, I'll leave your ass over there. Imagine being alone in a country with no money, no I.D., no common language, no friends, and no way home. In fact, your skin color's your worst enemy right now."

Lewis chuckled again. "I see into your mind, Conrad. If you're wondering why the CIA would condone this mission…who says I'm still an agent? Consider that, if you will." With that, Lewis closed his eyes for a nap.

Von Honig turned his attention to his meal, chewing carefully, slowly. He hoped Lewis hadn't noticed the ripples appearing in his coffee as his hands shook ever so slightly.

~ ~ ~

Several hours later, the airplane bounced off the western edge of the China Sea, ultimately coasting to a halt on the sands of a deserted beach.

Lewis carried two backpacks from the aircraft as von Honig disembarked via a well-worn rope ladder into the shallow but chilly water.

As the airplane turned in the water and accelerated towards the clouds, Lewis smiled broadly. "Welcome to The Republic of Viet

Nam, just north of the Demilitarized Zone."

Von Honig muttered under his breath as he slogged towards the beach. Suddenly, he felt Lewis' hands grip both of his wrists and force them upwards. As the writer tried to regain his bearings, he felt something sticky tighten around his wrists.

"Don't struggle," Lewis advised. "I've bound your wrists so you can't go wandering off easily." Von Honig stumbled in the shifting sands under his boots as he unsuccessfully attempted to pull his wrists apart.

"It's an adhesive tape America created during the Second World War," Lewis explained. "The Army used it for quick repairs. Since it's waterproof and tough, it's often used in duct work. You won't break it any time soon."

Lewis seized his prisoner's collar and led him toward dry land with stern purpose.

With both backpacks over one shoulder, Lewis cast his dead grin at von Honig. "Let's get busy. March!"

5.

"They are leaving the beach now," Huy stated by way of the morning's greetings.

Colonel Trahn nodded. "As you knew they would."

Huy smiled softly. "Like a dream come true."

~ ~ ~

"Yes," Rob Lewis said with a sigh, "you are angry at me. I got that several obscenities ago."

Conrad von Honig listened to the tall, dry grasses crunch under his boots as the two men marched alongside a rut-filled dirt path that passed for a road. "And why am I walking in front of you?" He swallowed hard. "I take it I'm a meat shield?"

"More of a distraction than a defense," Lewis admitted. He

checked a well-folded map once again, then glanced at a small compass, both of which he dropped into a jacket pocket when done.

Von Honig heard his captor rifle through one of the backpacks, but didn't turn around. "I hate to be negative," he said, "but your face is every bit as pasty as mine."

Lewis chuckled. "Not necessarily."

The writer whirled around to see Lewis applying makeup to his face and arms, covering his moderately tanned skin with a color more appropriate to the locals. A military jacket—von Honig assumed it was of Vietnamese manufacture—rested over Lewis' shoulders.

Von Honig stopped in his tracks. "Hey! Where's *my* disguise?"

"Like I said, distraction," said Lewis. He gave von Honig a gentle nudge and the writer resumed his march toward what appeared to be a small village.

A dozen poorly-constructed huts lined the dirt road that bisected the community. "You probably had more in your wallet than any one of these people earned in a lifetime," Lewis said softly to von Honig. "They've survived through barter, catching the crumbs from the foreigners' tables, or crime."

Von Honig avoided the curious stares of the natives as they peered at him through mesh-covered windows or from the safety of their front steps. "Survived everything but our leaving them, it seems."

Sighing, Lewis motioned for his captive to pick up his pace. "These people hoped reunification with the North would become one big party. You know, all is forgiven and all that bullshit."

A flock of dark birds erupted from the top of the trees like a screeching boil suddenly lanced open. After a minute's contemplation, von Honig grumbled, "You talk too much."

Lewis grinned. "I've spent too many years keeping secrets," he said. "To be able to talk about my work is almost cathartic."

Von Honig looked around frantically, his senses alert. He whispered, "Can you hear –?"

"I hear everything," Lewis stated loudly. "Haven't you figured out that I'm inside your head? Inside everyone's? I know your thoughts before you do."

"Shut up!" von Honig whispered as the sound of an engine grew louder. "We're not alone."

Looking towards the curve a couple hundred feet ahead, a left-over American Jeep took the corner with deliberate slowness. But once the officer riding shotgun caught sight of Von Honig and Lewis, he motioned for the driver to accelerate, which the man did without hesitation.

By the time the vehicle ground to a halt, sending up a spray of gravel in von Honig's direction, all four North Vietnamese soldiers had pistols in their hands, all covering the two strangers.

~ ~ ~

Huy's eyes widened.

"There is a complication," he informed Colonel Trahn. "One that could be beyond my control."

6.

Rob Lewis stepped forward with his hands by his side, not palms up in a sign of surrender. A trepidatious von Honig watched his smiling companion approach the soldiers.

"I trust you have your papers, Comrade," the officer said curtly. He extended his free hand to accept Lewis' identification.

"You have seen my papers," Lewis said confidently in perfect English. "You are satisfied with them and will allow us to go on our way."

The soldiers collectively furrowed their brows as they stared at Lewis' running makeup. The officer wrapped his finger around the trigger of his pistol.

Lewis stepped forward, covered his mouth with his right hand, then swept his gaze across the passengers of the Jeep, whistling softly.

Suddenly, the driver clutched his face in an attempt to stem the flow of blood from his nostrils. As the other three in the Jeep turned their attention towards their comrade, Lewis reached forward and seized the pistol that dropped onto the driver's lap. Three shots later, the driver and the two soldiers in the rear seat fell backwards, propelled by the momentum of the bullets that entered their brains.

The officer held his handgun with both hands in a desperate attempt to steady it. However, the effort taken to overcome his terror left him unable to draw a sleeve across his eyes to clear the blood oozing from them.

Unencumbered by such concerns, Lewis squeezed the trigger of the stolen firearm once more, allowing the rest of the officer's blood to drain from his body.

"You okay, Conrad?"

But when Lewis turned, von Honig was nowhere to be seen.

~ ~ ~

Every breath sliced into von Honig's lungs as he sprinted through the trees. However, "sprinting" was far too generous a word for the writer's version of locomotion. With his arms bound behind his back, Von Honig found his speed and agility severely hampered.

After a few minutes, the man slowed to catch his breath. Panting like a dog on a hot day, von Honig attempted to control his breathing in the hopes of hearing any pursuers. However, the effort only made him feel light-headed so he allowed himself the indulgence of deep, quick breaths just as the sound of four gunshots tore through the greenery.

Despite his exhaustion, von Honig pressed on. He tried to be as silent as the dried grasses underneath his boots would allow, hoping his march would be towards safety, if such a thing existed over here.

~ ~ ~

Lewis gave up on brushing the blood from his jacket. Centering himself, the agent extended his senses, both physical and mental. Voices whispered on the breeze, entering his skull and whirling around his brain. Lewis smiled as he savored the stimulation to his mental palate.

After several minutes of intense concentration, Lewis opened his eyes. "Going to make this difficult, are you, Conrad?" He spat twice, then checked the ground where he discovered the grasses pressed flat by von Honig's hasty exit.

~ ~ ~

An hour later, Conrad von Honig knelt, pausing to cast a glance at the sun through a clearing in the trees. *So much for telling the time.* Eventually, he rose to his feet, both knees cracking in protest.

What little saliva he could summon up tasted like library paste. Again, the writer tested his industrial tape bonds but he still couldn't slide either hand free, nor rip his bindings in two. In fact, his wrists burned from countless attempts.

Von Honig looked about warily. He had no way of knowing what snakes, poisonous or otherwise, might conceal themselves in the tall grasses. But if their venom didn't do him in, the lack of water and food certainly would. *And this is where my ego has brought me.*

He knew that walking in the wrong direction, or in circles, would mean his demise. However, there existed the slimmest chance of finding provisions in another village or even the one he just passed.

A slim chance beats the hell out of none at all. Von Honig looked up at the sky, made his best guess as to which direction the village lay, and trudged off towards what he hoped was salvation.

7.

The aroma of burning wood and cooking food rode the humid breezes that wafted through the village. Numerous iron kettles suspended over yellow flames brimmed with broth, vegetables and whatever meat a family could secure. Children chased each other in their underwear between the huts, laughing as the sun moved towards the horizon while a rhythmic *clang-clang-clang* split the relative quiet of the late afternoon.

Behind one of the huts, an anvil stood on an old tree stump, just as it had for thirty years. In the center of a barren dirt circle ten feet away rested a small smelting oven, now fired up to where its heat could be felt in any direction from several feet away.

Duong Tad dropped the newly-hammered chisel into the coffee can full of motor oil at his feet. The chisel hit the lubricant with a loud *hssss*. After a long morning's work, Duong had enough tools made for his father to take to town and sell in the marketplace.

The teenager silently thanked God, as the missionaries taught him to do when he was still a child. A part of him wondered if their deity fled Viet Nam along with the nuns two years ago. But hedging his theological bets, Duong thanked God again–adding "and to whom it may concern," just in case–for his metalworking skills and the equipment he inherited from his late father.

"We stand for self-reliance," Duong whispered in unison with the soft voice in his mind. "We hope for foreign aid, but cannot be dependent on it." The young man knelt beside his anvil, resting for a moment. "We depend on our own efforts, on the creative power of the whole army and the entire people."

Squinting towards the first row of trees, Duong called out in Vietnamese, "And upon whom do *you* depend?" Then in English, "I see you. Come here."

Conrad von Honig grumbled as he half-walked, half-stumbled into the clearing, his arms still secured behind his back. As he approached, the writer spun around to show his bonds before facing the young man once again.

"You should take that off," Duong declared.

Von Honig suppressed his frustration. "I don't suppose you would want to free me."

Duong shrugged. "I don't have a knife on me."

"Then we appear to have something in common. I'll wait here until you find one."

Rising to his feet, Duong frowned. "How do I know you won't

kill me once your hands are free?" he said. "You have a gun?"

His patience at an end, von Honig vented, "I don't even have my wallet. It's been hours since I ate or drank and I am exhausted." His shoulders slumped. "If you can't–or won't–help me, I will simply wander off into the forest to die, all right?"

Duong moved cautiously so the anvil was now between him and this stranger. "Fine. But if I was to free you and one of the government soldiers saw me, I would be shot. Or worse."

Von Honig shook his head with disappointment. "Bah," he spat. "I have better things to do than engage in small talk." Von Honig turned as if to leave.

"You don't speak our language?"

"No Vietnamese." He inhaled deeply. "Your English is quite good."

"Thank you. So is yours." Duong bent down to pick up a hammer, just in case. "Many of us know your language as well as our own, maybe some French too. Why are you alone?"

Von Honig grimaced. "I escaped from my kidnapper. He dragged me from America on a fool's mission." He deliberately neglected to add *And killed four of your country's soldiers.*

Duong nodded slowly. "He sounds like a poor friend."

"I would have to agree. I can't decide what I would say to him, should I see him again. But I believe I could communicate more effectively if my hands were free." Von Honig paused. "I might need my thumbs on his windpipe, you understand."

Duong smiled. "So where do you think he would be?"

Von Honig ran a dry tongue over his lips. "Nuh ideah." The American marshaled his energies to speak clearly. "Sorry...looking for...water ..."

Blank-eyed, Duong stated in Vietnamese, "Words and actions should help to unite, and not divide, the people of our various nationalities."

"They should be beneficial," von Honig agreed in flawless Vietnamese, "and not harmful, to socialist transformation and socialist construction."

Duong's gaze regained its warmth as von Honig's blood iced in his veins. Somehow, the American knew the words came from the blueprint for Chinese Socialism, *The Quotations of Chairman Mao.*

And not only did Conrad von Honig understand every word he just uttered, he believed the sentiments with all his heart and soul.

8.

"I need to know!" von Honig shouted as he stepped forward. He probably moved too quickly for Duong's comfort, as evidenced by the young man lifting his hammer defensively.

"You are crazy, American. I should look for a patrol."

"No!" Von Honig took a step backwards, almost falling over the uneven ground. "I'm not crazy." He selected his words carefully. "Have you had odd thoughts since the Americans abandoned you?"

Duong looked up at von Honig with haunted eyes as he lowered the hammer. "Many of us hear crazy things in our heads," he said, "but we do not talk about it."

Von Honig shook his head. "Not crazy. I've seen strange things before, more than you know." He thought for a moment, then spoke slowly. "I cannot explain how. Not yet, anyway. But someone's mentally drilling propaganda directly into our brains. I need to find him and stop him. He's dangerous."

Duong lifted the hammer once more, his voice filled with determination. "Perhaps I changed my mind about the Americans and democracy?" He searched his memory, then allowed the hammer to drop to the ground. "I didn't always feel like this."

"Yes, but now we are enlightened." Von Honig stopped himself. "Repeat a lie long enough," he stated solemnly, "and it will become someone's truth. Please help me. I need to stop this violation."

Duong frowned as he contemplated the hammer in his hand.

~ ~ ~

Inside the edifice, Huy swallowed the last bite of his dinner. In response to the boy's mental summoning, Colonel Trahn entered the small room. "All goes well, Huy?"

Huy smiled broadly. "My father tried to teach me chess once. I begin to see the appeal of the game when the pieces move into place."

9.

Conrad von Honig stumbled through the jungle, hoping he was heading north. At this point, he gave less than a full shit about encountering any snakes or hostile locals along the way. Confronting Huy outweighed any other considerations.

Despite his new misgivings, Duong brought the writer some warm water and a dented steel ladle. However, the young man's new brainwashing wouldn't allow him to slice the tape from the American's wrists. *One hurdle at a time*, von Honig reasoned.

Emerging from the trees, von Honig paused to study the fields that blanketed the nearby landscape. A lone woman, her face aged by the sun and hard labor, looked up from her work in a rice paddy, the edge of which almost touched the crude road where von Honig found himself.

The American stopped, rising up to his full height. "Madam, I know I must look a fright," he said. "However, I could use some directions."

By way of reply, the old woman waved her index finger at von Honig and screamed in her native language for what he could only assume was help. In response, the writer took off at a run, his gait rendered more awkward by his hands still behind his back.

The air in his lungs turned acidic as the strain of jogging became too much for him to endure. Von Honig slowed down again, coughing from the dust raised by his sprint. Blood roared in his ears like a freight train and his heart pounded against his ribs as if it was trying to escape.

Von Honig stumbled off the pathway into some overgrown

grasses. He dropped to his knees inside the verdure, then half-rolled onto his back. Once concealed, the investigator closed his eyes, hoping to get his breathing back under control.

But his eyelids barely closed when the shouting resumed. With curiosity motivating him far more emphatically than self-preservation, von Honig sat up.

Duong stood at the forefront of the openly angry villagers. They held scythes, rakes, pry bars, anything that could be used as a weapon. The old woman from the rice farm held her hoe tightly as she declared, "In the fight to wipe out the enemy and to restore and increase industrial and agricultural production –"

Holding up his hand for quiet, Duong spoke softly, "You have overcome many difficulties and hardships and demonstrated immense courage, wisdom and initiative."

Von Honig felt oddly taken aback by the compliment. He spoke calmly in Vietnamese, addressing each member of the mob. "You are models for the whole Chinese nation, the backbone of the victorious advance of the people's cause in all spheres."

Von Honig felt an odd sensation of pride as he rose to his feet, a fire in his chest that erupted like a volcano. He grinned as the once-hostile crowd applauded in unison, nodding vigorously with approval. Looking beyond his audience, the nearby trees took on the look of a painting done in pastels, devoid of detail and shading. *An illusion? Quite a good one.*

Suddenly, a coldness washed over von Honig as he realized what he'd just said, every word that came from his mouth without hesitation or reservation. His mouth went dry as the illusion of the crowd vanished, leaving an image of a boy – no doubt another illusion – who had to be less than ten years old, but with the eyes of a man several times his age.

"Please forgive me, Mr. von Honig, but I wanted to make sure you were surrounded by familiar faces. With such short notice, all I could find were your memories from the last few hours. I hope you don't mind. I'm still learning how to use my talents."

The writer found himself staring at familiar scarring around the youngster's left eye. "You are Huy, I take it?"

The boy bowed slightly and spoke respectfully in perfect English. "Welcome to the Republic of Viet Nam, Mr. von Honig. You are thinking the markings around my eye resemble those you saw in Majavaca?"

Nodding, von Honig fought the urge to bow in return. Instead, he glanced at the odd ring suspended from the boy's throat. "We have much to discuss when I arrive at...I guess it's your home?"

Huy held up a hand. "We shall, Mr. von Honig." He chuckled. "In fact, you are closer to my home than you know."

Without apology, von Honig stated, "A man claiming to be your father brought me here."

Huy grinned. "Yes, as I guided him." He gestured for the older man to approach and the writer complied without a moment's deliberation. Mere seconds into their stroll, a mist formed, enveloping them both completely. Even though he couldn't see farther than the length of his arm, von Honig walked forward confidently, his aches, his hunger, and his thirst momentarily forgotten.

"Remember how I said you were closer to my home than you knew, Mr. von Honig?" said Huy. He turned around and with a wave of his hand, the fog dispersed to reveal a prison camp on their right. Von Honig saw beyond the barbed wire fencing where a group of people tilled a small garden, their mouths moving in unison. If they were aware of his presence, they gave no outward indication.

Huy gestured towards the top of a nearby mountain. There, a small bullet-shaped edifice was visible at the end of a well-worn pathway.

Huy smiled mischievously. "You've been sleepwalking under my guidance since you laid down to rest your eyes," he said. The boy's image shimmered like a mirage before vanishing entirely. "Please make your way uphill, Mr. von Honig, so we can talk."

As the writer moved forward, Huy continued to speak inside von Honig's head: "You would have fought me yesterday. But now, you are more agreeable, less rigid in your western thinking."

Von Honig bit his lower lip as he made his way up the path towards the edifice.

Meanwhile, concealed in the tall grasses, Lewis grimly watched the American stumble uphill. Once his former captive disappeared among the stones, the agent stashed the map in his pocket before moving swiftly in pursuit.

10.

Upon entering the edifice, von Honig delighted in the height of the entryway. Its dimensions could accommodate the alien life forms that he'd conjectured and even obsessed about for years. The writer turned to press his palms against the wall, feeling a chill emanating from the rough surface.

Colonel Trahn stood at the base of the steps. The officer smiled warmly, although von Honig noticed one hand resting on the pistol strapped to his hip. Trahn didn't blink as he stated in halting English, "Citizen Huy requests your company upstairs." He punctuated his sentence with a shake of his head.

Von Honig ascended the steps, his eyes wide with childlike amazement, his pulse racing. *I'm surrounded by evidence. If I can find a way to get this back to civilization–...*

"And who's to say who is genuinely civilized?"

As von Honig stepped onto the upper level, Huy smiled at him from atop his mattress. The boy rose to his feet and moved across the room to shake his visitor's hand with mature confidence.

Huy chuckled. "Sorry. I have a habit of answering unspoken questions both aloud and in your head."

"Except one," von Honig stated.

Huy's face turned serious. "Not just one, sir. No, I don't know how old this building is." The boy paused, looking directly into his guest's unflinching stare before wrapping his hand around the ring hanging from his throat. "My mother found it when she and my father were doing something adult that my keepers say they'll discuss with me when I am more mature."

You're very mature right now.

"Thank you, sir." Huy slowly ran his thumb along the edge of the object suspended from his neck. "I don't know if this coin granted me these talents, or if I was born with them." The boy looked at the artifact. "I haven't seen Mother since the country became one again."

Von Honig cleared his throat. "Well, I could –"

"And hand it back when you're done?" Huy's face turned dark, untrusting. "Don't make the mistake my *original* handlers made with that offer." The boy allowed the threat to hang in the air for a few heartbeats before he added, "I can transmit all kinds of bad things." His eyes met those of the older man.

In response, von Honig pressed his back against the wall of the building, his hands still behind him.

Huy probed his guest's mind. "You truly believe space gods built this? And mankind needs to be...worthy of them?" Huy's grin startled von Honig with its brightness. "Then I am doing the work of the gods."

Von Honig's eyes narrowed. "How so?"

"With my talents, I can bring people around to Mao's thinking, united in the Socialist way; sharing, working for the common good." The boy appeared ready to jump up and down with delight like any other child his age. "Soon, everyone will know the wisdom of Mao. All hate will vanish."

~ ~ ~

Downstairs, Colonel Trahn lay on the floor of the edifice. His body trembled as saliva poured from the corner of his mouth. Inside his head, every demon he could never imagine assaulted his defenseless psyche with dozens of chilling thoughts and images that left him terrified, helpless, broken.

Gently wiping the blood from his victim's eyes, Rob Lewis slowly moved towards the steps, attracted by the voices upstairs, including a familiar one that echoed inside his own head.

Moving quietly, Lewis reached the top of the steps. The first person he saw was Conrad Von Honig, the writer's back pressed against a wall, his arms still behind him.

Sweeping the room with his eyes, the agent found Huy. The boy stood with his arms folded, whispering inside his father's head, *I waited for you.*

"Since seventy-five, right?" Lewis withdrew a pistol from the waistband of his trousers and leveled it at his son. "Probably not the reunion any of us anticipated, right?"

Huy chuckled. "Actually, *Father,*" the boy said venomously, "you've behaved just as predicted."

11.

Rob Lewis turned to see Conrad von Honig coming as close to a smirk as he'd seen in their brief time together. "You find something amusing, scribbler?" Von Honig noticed a subtle change in the man's accent to something other than American. Lewis shrugged in response to the question. Lewis added: "Locate any other artifacts?"

"The only one I've seen is around your son's neck," said von Honig, "and I wouldn't even contemplate its appropriation."

The boy gripped the circular artifact tightly in his left hand. "Where is Colonel Trahn?" he demanded of his father. "What did you do to him?"

"He's downstairs, drooling," said Lewis. "Praying for death's sweet release." He reached into his pants pocket and pulled out what appeared to be a small, clear plastic pillow not more than an inch square. "I used my own talents on him. First, I clouded his mind, made myself invisible to his senses. Then I took him into Wonderland." The agent chuckled as he bounced the "pillow" in the palm of his hand.

Lewis' pistol now swung towards von Honig. "If there's no alien artifacts here, I guess your existence is rather superfluous."

"*No!*" Huy commanded. He stepped forward, halted by the sight of the handgun now moving towards him. "Please, no killing." He squinted at his father. "What is that grease on your face?"

"Son," Lewis said derisively, "killing is the one thing I'm best at." He pulled back the hammer and aimed the handgun at a point between Huy's eyes. "You didn't always consider the time difference between Viet Nam and Langley." He grinned like a chess master about to announce checkmate. "I wasn't always asleep when you touched my mind so I kept a dream journal as it happened." Lewis' eyes narrowed, "However, we *will* discuss your results when I slipped up."

"I hate to interrupt, but why me?" ask von Honig.

A corner of Huy's mouth rose slightly as he faced the writer. "Your expertise in relics is well known, even over here."

"What," growled von Honig, "you couldn't just ask me to drop in?"

Huy indicated his father with a tilt of his head. "Our common blood allowed me to enter his mind from a distance." Huy took a deep breath. "I needed someone who could get you here, someone who didn't respect borders." The boy grinned. "And then I remembered my father." The boy broadcast, *Which is more than my father did me.*

Lewis' lips twisted into the most vicious snarl von Honig had ever seen. "*No one violates my mind! NO ONE!*"

"No one but your son, Lewis," von Honig taunted. The writer didn't even see Lewis' backhand coming as it met his temple, just above his left eye. All the strength left his legs and he slid down the edifice's wall, both wrists scraping against the rough surface.

"You just sit right there, von Honig," said Lewis, "or I paint the wall with your brains." He turned to Huy and pressed the barrel of the pistol against the boy's forehead. The agent spoke in English, but with an accent that von Honig now recognized as Russian: "Don't run me around. My spies surround you." Then he popped the small pillow into his mouth and pushed it behind his molars with his tongue.

Huy looked at von Honig with a serenity that was frighteningly mature. "This man has lied to you, sir."

Von Honig pushed his back against the wall and with his shoulders and the limited use of his hands, he struggled to get to his feet again. "Every opportunity he got, I'd imagine."

A glare of defiance filled the boy's dark eyes. With the rapidity of thought, Huy transmitted, *The name "Rob Lewis" is merely one of his covers. His name is really Rostislave Makar, and he's with the Russians.*

The pistol wavered for a moment. "Ex-KGB, if you must know," said Lewis, now revealed as Makar. "Since World War Two, our governments have worked to battle each other on a psychic level, rather than physical." A terrifying leer crossed Makar's features. "I'm the reason for your MK-Ultra program."

Von Honig shook his head. "So your genetics are responsible for Huy's abilities?" He added with no small measure of disappointment, "Not the visitors?"

Madness danced in Makar's eyes. "I use special chemicals that trickle through my skin, unlocking my abilities." He paused to grin again. "My little time-release pillows."

Makar then rushed towards von Honig and pushed the barrel of his pistol hard against the bottom of the writer's chin. Wrapping the palm of his free hand onto von Honig's temples, as if to unscrew the top of the man's skull, Makar whispered so only the writer could hear him.

Von Honig smelled that chemical again, just as he had back on the airstrip, a moment before the bottom dropped out of reality.

12.

Flailing against the walls of a tunnel made completely of darkness and disappointment, Conrad von Honig plummeted into the darkest depths of his own mind.

Sliding down the ebony walls of his imagination, he saw various oddly-shaped objects, all constructed from the peculiar substance that comprised the walls and floor of the edifice. He reached for them in his descent but the very act of wanting them pushed him farther away.

A fitting metaphor for my existence, he noted with a surprising calm.

While he fell, von Honig felt the presence of another mind. *Lewis? Makar?*

And a calm voice replied, No.

~ ~ ~

Makar watched Conrad von Honig's legs twitch as if in the throes of some impossible-to-cure muscular disorder. The first few drops of saliva trickled from the corner of von Honig's mouth, much to the Russian's delight. The Russian turned his icy glare towards his son. "Leave the lying to the pros," he said. "You stink at it. Now take me to the artifacts that aren't supposed to be here."

Huy fearfully retreated to his mattress, where he lifted the down-filled rectangle, revealing almost three-dozen objects of varying sizes, all of them made from the same mysterious substance as the edifice.

Suddenly, Huy's eyes went wide and he whispered, "No."

Makar aimed the handgun at the base of his offspring's skull. "You shouldn't say no to your father, young man. You could wind up with scars around more than just your eye."

Huy's stare was dark and defiant, yet tinged with a child's fear. "I wasn't talking to you...Father."

~ ~ ~

Von Honig was still in free-fall. Serpents wrapped around his body, constricting his breathing and sweating venom. Maggots burst from his flesh, nibbling their way into his guts.

He knew this was real...Lewis/Makar told him it was true. He was a true psychic, wasn't he? He could translate foreign languages and torture with the power of his mind, right?

Huy's voice thundered inside his skull. *He has the items. I am sorry.*

Von Honig forced his mind to still itself. "What is your father doing?"

Without warning, the writer felt a hollowness in his chest and a sharp pain in his right wrist. *Father has my wrist. He's so strong.* A moment later, Huy's voice was almost on the verge of weeping. *ONLYBABIESCRYONLYBABIESCRY! What do I do?*

As snakes exploded from his fingernails and his blood turned into bleach, von Honig gritted his teeth and stated with absolute conviction:

"Hold tight, Huy. Help is on its way."

~ ~ ~

Rostislav Makar gripped a rectangular object tightly as if to shatter it in his grasp. "It doesn't work, brat. I have no more power than I did before."

Tears of pain and frustration poured down Huy's face. He pulled at his father's fingers, but to no avail. "I don't know what they do. Ask von Honig."

Makar spoke calmly. "Tell me how to make this work, boy, and I'll make sure the flight home is pleasant for you."

"I am home!" Huy cried. "I won't go to America."

"America?" Makar laughed. "Once you tell me how these damn objects work, you might wind up living in Paris or Moscow or wherever the highest bidder wishes to place us." An edge crept into Makar's voice. "Now behave, you little bastard, or you'll spend the flight in a coma." He reached into his pants pocket for another chemical-filled pillow. "Want a taste of *my* powers?"

"You...have...no...powers..."

Makar and Huy turned. Conrad von Honig rose to his feet, however unsteadily, pushing himself upwards with his hands still behind his back. He squinted at the pair and spoke slowly. "Get away from him, Lewis—or Makar, or whatever the hell your name is. It ends here."

"Screw you, von Honig." Makar reached into his pocket and withdrew at least a half dozen of the pillows. "I'm going to send you straight to hell."

Surprised at the clarity in his own voice, von Honig announced, "I'm onto your psycho-chemical scam, Makar."

"Say goodbye to your sanity, von Honig," said Makar, and he smiled as he dropped the pillows into his open mouth.

As Makar positioned the squares in his mouth, von Honig charged toward him, head down like a bull racing towards the matador. Makar's eyes widened with mad anticipation as he drew in a full lungful of air, ready to spit lunacy at his foe.

But just as Makar's lungs expanded, a *snap!* sounded from behind von Honig, who immediately brought up his right fist in a flawless uppercut to his kidnapper's chin. Makar's head flew backwards.

"Y-your hands..." Makar shook his head, swallowed instinctively, then pointed at von Honig's fists. "They were bound..."

"I scraped the bonds against the wall when I slid against it," said von Honig, "just enough to weaken the tape." Makar stole a quick glance at the wall where his former captive stood just a moment before and saw the shreds of adhesive tape on the floor. "Do your so-called 'powers' not include precognition, Lewis?"

Makar's eyes blazed with fury. "Shut up, von Honig." He lifted the pistol. "I'm still in charge here." He indicated Huy with the barrel of his handgun. "I'm taking my bastard to America so we can brainwash key people in Washington, then the Kremlin, then every capital of the world until people start...start...seeing things...muh... my way..."

Von Honig calmly removed the pistol from Makar's hand. He watched a line of chemical-infused saliva slowly trickle from one corner of Makar's half-open mouth. Less than a minute later, the Russian's knees gave way, and he crumpled to the floor.

Von Honig allowed himself a *Hmmph!* of disgust. "The chemicals entered Makar's system slowly," he recounted, "absorbed through the flesh of his mouth. I gambled that swallowing the pure stuff would overwhelm him."

He turned towards Huy. "Now about the artifacts, young man. I'd like to take a –" The writer looked down at the palm of his hand where Huy had pressed a nine-sided star into its center.

A moment later, the world turned dark and Conrad von Honig knew no more.

13.

When he finally awoke, Conrad von Honig didn't realize the airplane had been in flight for more than two hours.

He looked outside and saw nothing but a sea of ivory fluff in the bluest sky he could recall in quite some time. A glance onto the seat beside him revealed a wooden box. He slowly opened it to find a pair of cylindrical containers.

Von Honig lifted a large grape jelly jar packed full of lukewarm, sticky rice. Unscrewing an old thermos revealed a bright yellow broth, still steaming hot, that contained a number of local vegetables and the heady aroma of chicken. In less than five minutes, he gratefully consumed the contents of both vessels.

When von Honig turned his attention to the wooden box, he noticed something else at the bottom—a leather strap threaded through a circular medallion with a hole in the center. It was a piece of crude jewelry constructed of no metal or stone known on Earth.

Huy's artifact ... or its twin, more likely

Von Honig lifted the strap and watched the medallion swing freely in the gently-rocking aircraft. Struggling to prevent his hands from shaking, he wrapped his hand tightly around the pendant.

I trust you enjoyed your meal, sir...

"I did," von Honig whispered to the familiar voice in his head. "Thank you for your consideration." He gathered his thoughts. "Kindly explain how I got here and where I am headed."

You were guided to your aircraft, just as I led you across the jungle. As for your destination, you are going home. Colonel Trahn's pilot will ensure your safety.

Before von Honig could frame an intelligent question, the boy transmitted into his brain: *Your time with us has been quite instructive, sir. I now know how to increase the range of my telepathy with minimal effort as well as some new uses for my talents.*

Von Honig bit his lip, uncertain if he should ask his next question. However, his head filled with gentle chuckling. *You are worried that I've turned you into a Communist? The teachings of our beloved Chairman will fade in time. Unless you want me to make them more a part of your—*

"I'll get back to you about that," von Honig interrupted. "What of your father?"

An image of Rostislav Makar – or Rob Lewis – appeared in von Honig's mind. The Russian rested on a thin mat inside the edifice. His eyes and mouth lay open, unmoving, his senses overwhelmed, and his mind vulnerable.

He will be treated...in time. Colonel Trahn responds well to my attempt to recover his sanity. I have every faith that my father will as well. He added, *When I get around to it.*

Von Honig briefly "saw" a younger version of the agent as Huy continued his narration. *Father used research chemicals that affected his mind. He had no talents for me to inherit. To please his Russian masters, my father infiltrated the CIA, looking for more mental soldiers. Instead, he birthed one.*

"And after he abandoned you?"

Von Honig's eyes stung from tear drops shed several hundred miles away. *The Americans saw through his deception upon his reassignment to Washington, D.C. Unable to return to Moscow as a failure, he went freelance.* The boy sniffed loudly. *Thanks to the artifacts, I now know my father even better than he knows himself.*

Drawing a long breath, von Honig focused on the circlet in his hand. "Now, as for me?"

At that moment, von Honig saw the inside of an inexplicable edifice a continent away. Huy stood, his arms crossed, a funereal expression on his youthful face. With one hand clutching his artifact, Huy reached out with the other and the world went dark once more.

When the writer opened his eyes again, he found himself lying on a bed inside a hotel room back in Hawaii. For all he knew, it was the same room rented for him by Lewis–or Makar, or whoever he was supposed to be.

Rolling over, von Honig noticed his wallet, his keys, and a ticket for a first-class flight to New York City on the bedside table.

However, the companion to the trinket that had hung from Huy's neck was gone.

Von Honig sat up on the edge of the bed, noticing that his own clothes had replaced the fatigues that had been previously supplied to him.

Huy's voice was faint but still discernible from across an ocean. *Thank you again, sir, for your help in deducing what the artifacts can do. I look forward to our next meeting, when you will remember all we have accomplished together. But until then...*

Von Honig felt his heart pounding while trembling fingers stroked invisible scars over his left eye—no, not *his* scars, but those of a phantom, thousands of miles away. The writer's hands shook in rage and bewilderment. *How many times must I allow myself to be duped? To be manipulated? I need to stop nipping at every worm in the water.*

He searched any memories of Huy, but there were few to be found. What the investigator did find was a lingering hole filled with the gentle chuckling of a dust child that continued to haunt his mind – and his dreams – for a long time to come.

(NOTE: All quotes attributed to Mao Tse-Tung are from The Quotations of Chairman Mao Tse-Tung, Foreign Language Press, 1966)

THE IRON DOOR

by Terry Alexander

The jarring ring of the telephone invaded Conrad von Honig's mind. He broke off his meditation, opened his eyes and stared at the offending instrument across the room. He found himself counting the rings, and when he reached twelve, he unfolded his legs from the lotus position and rose to his feet. He crossed the floor and lifted the phone, cradling it to his ear.

"Von Honig."

"Conrad von Honig, this is Clay Wallace." The voice on the other end spoke rapidly with a thick southern accent. "I want to talk to you about some things I've seen here in Oklahoma."

"How did you get this number? Only a few people have it. Who gave it to you?"

"One of your friends thought that I should talk to you about what I saw."

"Tell me your story, and be quick about it. You interrupted my meditation."

"Are you familiar with the Heavener Runestone? It's a huge boulder, and legend says there are Viking letters carved on it."

"I'm familiar with it. I've heard a homesick Swede carved those symbols in the rock when he was working for the railroad."

"So you don't believe that Vikings carved those symbols?"

"You're wasting my time, Mr. Wallace." An annoyed tone crept into von Honig's voice. "If you look closely enough, you'll see the tool marks on the boulder."

"Those aren't the only symbols carved into rocks in southern Oklahoma. Poteau has some rock carvings."

"True. And they are even newer than the ones near Heavener. I don't know which one of my friends gave you my number, but when I finish with them, no one will ever give it to another charlatan."

"There is another rock carving at Heavener that very few people know about. It's back in the hills, and it shows a large man with a balloon head standing with what looks like a normal-sized family—a man, a woman and two children. Considering the age in which it was carved, it's in remarkable condition."

Von Honig paused for a second and licked his lips. "Tell me more about this carving."

"Considering the relative size of each figure," Wallace went on, "the balloon man must have been nine feet tall."

"Take a picture of this carving and send it to me, with the negative, so I can study it at my leisure."

"I can send you a picture, but I'd like for you to come to Oklahoma and see the carving for yourself," said Wallace said. "Have you heard of the cave with the iron door?"

"Naturally. One legend is that Belle Starr or some other criminal from the Old West robbed a train near Hobart and took a sliding metal door from the box car and dragged it out into the wilderness and put it on a cave where they hid their loot." Von Honig paused for a moment. "But that story is pure rubbish."

"That's true," said Wallace. "That story is a crock of bull. Back in the sixteenth or seventeenth century, there was a small Mexican settlement in what are now known as the Elk Mountains. These Mexicans were mining the ore in the mountains and sending it by burro back into Mexico."

"Mr. Wallace, I'm a busy man," von Honig interrupted. "I don't have the time or the inclination to chase ghosts and myths in Oklahoma." He paused for a moment. "There are examples of rock carvings all over the United States. There are some very interesting ones at Massacre, Nevada."

"After the Mexicans died out," Wallace went on, "Jesse James and his gang hid about a hundred thousand in gold inside the mine, and after that Belle Starr added another two hundred thousand." Wallace paused, then added, "If you can believe those stories."

"You're a treasure hunter, Mr. Wallace?"

"I am, but I know when I'm involved in something over my head. The rock carvings near the iron door show the tall man with the balloon head. Only this time, he's standing close to a large plate-shaped object. Whatever it is, it makes him look small."

"Really." The tone of von Honig's voice changed. "How can you be sure it's the same figure?"

"There's a marking on the right arm of balloon head, near the wrist, it looks like three horizontal stripes," said Wallace.

"Three stripes? You're sure it's three stripes?"

"I'm sure, and I've got pictures to prove it." An awkward silence stretched for several seconds. "When can I expect you in Oklahoma?"

"Are there any airfields close to you?"

"Tulsa and Oklahoma City both have major airports. So does Fort Smith, Arkansas. Tell me where you want to go and I'll pick you up."

"No need," said von Honig. "I have a friend who's a pilot. He can land his plane on any field that's available. If you're close to a crop dusting operation, he can land on their runway."

"If it's all the same to you, Conrad, I'd rather meet at one of the bigger airports. There are some other interested parties, and they would love to get their hands on the gold in the cave."

"Let me guess. Some of your treasure hunting friends have taken a dislike to your methods, and they want to cut you out of the pie?"

"Something like that. Let's just say they don't have reason to love me."

"I want to see the carving at Heavener. If I'm convinced that it's authentic, I'll accompany you to the site in the Elk Mountains."

"Catch a plane for Fort Smith and I'll pick you up there," said Wallace. "Bring hiking clothes and some good boots. We'll be going into some rough country."

"Mr. Wallace, I've recently returned from the Balkans. I doubt anything in Oklahoma could be rougher than what I've experienced."

"If memory serves me right, there should be a plane arriving from the East Coast tomorrow at two in the afternoon. I'll be waiting for you there."

"How will I know you?" von Honig asked.

"I'll be wearing a sweat-stained white cowboy hat. Come ready for a campout. Where we're going may not be as rough as the Balkans, but it's rough enough."

The phone clicked and went silent in von Honig's ear. He slowly placed the receiver back on the cradle. "I hope this trip is worth it," he mumbled, and headed down a hallway to pack his duffle bag.

~ ~ ~

Von Honig walked down the steps from the Boeing 727. He crossed the tarmac with a line of people and passed through the glass doors to the cool interior of the Fort Smith Regional Airport. His eyes shifted through the small crowd gathered inside, and then he spotted the stained cowboy hat.

A big broad-shouldered man with red hair and a matching mustache and goatee walked toward him, his hand extended.

"You look just like your picture, Mr. von Honig."

"You're Clay Wallace?" von Honig asked.

"The one and only."

"Do you have any identification?"

The big man grinned. "It pays to be cautious." He reached into his back pocket and pulled his wallet free. He flipped it open and removed the license. "You can see my description there."

Von Honig grinned. "It does say your name is Clay Wallace and you have red hair, but this says you only weigh two-hundred pounds."

"Yeah, I haven't updated my weight in a while." He reached for the duffle again. "Let me help you with your gear?"

"Sure," said von Honig. "Did you bring the pictures and the negatives?"

"They're in the pickup, in the glove box." Wallace swung the duffle onto his shoulder. He looked at the crowd around them, searching for faces. Three men walked inside and lounged around the exit doors. "Damn."

"What is it?" von Honig asked. "What's wrong?"

"Them three birds standing by the doors. They're Bryce Reynolds' men."

"Who's Bryce Reynolds?"

"One of those fellas that doesn't have any reason to love me." Wallace grabbed von Honig's elbow. "Come on," he said. "They haven't seen us yet. We'll go out the side door." He steered him across the crowded building and out into the bright sunlight.

"Come on," Wallace said again after a few steps. "We have to hurry, ten dollars says they have someone watching my pickup." He broke into a fast trot.

Von Honig matched his pace. "How serious is the disagreement between you and Reynolds?" he said.

"Scrious enough that he took a couple of shots at me last year." Wallace rounded the corner and stopped. "That blue pickup with the white top is mine." He gazed up and down the rows of parked vehicles.

"What are we waiting for?" von Honig urged. "Let's go before the others show up."

Wallace scratched at the whisker stubble along his chin. "Something's not right," he said. "Reynolds wouldn't make a mistake like that. He'd have someone watching my pickup."

"You didn't see Mr. Reynolds inside. Maybe his men forgot to place a sentry around your vehicle."

Wallace shook his head. "Not Reynolds," he said. "He never forgets a thing."

"Mr. Wallace, I insist we go forward at once, or I'll call off my part of this adventure."

Wallace nodded. "All right," he said. "Move fast, toss the duffle bag into the back and get inside as quick as you can."

The two men broke from cover, the soles of their shoes smacked against the asphalt as they raced toward the two-toned vehicle.

"Damn it!" Wallace cursed as they approached the truck. "The window's broken. I'll bet anything that Reynolds has the pictures."

Von Honig slowed to a stop and shook his head. "That's very convenient, isn't it? Someone breaks into your pickup and steals the evidence."

Wallace stopped and stared at von Honig. "What the hell are you trying to say? Do you think I vandalized my own vehicle?"

"Desperate men are known to do desperate things." Von Honig gazed around the parking lot. "Where are these men you spotted inside the airport? Where are they now?" He dropped his bag to the asphalt. "I think you brought me here under false pretenses to aid you in a search for outlaw gold."

"Don't fancy yourself so highly," said Wallace. A fluttering bit of paper caught his attention. He walked over and stooped to pick it up, and his expression was suddenly triumphant. "I'm a liar, huh? Brought you here under false pretenses?" He walked back toward von Honig and shoved the paper at him. "Then explain this!"

Von Honig glanced at the paper, a black-and-white photograph of a rock carving. The resolution of the image was sharp enough to capture the precise detail work in the carving. It showed four figures standing with a giant in a bulky suit with a huge round head.

"My apologies, Mr. Wallace," said von Honig after a moment. He reached down and grabbed the strap of his duffle bag. "It appears that I've done you an injustice."

"I'm tempted to tell you what you can do with your apology," said Wallace as he walked to the pickup and tossed the duffle bag in the back. "It'll cost me a hundred bucks to get this window fixed."

"Hey, Wallace, did you lose something?" It was a high-pitched voice, shouting to them from behind.

Wallace turned quickly. He pointed at the small man standing near a dull gray Jeep. "That is Bryce Reynolds."

"I heard you were bringing in some big shot to help you find the lost mine," Reynolds shouted. "It won't help you at all." The three thugs from the airport appeared, forming a semicircle behind him. "See, I've got the inside track on everything."

A tall shapely woman in a tight-fitting dress walked from the vehicle and took Reynolds' hand.

"Alice," Wallace whispered.

"Who's Alice?" von Honig asked.

As they watched, the dark-haired female wrapped herself around Reynolds and kissed him hard on the mouth.

"Alice Penney. We used to be friendly."

"Looks like she found a new friend." Von Honig threw his bag in the back of the truck. "Let's go. I want to look at the rock carving in Heavener."

"Conrad, we need to go straight to Hobart," said Wallace. "They have all the information on the canyon and the map and directions. All I have is my memory." The driver-side door on the truck screeched as he tugged it open. "We need to go to the Elk Mountains and find Devil's Canyon."

Von Honig grabbed Wallace's arm as he tried to climb into the truck. "Wait a minute," he said. "What do you mean *find*? I thought you knew where we were going!"

"I've been there. Eight months ago, I found the iron door." Wallace grabbed the steering wheel and looked down at von Honig's hand on his shirt sleeve. "I went back three months ago, after a big storm rolled through, and everything was different. My compass wouldn't work right. Nothing worked the way it was supposed to."

"What makes you think you can find it now?" Von Honig released his grip. He watched as Wallace took a set of keys from his pants pocket and climbed in behind the wheel, sliding the key into the ignition.

"I've rented a mule from a guy named Rudy Salina. That mule came in after a week of roaming, it had a chunk of gold caught in the hoof. It had been to the old mine."

Von Honig shook his head. "You rented a mule?"

"We're going to ride into the Elk Mountains. Rudy's mule is one of the best pack animals in the area." Wallace started the engine and shifted the column lever into first gear. "That mule has roamed all over those mountains. He can take us right to Devil's Canyon."

Von Honig stepped around to the passenger side of the truck, shaking his head the entire way. He climbed into the passenger seat and said, "We're depending on a mule to lead us into the mountains in search of a magical door."

When Wallace didn't answer right away, von Honig said, "We're going to Heavener first. You're going to show me the rock carving where this picture was taken. If I'm convinced it's genuine, then I'll go with you and we'll look for the lost mine."

"Conrad, we can't do that," said Wallace. "Reynolds and his people will beat us to Hobart." He released the clutch and drove through the parking lot toward the highway. "We need to be on the trail for the canyon at first light."

Von Honig grabbed the door handle. "Stop the vehicle," he demanded. "Let me out and I'll go back home. I have better things to do than get involved with a fortune hunter and a get-rich-quick scheme."

"Okay, you win," Wallace conceded. "We'll go to Heavener. I'll show you the carving, but that's going to really put us in a bind." He shook his head. "We'll have to drive all night to get to Rudy's place. I'll go the first hour or so, then you can take over for a while."

Von Honig frowned and shook his head. "I don't drive."

Wallace stopped and stared back at him, his expression suddenly incredulous. "What?"

Von Honig shrugged. "I don't drive."

"What, you mean you don't even have a license?"

"Nope."

Wallace kept staring, then finally looked away and shook his head. "Unbelievable," he muttered. Then he let out a sigh and said, "Okay, let's go. And make sure I don't fall asleep on the way."

~ ~ ~

"Wake up, Conrad. We're here." Wallace shook his shoulder.

Von Honig stretched. "What time is it?"

"I don't know. Five-thirty, maybe six. We need to hurry. It'll be dark before we can get to the rock carving you want to see." The driver side door opened with a loud squall. Wallace stepped to the ground and stretched. "My butt is numb."

Von Honig stepped from the pickup to the ground. "Any sign of Reynolds or his men?"

"No." Wallace scratched at his whiskered jowl. "They're driving west. They'll be in Hobart long before we get started." He pulled a snub-nosed .38 from the glove box and stuffed it in his back pocket. "Grab a flashlight. We'll need it."

"Is the gun necessary?" von Honig asked. "I just returned from an area where two armies were carrying fully automatic weapons. It didn't feel very safe."

"I'm a graduate of Vietnam," said Wallace. "Class of fifty-nine." His hands wrapped around a long four-cell flashlight. "It's better to have a gun and not need it than it is to need it and not have it. Don't worry. It's not that heavy." He grabbed a small backpack from behind the seat and passed it to von Honig. "We better take this with us. Medical kit and a few tools."

Von Honig strapped on the backpack and together they made their way down the narrow path, moving in silence for several minutes along a gentle incline. They came to a gate and Wallace opened it. Presently they crested the hill and started down. Wallace turned the beam of his light on a huge boulder. "There it is. The Heavener Runestone."

Von Honig stepped forward and let his own light play over the surface.

"Do you see the marks?" Wallace asked.

"Yes, I do," said von Honig. "I'm convinced a homesick Swede carved those letters into the stone." He brushed dirt from his fingers. "I hope the other rock carving is of better quality."

"It is. The carving is much deeper into the surface of the rock, and you won't see a hint of a tool mark. It looks as though each figure was drawn in a single motion."

"I'll believe it when I see it," said von Honig. "I've seen one carving with as much detail as you claim that this one has, and it was destroyed by a madman." He played his flashlight along the ground. "I hope you know where we're going."

"It's maybe forty-five minutes away. Not much of a trail though, and the path is overgrown. And you need to keep a lookout for snakes."

"Please. I've been in mountains where the only trail was a ledge that was barely six inches across, and I've seen Burmese pythons nearly twenty feet long." They started moving again, and von Honig matched Wallace step for step.

"I saw big snakes when I was one of the advisors in fifty-nine and sixty," said Wallace. "They had a smaller snake called a two-stepper. If it bit you, you'd manage to take about two steps before you died." Wallace went quiet for a moment. "We need to be quiet," he whispered. "Reynolds may have someone waiting for us." He aimed the flashlight toward the ground and moved forward silently.

Von Honig played his light on the ground. He saw a large black snake moving through the grass. Recognizing it as non-poisonous, he paid it little mind. Sweat collected under his hat, ran down his face and dripped onto his damp shirt. A mosquito buzzed around his face and settled on his nose. He waved it away and kept moving.

He glanced at the trees surrounding them, his internal clock telling him that he had been walking for more than a half-hour. "How much longer?" he whispered.

"It's just ahead." Wallace moved to a huge boulder half-buried in the hillside. He reached for a flat rock that was leaning against a side of the boulder and moved it away. "There it is."

Von Honig stepped forward, his light illuminating the rock carving. "You're right. This has been here a long time." He ran his fingers over the surface. "Very smooth. No rough edges at all. The human figures aren't wearing any clothes. Why didn't you tell me that earlier?" He turned and looked at Wallace.

"I didn't think you'd believe me."

Von Honig shrugged "This is amazing," he said. "I've seen a figure similar to this in South America." His hand played over the Balloon Man. "This figure–you're sure it's the same one you saw in the Elk Mountains."

"The very same."

"How can you be sure?" Von Honig swung the light toward Wallace.

The treasure hunter blocked the light with his hand to shield his eyes. "Take a close look at the right arm on Balloon Man, near the wrist."

"What am I looking for?"

"Don't play stupid," said Wallace. "You saw that mark on the sleeve. It's the same mark on the carving in South America, and the same mark is on the carving in the Elk Mountains." Wallace pulled a stem of grass from the ground and stuck it in his mouth.

"You've studied my work?" Von Honig straightened. "You knew about the South American carving."

"I did," Wallace admitted. He tossed the grass stem to the ground and stood. "Have you seen enough?"

"I need to measure these figures, take some decent pictures in the daylight. This discovery must be documented and shared."

"We need to get the hell out of here," said Wallace. "I know the guy who owns this property. He doesn't mind if I come up here and poke around, as long as I don't tell everybody what's up here." He lifted the flat rock and put it back over the carving. "He doesn't want this to be documented. He doesn't want news people and scientists and gawkers running around on his property. He wants to be left alone."

"This is an important discovery," von Honig argued. "If this carving depicts the same traveler as the one you claim is in the Elk Mountains, and it's certainly the same as the one I documented in South America, then it shows that this being traveled to far distant lands. It could be the lynchpin in my theory of beings from outside our world coming to Earth."

"When we find the iron door and get it open," said Wallace,

"and if we find some old Spanish gold inside, then we can talk to the owner here. Maybe we can convince him to change his mind at that time." He drew in a deep breath. "We need to get started for Hobart. It's a long drive."

Wallace headed back along the path toward the truck, and von Honig followed reluctantly.

"You didn't open the door when you were there before?" said von Honig. "Why?"

Wallace shook his head. "I can't really explain it," he said. "Something happened. A purple mist came from some odd-looking flowers. I remember thinking how pretty they were and how sweet they smelled." He took a few more steps without speaking, as though he were trying to solve a puzzle that had been eluding him for some time. "I woke up two days later. My tent and my other camp supplies were torn to bits and scattered around me. I didn't know where I was, and I didn't have any idea how to get back to camp or find my truck. I walked for three days before I found a road, and another half day before I found a house with a phone. Thankfully, the old timer at the house let me call Rudy. It was a party line, so I had to wait for two old biddies to stop gossiping long enough for me to make my call."

"Flowers and purple mist?" Von Honig's voice rose. "What kind of idiot do you take me for, Wallace? Did you even find the iron door, or is that a lie too?"

"I found it," Wallace insisted. "Rudy came and picked me up and took me to his place. Then the storms came in and it rained for three days. When it was over, I couldn't get to Devil's Canyon. I made another attempt a several months later, but I couldn't retrace my path."

"You couldn't find it then. Why are you so confident now?"

"I flew over the mountains in a Piper Cub. The pilot kept the plane at a low altitude, just above the tree tops and the electric lines. I spotted the door." Wallace paused for a moment. "The storms had knocked some trees down and they blocked the trail that I should have taken. The trail I followed took me in the opposite direction, away from the door."

"And you'll recognize the right trail when we approach it from the ground?" said von Honig.

"I can. We'll have to leave our horses behind for the final stretch and walk in on foot." He came onto a patch of level ground. "If I'm right, we'll get there late in the afternoon, set up camp, and then open the door early in the morning. Then you can get all the pictures you need for your next book."

"What are you going to be doing during this time?" von Honig asked.

Wallace grinned. "I'm going to look for the gold that the Mexicans left behind when they died out."

"You know the tales of gold and riches are just a pipe dream."

Wallace caught von Honig's arm. "Hold up a second," he said, pulling him behind a large pine. "There's someone around my pick-up."

Von Honig peered around the side of the tree. "Are you sure? I don't see anything."

"Look toward the rear quarter-panel. Someone moved back there, I'm sure of it."

Von Honig peered into the darkness and waited for several seconds until a movement near the truck caught his eye. "Yeah, I saw it," he said. He glanced at Wallace. "I think it's a woman."

"I think you're right, but I can't tell for certain."

"We can't stay here all night," said von Honig, scratching at the whiskers along his jaw. "I'll keep walking down the trail. You circle around and come up behind her."

"Sounds good," said Wallace. "Give me a couple of minutes before you start moving." He disappeared into the night.

Von Honig stared at the pickup, occasionally noticing a bit of movement.

"Clay, I know you're out there. You and the Con Man. It's Heather. Why are you here? Reynolds and the rest of the crew are driving to Hobart."

Von Honig's resentment got the better of him. "Young woman, that name offends me," he said. "I want you to stop addressing me that way."

"You must be the dude they told us about." Heather stepped away from the pickup. "Come over here, I want to talk to you."

"I'll be there in a second."

"Where's Clay?" she asked. "And don't tell me you don't know. I won't fall for it."

"Actually, he should be coming up behind you at any time," said von Honig as he approached the pickup.

"If he tried to circle around me, Larry would find him and bring him here." A pistol appeared in her hand. "I can't figure out why you came here. Reynolds knows about the gold in the lost mine." She grew silent for a second. "It doesn't make sense."

He raised his hands and edged closer to her. "Wallace wanted to show me something. Can I remove the backpack? It's very heavy. The weight is straining my shoulders."

"What is it?" she asked. The flashlight beam glinted off the pistol barrel as it quivered in her hand. "Is it gold? Did you two find gold up there?"

"It's the stuff that dreams are made of," said von Honig, coming to a stop. "Let me take it off, and you can look in it all you want. We may even cut you in for a share."

The sound of a snapping twig behind her drew her attention. She half turned her head. "Did you hear that, Larry? He said they might cut me in for a share."

"I don't really think that's going to happen," Wallace said.

Wallace's voice in the dark created enough of a momentary distraction for von Honig to reach out and snatch the pistol from the woman's hand. "I don't think you'll need this," he said, releasing the hammer and stuffing the weapon in his pocket.

"Relax," she said. "It isn't loaded." She leaned against the pickup. "Sure didn't figure you'd get around Larry. He's a great man to have in the woods."

"He got careless," Wallace said with a grin. "A skunk got too close and he moved to get away from it. He gave himself away."

"You didn't hurt him?" Heather asked.

"He'll live," said Wallace. "Might have to spend some time in a hospital though." He circled to the driver side of the pickup and yanked open the door. "He's hard-headed."

He rested his hands on the door. "Get in, Heather. I'll drop you off in town. You can call someone to come up here and get Larry."

"Do you trust this woman?" von Honig asked.

"She and Alice are running with the wrong crowd, but I know Heather well enough. I won't leave her out here with no transportation and force her to walk back to town."

"I always liked you, Clay." She grabbed the door handle on the passenger side and pressed the button. "I think my sister made a big mistake when she left you and took up with Reynolds." She climbed into the seat and scooted to the middle.

Von Honig settled in next to her and slammed the door. "Let's get started," he said. "We have a long way to go."

"They've got a big lead on you," said Heather. "They'll be at that farmhouse and be on the trail a long time before you get there." She shook her head. "Still can't figure out why you came here, though."

~ ~ ~

"What the hell happened here?" von Honig nudged the door open and stepped to the ground. He stared at the smoldering remains of the house.

"Rudy? Oliva? Where are you?" Wallace opened the driver's door. "Can you hear me?" He wiped tears from his eyes. "Damn it, they're not here." He stared at the two vehicles parked in the driveway. "That black Plymouth belongs to Reynolds."

"They took your friends with them," von Honig said. "Would Reynolds take them to the Mountains?"

Wallace grew silent for a moment. "Gotta check the corrals. Maybe they didn't run off all the horses." He broke into a run toward the holding pen.

The gates were opened wide and the corral empty. Wallace stopped at the gate and stared at the tracks dotting the ground. "We're afoot."

"How far away is the mine?" von Honig asked.

"It's a least a two day ride, part of it over some brushy country." Wallace shook his head. "It'd take us five days to walk there."

"Reynolds didn't want us behind him," said von Honig. "Is there anything else we can use for transportation on this place?"

Wallace snapped his fingers. "Wait a minute. I need to check on something." He ran to the edge of the barn and disappeared around a corner.

Several minutes later, von Honig heard the pop and sputter of a motor. The sound grew louder as Wallace rounded the corner driving a faded green John Deere tractor with a narrow tricycle front-end. "They missed this," he shouted to von Honig over the chug of the engine. "Good thing Rudy parked it in the barn. We can throw our gear on the trailer and drive as close as we can, then we'll carry the gear the rest of the way."

Von Honig shook his head. "We're not going to sneak up on them," he said. "That's for certain."

"This Poppin' Johnny is a tough tractor. It's low geared and we can take it in some really tight places before we have to park it." He drove the tractor closer to the pickup, killed the engine and hopped to the ground. "They have a big lead on us, but we might be able to narrow the distance. They'll have to rest the horses and we can just keep on going."

Von Honig threw his duffle bag on the trailer, then grabbed Wallace's bag and placed it gingerly on the rough boards. "Can we catch up with Reynolds in time to save your friends?"

"If we don't, and Reynolds gets that door open, he'll leave their bodies in that old mine," said Wallace. He pulled a pistol from the glove box and a sawed off double-barreled shotgun from behind the bench seat. "Take this," he said, passing the shotgun to von Honig along with a box of shells. "If things get bad, don't hesitate to use it."

"I don't like these things," von Honig grunted. He climbed aboard the trailer and held on to the angle-iron railing as Wallace mounted the tractor seat, started the engine and released the clutch. The tractor jumped forward, and the front wheels left the ground for a brief instant and then settled back to the earth. A column of smoke came from the exhaust stack and settled around von Honig and the trailer. Wallace passed through the gate and pulled the gas feed lever toward himself. The tractor increased in speed, and the smoke hung low to the ground.

"Is this the top speed?" von Honig shouted.

"This is it, but this tractor will go on as long as we have fuel." Wallace glanced over his shoulder. "I filled the tank and I've got an extra ten gallons in those two cans. I think we'll be alright. You can lay back and take a nap if you want."

"How can anyone sleep with all this noise?" said von Honig. He pulled his hat down over his eyes and used the duffle bag for a pillow. Within seconds he was snoring.

~ ~ ~

"Conrad, wake up." A hand touched his shoulder. Von Honig reached out and grabbed the fingers, giving them a savage twist.

"Damn it, let go," Wallace grunted, retracting his right hand and shaking it. "What's wrong with you?"

"Sorry," said von Honig. "I was dreaming about another place. Why did you stop?" He glanced around and frowned when he realized that Wallace had parked the tractor on the outer edge of a massive briar field. A wall of hanging vines grew into the trees around the edge of the briars. Flowers grew along the vines and brilliant reds, dark blues and rich purple blooms colored the living ring.

"We have a problem," said Wallace. "I saw the flash of a scoped rifle in those trees. Reynolds has a guy working for him named Skip. He's a crack shot. He can hit anything up to three-hundred yards." Wallace leaned on the angle iron railing.

Von Honig shook his head. "Guess they heard this monstrosity and knew we were behind them," he said. "I'm assuming you have an idea."

"Yeah, I do. But it's not a very good idea."

"You want me to drive the tractor through this mess and keep our visitor focused on me while you circle around and get behind him."

"Yeah, I know it's a bad idea," said Wallace, with an edge of irritation suddenly creeping into his voice. "Especially with you not being a driver and all. I need thirty to forty minutes to get into position."

"You'll have to show me how to start this thing," said von Honig, "and how to operate it, for that matter." He paused for a moment, then said, "And you need to understand, if I see the flash in the trees, I'm jumping off."

The wind picked up before Wallace could answer. It swirled through the briars and plucked the plants up by the roots, carrying them high into the bright sunshine.

Von Honig shielded his eyes from the debris. "I've never seen a whirlwind like this."

"I've never seen one this strong," Wallace answered. "It's like a miniature tornado."

A column of vapor rose from von Honig's mouth. "The temperature's dropping," he said. "We need to find shelter."

"Get under the trailer." Wallace dropped to his belly and rolled under the rough-cut boards. Von Honig joined him, positioning himself near the single axle.

"I've never seen the temperature drop so fast," said Wallace. "It's at least thirty degrees cooler."

"I was hiking through the South African jungle once, when a weather inversion occurred," von Honig recounted. "Three members of our party froze to death before we could find shelter, but it was a fast moving event without a whirlwind."

The first hail stone struck the angle iron frame and shattered. The resulting chunks of ice scattered over the trailer. A second and third followed immediately. Then the sky opened up and an onslaught of hail stones battered the trailer.

The heavy thump of ice made conversation impossible. Von Honig covered his ears and curled into a small ball. The hail storm ended as quickly as it came, passing within seconds. Von Honig opened his eyes, a wall of hail stones surrounding the trailer. He reached out and pushed against the wall, feeling it give slightly.

This is impossible. His hands ran over the icy surface.

"Damn," Wallace breathed. "I've never seen weather like this."

"We need to kick our way out of here," said von Honig. "I don't fancy staying here until this melts." He kicked at the icy wall. Several hail stones dislodged and rolled under the trailer.

Wallace followed von Honig's lead and presently they found themselves standing outside the trailer. A mound of melting hail stones surrounded them.

Von Honig shook his head. "We're lucky it didn't beat through the wooden boards," he said. He glanced up at the tractor. The icy balls had crushed in the shroud and the gas tank, and bent the seat into a misshapen mass of twisted metal.

"Check the gear, see what you can salvage," said Wallace. "I'm going to check on our guest."

Von Honig watched as Wallace departed. He shook his head and raked the ice away from the supplies. The hail stones had beaten holes in the duffle bags and bent the cans of food and coffee. The replacement clothes he had brought were soaked from the melting ice. "That was a very strange weather pattern," he muttered to himself. He glanced toward the tree line, and a hint of movement caught his eye. He assumed it was Wallace.

How did he get there so fast? He just left a minute ago.

"You need to go back," a dull monotone chattered behind him.

Von Honig turned quickly, his fist up in a defensive posture. He stopped and stared at the pale-skinned man before him. Blood trickled from a massive wound on the man's head, the only suggestion of color in his complexion. His rain-soaked clothes stuck to his body.

"Turn around now, while you can," the pale man said. "It's not worth dying for." Spittle appeared at the corner of his mouth and dribbled past his bottom lip to the whisker stubble on his chin. "You'll die if you keep going."

"We're not going to turn back," Von Honig said. "I have to document the stone carvings."

"Reynolds and the others won't find the door. The old ones left several tricks behind to keep the iron door a secret. He doesn't want his gravesite disturbed." The inflection never changed in his voice.

"Gravesite," von Honig said, grabbing the man's shoulder. "You mean one of the visitors' remains are inside the cave?"

"Don't touch him, Conrad." It was Wallace's voice, with more than a trace of urgency. "Skip, get your hands where we can see them."

Von Honig's eyes never left Skip's face. "He's hurt, Clay. Those hail stones beat him badly."

Wallace moved forward slowly. He checked Skip's hands and found them empty. "I knew something was wrong when I found this in the tree line." He nodded to the rifle and pulled a shiny nickel plated .38 snub nose from his waistband. "Skip wouldn't leave his weapons laying around—not if he was in his right mind."

"They know you're coming, Clay," said Skip. "Reynolds is waiting to kill you." He stared at Wallace with wide eyes. "He's convinced there's gold in that cave. Alice believes he'll keep her around, but if he finds any gold, Reynolds will keep it all for himself."

"What about Rudy and his girlfriend?" said Wallace. "Are they still alive?"

Skip nodded. "They are for now. Reynolds is going to kill them and leave the bodies inside the cave after he takes all the gold." He glanced toward the wagon. "I'm sleepy," he said. "I need to rest for a few minutes." He walked to the flatbed and crawled aboard.

Wallace surveyed the tractor and shook his head. "Those hail stones beat the hell out of the Poppin' Johnny," he said.

"Think we can get it running again?"

Wallace glanced at von Honig and then at the unwanted passenger snoring on the flatbed. "I hope so. This thing may be slow and noisy, but it beats walking."

"We can't leave Skip behind," said von Honig. "Those hail stones have addled his brain. Someone has to keep an eye on him for his own protection."

Wallace moved to the tractor. "I don't like the idea of keeping him with us," he said. "What if he's faking?" He moved to the front of the tractor. "The fan shroud is bent. The blades will hit it when we get this baby running. See if you can find something I can use to get it bent back into shape."

"Did you see his horse back in the trees?" von Honig asked.

"No, I didn't. Figure it tore loose when the storm hit."

Von Honig shielded his eyes. "There's a spotted horse and rider along the tree line," he said. "Most people won't shoot from the back of a horse, despite what you see in the movies. Most horses would raise hell if that happened."

"Keep your eyes on them," Wallace said, then turned to focus on the tractor.

"The rider's hands are crossed on the saddle horn," von Honig said after a few moments. "Whoever he is, he's content to stare at us."

"Forget about him for a minute," said Wallace. "Find something I can use on this shroud."

Von Honig raked the melting hailstones to the side until he found a sizable rock that Wallace could fit into the small space. "I think this will work."

"That's perfect," said Wallace. "Take a look at the distributor cap. Make sure it isn't cracked and the inside is dry. There's a screwdriver in the tool box."

"I don't know anything about tractor engines." Von Honig moved to the front of the tractor kept an eye on the rider in the distance. "Our friend is moving."

"Figure he's going back to report to Reynolds."

"You'd be wrong," said von Honig. "It's a woman on that horse, and she coming this way." He rested his hands on his hips.

Wallace grabbed the screwdriver from the fender tool box. He let his foot rest on the front tire. "That's Alice," he said. "What the hell is going on here?" He fished a cigarette from his shirt pocket and stuck the filtered end in his mouth. He fished a Zippo from his pocket.

Von Honig scratched his chin. *Where did that cigarette and lighter come from?*

The horse and rider approached slowly. The pinto kept its head down, while its tired feet kicked at the hail stones. Alice pulled back on the reins and raised her head. "Everything's gone to hell," she said. Her eyes held a dull sheen. "The horses went crazy. They tried to turn around and go home. Rudy couldn't get them to calm down. Then the weather went screwy, cold wind and freezing drizzle, we couldn't even get a fire started when we camped."

"We had a hail storm here," said Wallace. He took the cigarette from his mouth and flipped a length of ash to the ground. He turned to the distributor cap and had it loose within seconds. "This looks good, just a small crack. It'll be alright."

Alice nodded. "I got separated from the main group and decided to ride along our back trail." She glanced at Skip, still sleeping on the flatbed. "Where did you find him? Did you have to rough him up so much?"

"I didn't touch Skip," said Wallace. "The storm got him." He glanced at Alice's horse. "That pinto's done in. Tie him to the back of the trailer and you can go with us. After a good night's rest, it should be able to carry you and Skip back to the Rudy's place. You can use one of the cars to get him to a doctor."

Alice nodded. "Sounds good," she said. "When are you going to camp?"

"If we can get this thing to start," said Wallace, patting the hood of the tractor, "we can go on for another hour or two." He turned to Alice. "Tie the horse to the trailer and take care of Skip," he told her.

Von Honig glanced at the woman, then back at Wallace. "I see you've changed your mind about taking people with us on this adventure."

"Me and Alice have a history," Wallace whispered. "She might be money hungry, but she wouldn't kill me."

"I don't want her or her friends to kill either of us," said von Honig. He pointed at the metal tractor seat. "Let me get that shotgun ready."

Wallace climbed aboard the tractor. "Are you having second thoughts about going on?"

Von Honig shrugged. "You have to admit, this places us in a delicate position," he said. "We have two people from the enemy camp in our midst."

Wallace put the tractor in neutral and hit the starter button. The engine turned over slowly, coughed once and started. A column of dark smoke rose from the stack. "I don't like the look of that smoke," he muttered. "Awful dark."

"Put it in gear and let's go," said von Honig. "We need to make up some time."

Wallace put the tractor into gear and popped the clutch. It jumped forward, leaving von Honig to chase after it and jump up on the fender well.

"You didn't have to do that," von Honig said, swinging his legs over the metal railing and into the trailer. He took a seat on the rough lumber and rested his back on the rail. "I could have misjudged my jump and broke my leg."

"This rig's really touchy now," said Wallace. "It wasn't acting like this before the storm." He glanced over his shoulder. "I can't figure it out."

"It's the storm," said Skip, who was awake now after the tractor's noisy, jerky start. He leveled his blank stare on von Honig. "The storm did it. It changed everything."

~ ~ ~

"Something's wrong." Wallace pressed the clutch pedal and let the tractor roll to a stop. "This isn't right," he said. "Everything's totally wrong."

Von Honig hopped from the wagon and walked to the side of the John Deere. "What now?" he asked, his hands gripped the shotgun tightly.

"The landscape is all wrong. We should have come upon a rock mound and made a turn to the left. Instead, we're in this canyon with solid walls on both sides and..." Wallace shaded his eyes and gazed into the distance.

"And the canyon is closing in on us, growing narrower as we go forward," said von Honig, finishing the sentence.

"Yeah," said Wallace. "I don't understand it. I've been in these mountains a hundred times and I've never seen this canyon before." He grew silent for a moment. "Think I see a break up ahead. If we push it, we can get there before dark. We can sit up camp and get some rest."

Von Honig nodded. "Good idea," he said. "I'll scrounge up enough supper for all of us."

"I could use some food," said Wallace.

Alice walked up behind them. "Hope the coffee pot made it through," she said. "I could use a hot cup of Joe."

Von Honig nodded. "It's been banged up a lot," he said, "but it'll serve."

"Horses." Alice pointed off into the distance.

A line of horses charged through the gap in the canyon. Dust rose from their pounding hooves as they ran toward the tractor.

"They're scared," said Wallace. "Something scared the hell out of them."

"The big black in the center is dragging something," said von Honig, shielding his eyes with his hand. "Might be a man."

"That's Whitlock's horse," Alice whispered. "They're on foot now."

Von Honig jumped to his feet. "They're running straight for us!" he said. "Get behind the tractor, between the rear wheels. That should protect us."

"Get to safety," said Wallace. "I'm going to stop that black horse. That man might still be alive."

"You can't get him by yourself," von Honig mumbled. "I'll go with you." He turned to help Alice to safety, but the glistening nickel plated revolver in her hand brought him up short.

"Does Reynolds give those shooters out to everyone in his group?" He raised his hands above his head.

Alice smirked. "Yeah, I guess he does. Now, put that shotgun down, real easy."

"I knew you were faking. I knew it. But I couldn't get Clay to see though your act."

"Clay and I were very special once, before I took up with Reynolds." She moved to a safe position and waved von Honig toward the trailer. "We were all friends. Clay and I were going to get married, and then we found the gold bars on Blue Mountain. That changed everything."

"Blue Mountain?" Von Honig glanced at the approaching horses. Wallace had positioned himself in the center of their path.

"Big steep hill down in Leflore County. There was a rumor of confederate gold buried there." She glanced over her shoulder. "Skip, get over here."

The man moved with slow ponderous steps.

"Hurry, Skip. Those horses will be here in just a second." Alice glanced at the man with the blank stare.

Von Honig followed her glance. "I can help him," he said.

"Keep your mouth shut and be still." Alice waved the pistol. "We need Clay alive. If you keep talking you could wind up dead."

"I don't understand. What's going on?"

"I said shut up." Alice cocked the hammer. "One more word from you and I'll give you an extra belly button."

Von Honig nodded.

"Damn it, Skip, get over here," Alice barked. "Those lumps on the head have scrambled your brain."

An uneven smile split Skip's face as he wandered behind the tractor.

Von Honig watched as Wallace jumped at the horse dragging the man shape. A cloud of dust obscured his vision for a brief moment as Wallace caught the reins and bridle.

"What the hell is going on?" Wallace shouted. "It's a dummy." He turned to look at von Honig and Alice behind the tractor.

"Actually, you're the dummy," said Reynolds, pulling the horse to a stop and bracing a sawed-off shotgun on the saddle horn. "Get your hands up, Clay. I don't want to shoot you."

How did he do that? von Honig thought. *That horse and rider ap-*

peared from nowhere. He glanced toward Alice. *This doesn't make any sense. How can I hear what they're saying at this distance?*

Wallace grinned. "You won't shoot me," he said. "You pull the trigger on that scatter gun, and that horse will buck you off and most likely stomp you to death."

Reynolds turned his head slightly and raised his voice to call into the distance. "Whitlock, can you hit him from your position?" he said, scratching the end of his nose.

"Yes, sir," a voice came back. "You give the word and I can nail him."

Wallace searched for the speaker but couldn't locate him.

"Arms and legs only," said Reynolds. "We need him alive." He pressed the safety on, and slid the shotgun into the leather scabbard on the saddle. "Whitlock isn't as good as Skip with a rifle, but he'll do in this instance. You have a choice, Clay. Work for me willingly, or be crippled for the rest of your life."

"Why do you need me?" asked Wallace, throwing the dummy to the ground in disgust. "Did you get lost?"

Reynolds nodded. "Yeah, we did," he said. "We took a break to rest the horses, and everything had changed when we mounted again." He slung his leg over the saddle and stepped to the ground. "Can you explain that?"

Von Honig licked his lips. *I hear everything they're saying,* he thought, *I shouldn't be able to make out anything.* He lifted his hand and scratched his head. Alice didn't react to his movement.

"Not really," Wallace said with a shrug. "It's just one of the odd things that happens here. "Other people have complained about the same thing happening to them when they were looking for the iron door."

"I don't want to hear stories about strange men wearing space-suits a thousand years ago," said Reynolds, scratching his chin. "The only thing I want is the gold that's in that cave. Take me there. My people and I will pack the gold on these horses and leave. We'll leave you and your friends at the mine on foot. By the time you walk out, we'll be long gone."

Wallace lowered his left hand. "You really expect me to guide you there?"

"Don't make any moves like that," Reynolds warned. "Whitlock could have shot you."

"You ain't going to shoot me," said Wallace, raising his left hand again. "You need me too much, but what happens if I lose the trail?"

Reynolds leaned in closer. "If you can't find your way there, I'll have to shoot your friends," he said, leaning in closer and flashed a wicked smile. "Might even start with Alice, then Olivia and Rudy."

"I know how you work," said Wallace. He raised his hands and turned to walk toward the tractor and trailer.

"Whitlock, get up here!" Reynolds shouted. "You and Skip need to catch those horses!"

"Skip's hurt," said Alice, snapping out of her doldrums. "He can barely stand." She grinned as the men approached. "I told you it'd work. Clay wants to see the good in me."

"I think he's learned his lesson this time," von Honig said.

"I think I've got it." Wallace turned and sat on the wagon's iron side rails.

"Shut up," Reynolds ordered. He turned his gaze on Alice. "What's wrong with Skip?"

"I don't know. I think those hailstones beat the hell out of him." She moved to Reynolds' side, and his arm circled her waist. "He's got knots all over his head and his eyes look strange."

Reynolds leaned over and kissed her cheek and nuzzled her ear. "Can he ride?" he whispered.

"I don't know." Alice moved from his embrace. "He can talk, but most of the time it's gibberish."

"He may have a concussion," said von Honig, moving moved away from the wagon. "He needs a doctor."

"Ain't a doctor out here, Con Man."

Even in the midst of his highly compromised situation, von Honig simmered at the sound of the nickname.

Whitlock rode up behind them. He was a big man with long brown hair, pulled back in a ponytail. He wore camo pants and shirt.

"Boss," he said, "I'm going to need some help getting those horses."

Reynolds looked at Alice and offered her the reins. "Take my horse and help Whitlock," he said. "We need those animals."

"I should stay here," said Alice. Her eyes glanced from Wallace to von Honig to Skip. "You might need help."

"We left Rudy and Olivia tied to a pair of trees over yonder," said Reynolds, pointing toward the end of the canyon. "You know he's trying to get loose. We need those horses quick." He pulled the sawed-off from the saddle and cocked the hammers, tilting his head toward von Honig and Wallace. "These two won't try anything. Ol' Pat here will put them down if they do."

"All right," said Alice. She stuck the pistol in her waist band, walked to the horse behind Reynolds and swung into the saddle. Her heels drummed on the animal's side, and it jumped forward into a gallop.

"She shouldn't run that gelding over this rocky ground," said Wallace, watching as Alice rode of. "It might split a hoof."

Reynolds grinned. "Sure would be a shame if she gets killed in this operation," he said. "You do what I say and everyone will get to go home after I get that gold." He turned to Skip. "Get in the wagon."

The silent man moved forward and sat cross-legged in one corner of the wagon.

Wallace nodded. "I want to check on Olivia and Rudy," he said.

"Get on the tractor," said Reynolds. "Drive through the gap. Rudy and Olivia are over there." He pointed the shotgun at von Honig. "If you try something funny, I'll shoot your new friend right in the face."

Von Honig stared at the canyon and noticed that it had changed. The gap had moved closer in seconds. He stared at Reynolds and debated the wisdom of jumping the man and wrestling the shotgun away. He gave the idea up, and instead scanned the trailer for his own weapon but couldn't find it.

"I won't try nothin'," said Wallace, climbing into the tractor seat and waiting while von Honig and Reynolds climbed in the back and sat down.

"You can take off now," said Reynolds. "Remember, though–slow and easy."

The tractor popped and wheezed before it started. Wallace eased the shifter into second gear and released the clutch. The tractor jumped forward, belching dark smoke.

Reynolds turned to von Honig. "Tell me something," he said, easing the hammers down on the shotgun. "What did Clay promise to get you here?"

"I wanted to study the rock carvings."

A half laugh passed Reynolds' lips. "I forgot," he said. "You believe that crap, or you want people to think you do. I've read about you, Con Man. You wrote a lot of science fiction several years ago, now you claim to be hunting the very things you wrote about then. You're nothing but a liar. At least I'm honest. I'm here to take all the gold I can carry."

"Even if you leave dead bodies behind you?" von Honig asked.

"I might take Alice with me. She's good for fun and games, if you get my drift." Reynolds winked. He craned his neck to the side, staring at the back trail. "Alice and Whitlock are coming back." His expression and tone changed suddenly. "They've got extra riders on the horses. What the hell is going on here?"

Von Honig glanced over his shoulder. Four riders galloped toward them leading a fifth mount.

"They saw it," said Skip, rocking back and forth. "They saw the Balloon Man." Spittle hung from his bottom lip. "They saw him. He was floating through the air, just like those balloons on Thanksgiving Day. We could put him in the parade. Yeah, yeah, they saw him."

"What the hell is he talking about?" Reynolds demanded.

Von Honig shrugged. "I don't know."

The tractor passed through the gap and stopped under the shade of a massive cottonwood tree. Wallace killed the engine and stared at his surroundings. "Where are they?" he said to Reynolds. "I thought you said Rudy and Olivia were here?"

Von Honig hopped from the wagon. Reynolds scraped at the

whisker stubble along his jaw and stared about nervously. "What did you do? This ain't where we left those two. What kinda game are you pulling?"

"I didn't do anything," said Wallace, raising his hands. "I drove exactly where you said to go." He went silent for a moment, then pointed to his left. "That little side canyon shouldn't be here. It's another two miles up the trail, before it splits off like that."

"You know better than that," said Reynolds, backing away from the trailer. "Trails don't just change."

"We're close," Skip mumbled. "We're close. The iron door is close. I can smell it." More spittle flew from his mouth.

"The trees are different," said Reynolds, turning in a tight circle. "We left Rudy and his girl tied to two small trees not thirty minutes ago."

"I don't think so," said von Honig. He pointed to the riders galloping toward them. "I'll wager those two in front are Rudy and Olivia."

Two riders reined up beside the tractor. Alice and Whitaker came up right behind them. Dirty foam coated the animals' chests and sides. They kept their heads down, sides expanding as the breathed heavily.

"What the hell are you doing?" Alice screamed. "Are you trying to run out on us? Cheat us out of our share of the gold?" The pistol in her hand centered on Reynolds.

"What's your problem?" Reynolds glared at the woman. "Get that damn gun out of my face. We've only been here for ten minutes." He glanced at Rudy and Olivia. "Where did you find those two? They should have been here."

"You're lying," said Alice. She cocked the hammer on the pistol. "We found these two right where we left them. We've been chasing you guys for two hours. Good thing that tractor is so damn noisy, or you might have lost us back there."

Whitlock rested his hands on his saddle horn. "Why didn't you wait for us in the canyon?" he asked. "Why did you leave in the first place?"

"I came over here to get Rudy and Olivia." Reynolds squeezed the shotgun's grip.

"That's bullshit!" Alice shouted. "We nearly ran these horses to death chasing this rig. We screamed for you to stop. I swear you waved at us once."

Von Honig walked toward Olivia's horses. He reached up and untied her hands from the saddle horn and helped her to the ground. She clung to the saddle, the muscles in her legs quivering uncontrollably.

"What the hell do you think you're doing?" Alice shifted the pistol to him.

"I don't want anyone to start shooting," von Honig said. "Bullets don't have eyes." He raised his hands above his head. "If you guys want to kill each other, I'm okay with that. I don't want anyone else getting hurt."

Von Honig moved to Rudy and untied the rope binding him to the saddle horn. "I don't want to see a bloodbath here."

"Con Man's right," said Alice, lowering the hammer on her pistol and stuffing it in her waist band. She turned her attention to Wallace. "How far are we from the iron door?"

Wallace shook his head. "I don't know," he said. "These landmarks are familiar, but there's something different about them."

"Don't lie," said Reynolds. "You're not very good at it. Are we getting close?"

Von Honig helped Rudy to the back of the wagon. "Do you need a drink?"

Rudy nodded. "I'm as dry as cotton," he said.

Von Honig passed him his canteen. Rudy snatched it from his hand and tilted the container into the air, his adam's apple bobbing vigorously.

"Don't hog the water," said Olivia. "Give me some." She snatched the canteen from Rudy's hands and gulped deeply.

"Why did you leave us out there so long?" Rudy asked, looking from Reynolds to Alice. "We could have died out there."

Reynolds shook his head. "What are you talking about?" he said.

166

"You were only tied up for an hour tops."

"Liar!" Olivia screamed. "We were there for half a day, tied to those trees and gagged. Were you planning on leaving us behind?"

Skip interrupted them with a laugh. "It's not what it seems," he said. "The Balloon Man controls everything in these mountains. He knows what we're after and he took steps to stop anyone from taking what he left behind the iron door." His eyes fastened on Reynolds. "You'll never see any of the Balloon Man's gold."

"Skip," Reynolds growled, "sit down and shut up."

"This isn't real," von Honig said, stepping in front of Reynolds. "This is like one big dream—one we're all sharing."

"Con Man, do you think I'm stupid?" Reynolds pointed the sawed-off at von Honig's mid-section. "Get on the wagon and sit down."

Von Honig clenched his jaw. *That name again*, he thought. He did what he was told and hopped back on the wagon.

"I know where the door is, but you'll never see it," said Skip, a wide grin splitting his face. "You'll never see the gold."

"We're leaving, Clay." Reynolds nodded. "The rest of you stay here until we get back. Clay is going to take me to the lost mine."

Whitlock shook his head. "Not unless I go along," he said, his hand resting on the butt of his rifle.

"You and Alice are going to stay here and watch Con Man and the two farmers," said Reynolds. He turned to Wallace. "I said come on."

Alice pulled the pistol from her waistband. "You're not going without me," she said. "I'm not going to be left behind."

"Alice, put that away," said Reynolds. The knuckles of his hands whitened around the wooden grip of his gun. He turned to Wallace. "Come on, Clay. I won't say it again."

"Why are you three arguing like this again?" said von Honig. He jumped from the wagon. "This doesn't make any sense. You're at each other's throats again. Does that seem normal to you?"

"It's the Balloon Man," Skip cackled. "He's controlling everyone's emotions. He doesn't want anyone to trust anyone else."

"Why can't we all go?" von Honig suggested. "Why can't Clay and Reynolds lead off and the rest of us can follow along behind."

Reynolds cleared his throat and spat. "I don't like it," he said. "Too many people, too much noise."

Whitlock slipped his rifle from the saddle scabbard. "That's the way it's going to be, Reynolds," he said. "I can put a round between your eyes before you can swing that sawed-off my way."

"We're going along with you, just the way Con Man suggested," said Alice. She looked to Wallace. "Get water and whatever you need, and get started."

"Okay," said Wallace. "I hope I can find it."

Reynolds tapped his fingers impatiently on the shotgun grip. "Let's move," he said.

"Keep the pace slow," said von Honig. "Rudy and Olivia can't travel fast."

"You know, people, this isn't a democracy," said Reynolds, glaring at von Honig. "This is a dictatorship, and I'm the man in charge. They can either walk, or I'll kill them right now."

"We can make it," said Olivia. She jumped to her feet, tugging at Rudy's arm. "We can make it."

Rudy climbed slowly to his feet. Sweat beaded on his pale face. He lifted the canteen from the trailer, took another drink and tossed it to von Honig. "I'm okay," he said. "Let's go."

"Con Man, get up here with Clay," said Reynolds. "I want to keep both of you in sight." He swung the shotgun toward Wallace. "This thing puts out a wide pattern, so when I say stop, you stop or else."

Wallace nodded. He and von Honig walked forward along the path. A cold wind plucked at their hats. Von Honig held his by the brim as they moved forward.

"I want to go," said Skip, jumping from the wagon and running up the path. He stopped after fifty feet and waved the others to follow. "Hurry! Hurry! It isn't far! It isn't far!" He passed the two men and continued along the path.

"Is this familiar to you?" von Honig whispered to Wallace.

"Yeah," said Wallace. "Skip's right. We're close to the iron door. It's impossible, but it's happening."

"What's going on up there?" Reynolds shouted. "What's all the whispering about?"

"We're talking about the trail," von Honig replied.

"No whispering," Reynolds warned. "I want to hear what you're saying. I don't like it when people keep secrets from me. It makes me nervous."

"Nervous?" said Skip. "Why are you nervous?" He appeared from the side and raced past Reynolds. "Why are you nervous?"

"I swear, he took one too many hailstones to the head," Reynolds muttered. "He's nuttier than a squirrel turd." He aimed the shotgun after the running figure. "It'd be easy, one shell and he'd be finished."

"So are you if you pull that trigger," Alice said.

Reynolds turned to see Alice and Whitlock aiming their guns his way. "I didn't say I was going to kill him," he said. "I just said it'd be easy."

"You need to get those thoughts out of your head," said Alice. She shoved Olivia in the back. "And you need to speed up, sister."

Wallace stopped at a small creek, scarcely five feet across. "This shouldn't be here," he said.

"What did you say?" said Reynolds. Anger colored his voice. "What's going on?"

Both Wallace and von Honig remained silent.

"I asked a question!" Reynolds barked.

"I'm not sure where we are," said Wallace. "This creek shouldn't be here, but then this entire path shouldn't be here."

"Don't get cute with me," Reynolds growled. He jumped to the side, scratching at the side of his face. "Damn webs! Damn things are everywhere!" He pulled a silken strand away from his face.

"Spiders, spiders, everywhere," Skip muttered. He jumped into the path and danced, giving a near perfect imitation of Reynolds. "I hate the damn webs." He turned and dashed toward the creek. He planted his feet at the bank and jumped to the opposite side. "Come on! Come on! It's just ahead! It's just ahead!"

"Can we rest for a little while?" Rudy pleaded. He collapsed to his knees, where he unbuttoned his shirt and wiped the sweat from his brow with the tail. "I've got to rest."

Von Honig approached him with the canteen. "Here, drink some more of this," he said.

"Stop where you are," Alice snapped, waving the pistol in his direction. "Toss the canteen, and I'll make sure he gets a drink."

Von Honig shrugged. "Whatever you say." He tossed the canteen to Alice. "Look at his face. He's pouring sweat."

Alice unscrewed the cap and gave the container to Rudy. "You need to worry about finding the iron door."

In answer to her statement, a growl of thunder sounded in the east. A dark mass of clouds formed across the eastern horizon.

Von Honig ignored her comment. "I don't like the look of those clouds," he said. "We may be in for another storm."

Reynolds shook his head. "Con Man, this is Oklahoma," he said. "I've only seen one storm move in from the east in my life. They come from everywhere else, but never the east."

"The one that came from the east, how intense was it?" von Honig asked.

Wallace answered for Reynolds. "It was a bad one," he said. "High winds, hail like we had earlier today. Lightning strikes and a toad strangler of a rain." He turned to face Reynolds. "We need to find shelter."

"Reynolds, look around you," said von Honig. "You know this isn't right." He shrugged, certain only of his uncertainty. "I can't explain it. I don't know how it's happening. We're sharing the same hallucination."

The thunder rumbled, shaking the trees. The wind ripped leaves from the branches and sent them swirling high in the air. Lightning danced across the sky and arced to the ground. The scent of sulphur hung heavy in the air.

"Hallucinations my ass," said Reynolds. "We'll find shelter when we get to the cave."

"The cave! The cave!" Skip chanted, dancing into the path. "We'll find shelter when we find the door." He stopped and stared at Reynolds. The color had drained from his face, leaving it a chalky color. "You won't see the door, Reynolds. You'll never see it."

Reynolds glared back at Skip. "I'm getting awfully tired of you," he said. He cocked the hammers on the sawed-off and lined the barrels on the injured man.

"He's right, you know," said Skip. "Con Man's right. This is all a dream. Just a dream."

"You're lying!" Reynolds shouted. "I know your lying!"

Wallace took a step forward. Reynolds spun quickly, the shotgun pointed at his middle.

Conrad caught Wallace's arm. "Stay still," he said. He glanced around and located the purple flowers to his right. Wallace's earlier story immediately came to mind. "Pull the trigger," he said to Reynolds. "You're not going to hurt him." He took a step forward. "Or shoot me, if you can. This is all an illusion. It's a protective barrier to keep people away from the iron door."

Reynolds aimed the shotgun directly at von Honig's face, his finger on the double triggers. "I'm going to kill you."

"Go ahead, shoot me. Kill me right here." Von Honig took a step toward Reynolds.

"I mean it. I'll kill you. Don't take another step." Reynolds struggled with the words. He pulled the double triggers. Flame spewed from the end of the barrels. Von Honig stood his ground uninjured.

"Look behind you," said Skip, stepping forward and plucking the weapon from Reynolds' hands.

Reynolds turned to see Alice and Whitlock fade into the wind. "It's not possible!" Reynolds shouted. "It's not possible!"

He watched as the outlines of Rudy and Olivia grew hazy and indistinct, and then vanished completely. Then he stared at his own hand. It slowly became transparent and melted away. "It's not possible," he mumbled. "It's not possible."

Skip dropped the shotgun to the ground. It quickly turned to dust. He nodded at von Honig. "You figured it out," he said. "No one has ever done that before. You will be waking up soon. When you do, drive the tractor as close as you can to the creek. You can still save Rudy."

"Skip, this isn't making any sense," said Wallace. He turned to Conrad. "How can we be sharing the same illusion?"

"I ran into something similar in South America," said von Honig. "It's like a presence has been left behind to protect the site until we're ready to find it. Until we're ready to understand what's there." He turned to look at Skip. "Am I right?"

Skip nodded. "You are a very wise man," he said. "You'll find this body up in the trees."

"The iron door, the gold," said Wallace. "They're out there, aren't they?" He took off his hat and brushed the hair away from his forehead.

"The time is not right, Clay Wallace." Skip waved, then his outline grew faint and he faded from sight.

~ ~ ~

Olivia leaned forward in the wheelchair and held onto Rudy's hand. "It's a miracle you found us," she said. "The doctor said he would have died if not for you two."

"It was my fault you were in this mess in the first place," said Wallace. He gazed at the floor. "I'll help you get your house rebuilt and pay for the John Deere. The engine seized up before we made it back to the vehicles."

"You don't have to do that," said Rudy, flashing a weak grin.

"You'll have a home and a new tractor when you get out of here," von Honig added. "I'll see to it."

A blonde nurse appeared at the door. "Gentlemen, I think these two could use some rest now."

"She's right," said Wallace. He leaned forward and patted Rudy's shoulder, then glanced down into Olivia's face. "If you two need anything, just let me know."

"Me too," said von Honig. He turned and walked into the hallway and waited a few seconds for Wallace to follow him out.

"Any news on Reynolds?" von Honig asked.

Wallace ran a hand through his hair and tugged his cowboy hat on his head. "He hasn't come out of the coma," he said. "The doctors can't explain it." He glanced around and lowered his voice. "I know it's connected to those purple flowers."

Von Honig nodded. "Could be," he said. "What are you going to do now? Are you going to keep looking for the iron door?"

Wallace shook his head. "I'm not going back to the Elk Mountains for quite a while," he said. "This is Oklahoma. There are hundreds of tales of lost treasure all over the state. I'll find another adventure down the line." He glanced at von Honig. "What about you?"

Von Honig pursed his lips. "Skip said it wasn't time yet," he said. "I think when the time is right, someone will find the door. It's a big world. There are hundreds of stories that I need to look into. I know I'll find what I'm looking for one day."

"I know you will." They passed through a set of double glass doors into the bright sunlight. "After I take you to the airport, I think I'll check on Alice, see if there's anything I can do to help her out."

"That sounds like a plan." Von Honig walked toward the two-tone Chevrolet pickup.

UTNAPISHTIM'S CHILDREN

by Fred Adams, Jr.

"There." Khakov pointed to a craggy hillside rising from the Siberian tundra. "That one."

The six-hour ride had been rough to the point of brutality, bouncing and jolting in Khakov's rattletrap Ya-5 flatbed truck, crammed three-wide into the front seat. Von Honig elbowed his friend and fellow passenger. "Marcel, wake up. We're there."

The little Frenchman drew back the fur-rimmed hood of his parka. "Thank heaven. I don't think I could take much more of this carnival ride." The truck, styled after an old Ford Model A and patched together with rivets and bailing wire, jounced over one of the outcroppings of stone that jutted like the knuckles of a buried fist from the rugged grassland.

"You don't like my little truck now, Frenchie?" Khakov said, wrestling the steering wheel as the Ya-5 heaved over ruts and rocks. The bearded bear of a man laughed. "You like her well enough when the road is smooth. She is not one of your fancy Citroëns or Peugeots." He slapped his palm on the dash. "But she gets you where you have to go, eh?"

Von Honig had hired Khakov in a small village between St. Petersburg and Murmansk to take them to a cave whose wall paintings

174

were whispered about in the circles of men like von Honig, who firmly believed that the gods of ancient myth were not from heaven, but from the outer circles of the universe.

"Another cave, eh?" Marcel had said when von Honig told him where they were going. "As if that one in Majavaca wasn't enough to cure you of spelunking forever." Marcel's words recalled the incident, the murderous killer known simply as "the butcher," and the young woman Susac whose memory still haunted von Honig's dreams.

Another cave. The Cold War made visas expensive and travel to this one even more so. Bribery was the order of the day, and von Honig had greased many palms, but finally they had arrived.

The truck stopped at the base of the hillside and Khakov shut off the motor. The engine gave a belch and a backfire and shuddered to a halt. In the absence of the truck's racket, the sudden silence was profound. Khakov elbowed his door open with a groan of hinges and climbed from the truck. In his heavy fur coat and hat, he looked more like a beast than a man.

Von Honig hired Khakov for three reasons: he knew where the cave was located; he had his own truck and would not have to borrow, rent, or steal one; and he was the sort of scoundrel who always skated at the very rim of the law, the kind of man who would not rat them out to the authorities, lest he fall into the net himself.

Von Honig pushed his door open and flinched at the bitter cold wind. He unfolded himself from the seat and stretched to his full height. At five-foot-ten, he was dwarfed by the Russian but stood almost a head taller than Marcel deLancre, his companion.

"Get the equipment from the back," von Honig said, walking around the front of the truck. Khakov turned his back to relieve himself, and when he did, von Honig reached into the exposed engine compartment and pulled the wire from the distributor cap, stuffing it in his pocket. The deal they had struck was half the money in advance and the other half on their safe return, but von Honig worried that Khakov might be the sort who'd settle for half a loaf.

The climb was brief, and behind a heavy stand of brush, they found the mouth of the cave. "There is your opening," Khakov said. "From here, you are on your own."

"You are not coming with us?" Marcel raised an eyebrow at von Honig, who acknowledged the expression.

"I do not do well in small places. What is your word?"

"Claustrophobic," von Honig said with a smile. "Very well, then, stay out here. But remember the second half of your money."

Khakov laughed. "I will not leave you," the Russian said. "You paid me well to bring you here, but not well enough for me to give up the rest."

Von Honig pulled a pair of heavy-duty flashlights from his knapsack and handed one to Marcel. He and Marcel each closed one eye so that when they entered the darkness of the cave, they could more easily adjust. As they climbed through the entrance, Khakov said, "Do not linger too long." He cast his eyes to the sky where leaden clouds were gathering. "A storm is coming."

The cave was a dry one, formed by water eons ago when the Siberian plain was undersea during the Cambrian era. Water poured through cracks in the limestone bedrock and eroded passages, leaving most of the lower ones filled with sandy residue. The triangular passageway, only four feet high at the opening, gradually grew taller, allowing the pair to walk upright as they followed its gradual slope deeper into the earth.

Approximately a hundred fifty yards in, the tunnel opened into a long room. Von Honig shined his light on the wall to his left and found what they sought.

The mural was breathtaking.

Twenty feet tall on the wall of limestone, the paintings depicted what most would interpret as the worship of gods by men. The postures, the frozen gestures, the bowed heads spoke of the humans' reverence for the five tall, powerful creatures who stood before them. And these were no stick figures daubed with harsh pigment on rough stone. The cave wall was smoothed to an almost mechanical regularity, and the colors were subtle.

Though the faces of the devotees were almost blank, the faces of their gods were executed in reverent detail, capturing as much nuance in expression as a Renaissance portrait. The foremost of the figures held out his hand, and what may be described as a ball of light rose from his palm.

"Amazing." One whispered word that echoed faintly through the winding passages.

"Yes, Marcel. And more than amazing." Von Honig shucked off his coat. In the constant temperature of the cave, his heavy cable-knit sweater would suffice. "Informative."

The pair stood in silence, awestruck by the sight before them.

"Turn off your light."

The little Frenchman blinked. "What?"

"Your light. Turn it off."

Marcel knew better than to argue. When von Honig gave an order, it was to be obeyed. He switched off the powerful flashlight, and gasped when he saw blue glow from the surface of the stone. The cave painting's ball of light and the eyes of the deities burned with cold fire.

"It appears the people who painted this masterpiece understood the properties of luminous pigment."

"*Mon Dieu.*"

"No, Marcel, *leur dieux.*" Von Honig was silent for a full minute. "Count the eyes."

"Seven, eight, nine."

Von Honig switched on his flashlight and shined its beam on the faces of the gods. Four stared directly at the viewer while the face of the most prominent figure – the giver of the light – was turned to the worshippers, showing only one eye in profile. "What does that suggest to you, Marcel?"

"I – I don't know."

Von Honig shined the beam of his light on each eye in its turn beginning with the Giver. "Mercury, Venus, Earth, Mars – do I need to go on? And I'd wager that when we measure the distance of each eye from that ball of fire – the sun if you will – the distances would be proportional to the orbits of the planets." His voice rose with excitement. "This is more than a painting. It's a map of the solar system."

Von Honig set down his knapsack and opened the flap. He reached inside and pulled out a Polaroid camera. "I'll take some quick shots while you set up the Nikon." He plugged in a fresh flash bar and began snapping photos of the mural. "The camera flashed and buzzed and pushed out image after image until the film pack was empty. He was reloading it for more pictures when the voice came from behind. Von Honig knew enough Russian to understand its imperative. "Do not move."

Three Russian soldiers clad in long coats and blocky fur hats came into the chamber, dragging Khakov with them. The guide's eyes were wide with fear. One of the men held a pistol on Khakov, and the other a vintage World War II Kalashnikov on von Honig and Marcel – an old weapon, but no less lethal.

The soldier who had spoken wore the red stripe and gold star of a junior lieutenant on his shoulders. "What are you doing in this place?" In English this time, spoken with the slow precision of a second language.

"This is a scientific expedition," von Honig said. "We are studying primitive art."

"This is a forbidden area. You are spies, American."

Von Honig shook his head and pointed at his chest. "Not American. Australian." He pointed to Marcel. "French."

"So you say." The officer said something in Russian to his companions and one of them seized Khakov by his elbow and roughly dragged him away, a pistol to his head.

The lieutenant looked von Honig up and down. "You have a passport, Australian?"

Von Honig nodded and started to reach under his sweater. The soldier with the rifle swung it from Marcel to von Honig and the explorer stopped and put up his hands. "Pouch underneath."

The lieutenant grunted and pulled up the bulky sweater. Under it was a flat canvas pouch on a thin strap. The officer opened it and looked inside. He stepped between von Honig and the other soldier, blocking his view before he pulled a thick wad of currency from the pouch. He ran a thumb over the edge of the bills. He kicked the knapsack. "More?"

Von Honig shook his head. "Only equipment and some food."

The lieutenant dumped the bag onto the cave floor and when he did, the Polaroids spilled out.

Before the lieutenant could reach them, von Honig scooped up a handful. He held two or three between his thumb and forefinger, showing them to the officer as he slipped another behind his back. "These are only photographs of the paintings on the wall. Nothing sensitive."

"Yet not permitted. I will have to take these from you." He pulled them from von Honig's fingers and tucked them into a pocket of his coat. He patted von Honig down, taking his Swiss multi-knife, a pocket magnifier, and his Breitling wristwatch. After a cursory search of Marcel, he said something in Russian about their papers being in order, but he didn't tell his underling to lower his weapon. "Go with your lives."

"At least let us have our food, or we'll die before we can reach a village," Marcel said.

The lieutenant turned a cold eye on him. "Go with your lives, or die with your food."

"Come, Marcel," said von Honig. "Don't argue."

As if to reinforce von Honig's argument, the sound of a pistol shot rang through the passageways. Apparently, Khakov wasn't co-operating, or perhaps his sins had caught up with him. Von Honig and Marcel climbed out of the cave and into the first flakes of snow falling from a darkening sky. The soldiers' horses were tethered to a skeletal tree beside Khakov's truck.

"The border is forty kilometers that way." The lieutenant waved an arm to the west. He waved his other arm to the east. "That way is death."

Von Honig and Marcel silently walked away from the cave mouth and kept walking until the Russian soldiers were no longer in sight. "We are lost, my friend," said Marcel, hanging his head. "Forty kilo-

179

meters on foot. We will freeze to death an hour after sunset."

Von Honig pulled the distributor wire from his coat. "Only if we have to walk."

An hour later, they returned to the cave to find the soldiers gone and the disabled truck waiting like a patient steed. Two more hours and they were negotiating with the guards at the Finnish border handing over the packet of money that the lieutenant had missed in Marcel's boot and the key to Khakov's Ya-5. An hour more and the two were warming at the hearth of an inn in Kelloselkä.

Marcel sipped his mulled wine and stared into the fire. "It is a shame that the soldiers came when they did. Now we have no proof of what we have seen."

"But we do." von Honig reached into his shirt pocket and drew out a Polaroid photograph. "There are some places even a Russian soldier won't put his hands."

~ ~ ~

"All of that money for one photograph?" Noel de Sapin leaned back in his chair and held the Polaroid between his thumb and forefinger. In his other hand he held an itemized statement of von Honig's expenses on his Russian expedition. He shook his head. "The accountants will have to be creative. There is no expense column for bribes. And the story won't even fill one of those 192-page book club editions Americans are so fond of unless I use a larger type font and expand the margins."

"But the story falls right into line with all of my other experiences – government suppression of evidence of extraterrestrial visitation. Noel, a man died for taking us there."

"And you looked at the cave paintings for how long? Five minutes? Ten? You had no opportunity to examine the physicality of it all. How do you know the mural wasn't painted a year ago, or a week before for that matter? I hate to say it, Conrad, but if I publish your account as it stands with no substantiation, it will play right into the hands of your detractors. I can hear them now: 'And once again,

180

Con Man von Honig makes a claim without evidence in a tale that reads like one of his juvenile pulp fiction tales.'"

"I wish I had never written those stories." As a youth, von Honig had written fanciful fiction about space travel, alien visitors, and intergalactic dominion that his detractors delighted in mentioning every time he published a new book about his theories.

"They are like Dickens' Ghost of Christmas Past, eh?" De Sapin rose from his chair and looked out his office window. In the Paris twilight, the illuminated facade of the *Arc de Triomphe* rose over the lesser buildings. "They are a thorn in your paw you can never remove, I fear."

The argument was an old one – one that von Honig and de Sapin had debated so many times it had become rote, and von Honig had always won in the end. De Sapin turned to face him, "Your books have made much money for *Édition Avancée*, it is true, but each new book costs us more. You must travel further, dig deeper."

"Bribe more officials. But my books have never failed to sell."

De Sapin's smile drew his thin moustache into a straight line. "True, but the market is becoming more crowded. This is 1976. You are no longer unique. Others are writing similar books, some aping your arguments almost to the point of plagiarism. It dilutes the market and hurts our sales. The story of the Russian cave is interesting, but it is not enough on its own. Is there no way to obtain more information about this cave?"

Von Honig reached into his briefcase and drew out a single sheet of paper. The embossed letterhead included the seal of the Russian embassy. "I won't read it all to you. In essence, it says that the Russian government cannot offer assistance in the exploration of something that does not exist. Official denial."

De Sapin drew a leather case from his pocket and extracted a cigarette. He lit it and turned back to the window. *That means he's thinking*, von Honig said to himself, and sat quietly for a moment. Finally, de Sapin blew out a lungful of smoke and turned away from the window. "I hate to say it, Conrad, but this time, until you can come up with more, the answer must be no."

"But there is more, Noel." Von Honig pulled a sheaf of papers from his briefcase. "Look at these enhanced images from the photograph. Von Honig swept an arm across de Sapin's desk, pushing items aside and knocking some to the floor. He laid the pictures face up, like a croupier dealing cards. "Look at the figures closely."

Von Honig had laid the images out left to right, in the order that they appeared on the cave wall. The supplicants knelt in subjection, but now they were the focus of attention.

"For what am I looking?"

Von Honig picked up a domed magnifier from the corner of de Sapin's desk and set it on the leftmost worshipper. "The amulet."

De Sapin squinted. On a thong around the kneeling man's neck was a medallion shaped like a curving letter M with an extra peak crossed by three waving lines, parallel sine curves.

Von Honig set the magnifier on the second worshipper. "And here. The same sigil." He moved the magnifier. "And here."

"And what significance does this have?"

"I have seen that symbol twice before – once carved into a stone in the Brazilian rain forest, and once on this map." He unrolled a photostatic copy that showed a white-on-black version of a crude map depicting mountain ranges, rivers, and lakes. Von Honig put his index finger in the center of it just below the worshippers' symbol.

"Where is it?" de Sapin asked.

"If I'm not mistaken, this is the Barrow Range, and that is Lake Disappointment," von Honig explained. "Unless I miss my guess, we're looking at the center of the Gibson desert in Western Australia."

"And the map?"

"Found pressed between the pages of a copy of Chapman's *Homer* in Cambridge Library. The map's origin is unknown."

"And the symbol?"

"I've never seen it anywhere but those three places, some of the most remote on the planet."

"I've never seen that symbol before. You'd know better than I what it could mean."

Von Honig sketched the sigil on a piece of note paper. "Three parallel waves are a universal symbol for flowing water if they're horizontal, for steam if they're vertical. The inverted, extended M could be mountains projecting out of water."

"Like volcanic islands," de Sapin offered." Or a group of islands in a river or stream."

"Possibly. Yet there are no mountains of any consequence in the Gibson Desert. The Altai range runs across the south of Siberia, but nowhere near the cave I saw. The Amazon jungle has mountains as well, but none near the ruins where I saw the sign carved into a stone the size of a Volkswagen."

"What about alchemical symbols?"

"An upward pointing triangle with a horizontal bar across it represents the hot and humid element of air," said von Honig, "but the bar is singular and straight, not curved. Two lines across the triangle with an odd sigil over the apex is the sign for Mercury, the planet and the element."

"Since water and mercury don't mix, that seems a remote possibility at best."

"Or the symbol could mean none of those. It's almost like those misguided science fiction movies about visitors from space who speak perfect English. 'We have been monitoring your radio signals for decades.' Television, I'd accept, but radio? Sound with no visual context can't teach a language. It's the same with these symbols. We have no context other than where they were found."

"So it's up to you to find it."

Von Honig nodded. "And here," he put his finger in the middle of the map, "is where I must go to find the correspondence among the three." He rubbed his hand through his hair. "The problem is that the map is anything but to scale. The needle could be anywhere in a very large haystack."

"How large?"

"The Gibson is over 150,000 square kilometers."

"That's a large area to search for something that may not exist for a book that may never be written."

Von Honig turned his hard blue stare on de Sapin. "Don't say no until I return."

"You'll need money."

"Not as much as other times. I'm going home."

~ ~ ~

Home was an ever shifting locale for Conrad von Honig in his childhood. Though his father avoided Hitler's death camps and spared his son persecution because of his wealth and position, he could not spare his wife. After the war, the widower married a woman who was part of the occupying American force. Her position took her to Italy, Japan, Egypt, and the United States, and the young von Honig traveled with her, living the transitory life of the proverbial Army brat until he reached his teens.

He had become accustomed to spending summers with his uncle Benjamin Katzeff, his mother's older brother, who emigrated from Germany in the late 1930s as Hitler's power was brought to bear on the "Jewish Problem." Although summer was winter Down Under, the boy loved Uncle Benjamin's farm in the Outback, and a life in one place. When he was of age to enter high school, von Honig asked to stay with Benjamin, and his parents grudgingly assented.

The farm work was hard. Uncle Benjamin maintained a herd of three-hundred sheep, but the young Conrad did his share and more, happy to finally have one place to live. The boy had to wake up every day before dawn, do his chores, and then ride thirty-two kilometers to the nearest secondary school on Benjamin's elderly Indian motorcycle.

A confirmed bachelor, Uncle Benjamin was a short man with a build like a fireplug and a full head of snow white hair. When the boy asked him why he chose the Outback, Benjamin answered with a laugh, "I wanted to get as far away from Hitler as I could, but Antarctica was just too damned cold." Benjamin had been a postal clerk in Stuttgart, and told von Honig more than once, "I'm glad I'm here doing real work. I'll live twenty years longer than I would have standing behind that counter in the post office." And work he did, turning a patch of scrubland on the edge of the desert into a successful farm.

When Uncle Benjamin died in 1974, he left the farm to his now famous (or some would say notorious) nephew, who hired Matthew Doone, a local sheep man, as overseer to maintain the farm. It rarely showed a profit, but von Honig kept the place running as a sentimental memorial to Benjamin.

Von Honig's trip to Australia could have been accomplished in a series of connecting flights and been over in thirty-six hours, but he opted to book passage on the luxury liner *Aphrodite* to Cape Town and from there, the cargo ship *Danae* to Port Hedland. Traveling by sea rather than air afforded him several advantages. First, he could take with him a large trunk packed with charts, maps, books, and papers and keep it in his cabin; second, the leisurely pace of the sea voyage would allow him eight days to read and research, to collate data and calculate locations.

On the third morning out, a knock at the stateroom door pulled von Honig away from photocopies of a handwritten journal by Samuel Schmidt, a 19th-century explorer who spent considerable time among the aborigines and cataloged their myths and superstitions. Von Honig had spent considerable time with the indigenous tribes himself, but valued Schmidt's insights.

Irritated at the interruption, von Honig rose from the stateroom escritoire and carefully picked his way across the carpet to the door, stepping over and around stacks of books and papers. He opened the door to find Hennig, the chief steward, standing at attention. Hennig was the epitome of propriety, his white jacket immaculate, his shoes polished to a high gloss, and every hair of his thick moustache clipped to uniform length. "Good day, sir." He bowed precisely ten degrees, and von Honig was surprised that he didn't click his heels in the bargain. "Captain Lombørg requests your presence at his table tonight at dinner."

Von Honig detected a hint of disapproval from the natty little man eyeing him in the doorway. He looked generally disheveled –

two days since his face had seen a razor, three days since his hair had seen a comb, and clothes that looked to have been slept in because frankly, they had. "Please tell Captain Lombørg that I would be honored to accept his invitation."

Hennig hesitated at the doorway.

"Is there something else?"

"Frankly, sir, I wish you would allow the staff to tidy your stateroom." He looked around von Honig at the cluttered floor and furniture.

"Frankly, Mister Hennig, I can't allow that. I am engaged in important research, and while all that you see here looks chaotic, there is method at work. I know where every item lies in the room. Should any of these books or notes be disturbed, I would lose valuable time locating them again."

"At least allow us to remove your food trays."

"I'll set them outside my door when I'm through eating."

"As you wish, sir, but I must point out that this is highly irregular."

The corner of von Honig's mouth crooked upward. "Tell your staff that I suffer from a malady peculiar to eccentric scientists: flat surface syndrome. I cannot tolerate a floor, a table, a chair seat, any level space that is not occupied. I hope that they understand."

Hennig nodded. "Good day, sir." He turned on his heel and marched off, his gait betraying his indignation at von Honig's insouciance. "Oh, Hennig."

The chief steward stopped abruptly. "Yes, sir?"

"Would you please send someone to pick up my tuxedo? It's in here somewhere and I'm sure it needs pressing."

"I am certain that it must." Hennig disappeared down the corridor, and with a chuckle, von Honig closed the cabin door and went back to work.

He had spent considerable time attempting to triangulate the Gibson Desert location from the Brazilian and Russian occurrences with little success. He learned that Ley lines ran through the Russian site, but not the Brazilian. Latitudes and longitudes were different for all three locations. It appeared that the sites were simply random, as such discoveries sometimes were.

Another knock. Von Honig cursed under his breath. He opened the door this time to find a different steward with an envelope in his hand. "Cable for you, sir."

Von Honig took the envelope with one hand while his other dug into his pocket for a suitable tip. He found a five-guinea piece, one of the last of his British coins. It was probably more than necessary, but von Honig pressed it into the steward's palm anyway, eager to be rid of him and read the cable.

"Thank you, sir," the steward said to the closing door.

Von Honig tore open the envelope. The cable was from Marcel: LOCATED FOURTH INSTANCE OF SYMBOL STOP URUK RUINS STOP WILL SEND PHOTOGRAPHS CAPE TOWN STOP MARCEL. Von Honig closed his eyes and took in a deep breath to calm himself. Uruk. The first city of Mesopotamia, the city of Gilgamesh in the Tigris-Euphrates basin, Civilization's Cradle.

~ ~ ~

If the ship's library had had a copy of *The Epic of Gilgamesh* in any translation, von Honig would have ignored Captain Lombørg's invitation, but since he did not have a copy in his trunk or one available elsewhere, he acquiesced to convention. He showered, shaved, and donned his tuxedo for dinner.

Von Honig had eaten most of his meals in his cabin since the *Aphrodite* left port and had not yet set foot in the ship's formal dining room. The opulence of the first class dining room lived up to the *Aphrodite*'s claim to be the finest luxury liner since Cunard retired the *Queen Mary* in 1967. Enormous crystal chandeliers blazed over a grand salon as large as the Waldorf Astoria dining room. The salon occupied two tiers connected by a grand staircase with hand-carved mahogany balustrades and rich royal blue carpet. A string quartet played Bach to the tinkle of silver and crystal.

187

The captain's table sat on that level, overlooking the floor below, and von Honig took the stairs two at a time because he was within thirty seconds of being officially late for dinner. He passed Hennig coming the other direction, and the chief steward did a double-take at his transformation from unkempt to elegant. If he weren't in such good shape, von Honig might have been out of breath, but he showed no evidence of hurry as he was shown to the table by a waiter just as the bell rang for the meal to begin.

Captain Lombørg rose from his chair and extended his hand. "At last we meet, Mr. von Honig. A privilege to have so distinguished a person aboard." He indicated the chair to his immediate right. "Please, join us."

Von Honig shook the captain's hand. The blonde, bearded Lombørg was nearly a head taller than he and in his formal uniform looked as if he'd been sent to the ship by Central Casting. His grip was strong, a commander's grip, but von Honig answered in kind. *Two "alpha males,"* von Honig thought, referring to the term coined by Aldous Huxley in the 1930s and enjoying currency in anthropological and sociological circles. For the pair, the gesture was one of mutual respect and recognition rather than challenge, each a dominant force in his respective arena.

In the chair to his right sat an attractive blonde woman in a midnight blue satin gown. "Mr. von Honig, please allow me to introduce – "

"The lady needs no introduction, Captain." Von Honig recognized her immediately from newspaper and magazine photographs; Margot Bane, the globe-trotting photojournalist whose pictures graced the covers of *Life, Time,* and most of the other prominent news magazines of the day. Despite her glamorous looks, Bane had a reputation for being tough, fearless, and absolutely relentless in pursuing a story.

She smiled. "Nor does the author of *To Seek the Space Gods.*" She smiled and shook his hand with a grip nearly as hard as Lombørg's.

The captain introduced the other five table mates in turn: Mr. and Mrs. Thomas Harrow, an older couple from London; New York banker Robert Wiegand; a Mr. Pakhomios, an Egyptian importer from Cairo; and Mrs. Evelyn Smith, a handsome silver-haired widow. Before conversation had a chance to begin, dinner was served.

The *Aphrodite* lived up to its reputation in the culinary department. Excellent lobster bisque and a Waldorf salad were followed by grilled swordfish over a wild rice pilaf. Dinner conversation revolved around travel and which countries had the best vineyards and local foods. As champagne was poured, the captain turned to von Honig. "You're the only one at the table who hasn't had a tour of the *Aphrodite*."

"Perhaps tomorrow, if it's convenient."

"I'll have Mr. Chambers, my first mate, contact you in the morning."

"Not only haven't you taken a tour of the ship, I haven't seen you in the ballroom or the bar," said Margot, looking at von Honig from the tops of her grey eyes. "In fact, I haven't so much as seen you on deck."

Von Honig smiled. "I've been busy, but if I'd known you were watching for me, I would have come out for some shuffleboard."

"If I may be nosy, what takes you to Cape Town?"

"Just a stopover on my way to Australia."

"Research for another book?"

Before von Honig could reply, Wiegand set down his third martini and said. "More of that flying saucer bullshit? Will the little men be green this time, or perhaps red or purple for the sake of variety?"

Lombørg set down his glass. "Mr. Wiegand." The barrows frowned in disapproval, and Margot's eyes betrayed her amusement.

Von Honig raised a hand. "That's all right, Captain. I never flinch at discussing my research." His face was impassive, but the challenge in his tone was unmistakable. "What of my work do you consider 'bullshit,' Mr. Wiegand?

"All of it, really. Gods from outer space. Preposterous."

"I'm curious," von Honig said. "If my theories are as preposterous as you say, how would you account for the confluence of mythologies around the world? Of evidence of science and method that

189

far overreach the state of technology of any ancient civilization? Of abandoned cities in inaccessible locations?"

"That's not for me to say. I'm a banker. I deal in the reality of finance and commerce, not some adolescent flight of fancy."

Mrs. Smith said, "How many of Mr. von Honig's books have you read, Mr. Wiegand?"

Wiegand stammered, "Well, none of them, but –"

"Then I hardly think it fair for you to criticize his ideas." She turned to von Honig. "I have read all three of your books. Frankly, as a Christian, I find them troubling. You make a good logical case, but I find it difficult to reconcile my faith with your assertions."

"If I may, Madame," Pakhomios interjected. "I appreciate your sentiment, but as a Coptic Christian, I do not find Mr. von Honig's arguments irreconcilable with the Judeo-Christian tradition. In the book of Genesis, chapter six, there is a statement, 'In those days there were giants in the earth.' Different translations offer different wording, yet the content of the statement is consistent, yes?"

"Yes," Mrs. Smith said. "I have read that passage many times."

Pakhomios continued, "The account has it that angels lusting for human women materialized into fleshly bodies to wed them, and their offspring were the giants, a race called Nephilim."

"Oh, this is ridiculous," Wiegand said.

"Are you a Christian, Mr. Wiegand? Never mind. It is no matter since the account comes from the Old Testament, the portion of the Bible written by the Hebrews." Pakhomios spoke with such quiet self-possession and understated authority that even von Honig hung on every word. "And if you were a Muslim, you would know that Mohammed regarded the Bible as a valid predecessor to the Koran. You are obviously an educated man. Tell me, how would you describe the deities of ancient Greece?"

"I'm no ignoramus," Wiegand said. "I've seen statues in the Louvre. They are all perfect, beautiful women and handsome men."

"Indeed, and if you were to present yourself to humans for the purpose of mating, would you make yourself ugly?"

"I don't follow you." A red flush was creeping from the banker's collar upward from his jowls to his cheeks.

Pakhomios smiled indulgently. "Let us assume that the gods of mythology were those fallen angels, and their children, the Nephilim, were the demigods of mythology – Herakles, Perseus, Theseus and others. The Bible calls them 'mighty ones' and 'men of fame.' And where do angels come from? The heavens. They come from space."

"I've had enough of this nonsense." Wiegand threw down his napkin and rose from his chair. "I still say it's all bullshit." He strode away from the table and down the grand staircase.

"That's a fascinating theory," Barrow said. He turned to von Honig. "But what did you mean by the 'confluence' of mythologies?"

"The myths and religious literature of every culture contain three common elements: a creation account, a story about The Great Flood, and some analog to the Tower of Babel story that explains the dispersion of people and the variety of languages. From that point, mythologies diverge rather widely."

Pakhomios picked up the thread. "And while these 'gods' were on the Earth, they would use their superior knowledge and abilities to achieve things far beyond the level of technology of an early civilization. When the world was flooded, they gave up their physical bodies and returned to the heavens. The Nephilim were destroyed, and when Noah and his family came out of the Ark, or Deucalion and Pyrrha in Greek myth – "

"Or Utnapishtim in the epic of *Gilgamesh*," von Honig added.

Pakhomios turned to von Honig and for just a second stared at him as if he'd said a magic word, and his fingertips touched his chest as if he'd felt a sudden spasm. Then his face relaxed into a smile. "Just so. When they came out of the Ark, or a hollow tree, or whatever provision was made for their survival, mankind was reborn." He turned to Mrs. Smith. "So you see, my dear lady, there is no need for consternation. Mr. von Honig's theories do not contradict your beliefs. Rather, they validate them."

"My," Mrs. Smith said. "You've certainly given me something to ponder."

"And myself as well," the captain said. "If you folks will excuse me, I must go the bridge. Thank you all for joining me."

As they left the table, von Honig took Pakhomios by the elbow. "I couldn't have stated the case more succinctly. You are a very erudite man."

Pakhomios shrugged. "The result of a long life. Disparate facts pulled together on reflection."

"Your name is unusual."

"It was common enough in ancient times, a Hellenization of the original from the days of the Alexandrian conquest. Perhaps not so common now."

Margot Bane appeared at von Honig's side. "Buy me a drink? Or shall I buy you one?"

"Will you join us, Mr. Pakhomios?" said von Honig.

"Thank you, but I have correspondence to attend to, cables to send. Another time, perhaps." He bowed slightly from the waist and walked away, leaving the pair alone.

Pakhomios turned as he descended the staircase and smiled at Margot. "He seems very fit for an older man," she said. "And that thick, dark head of hair. He reminds me of Omar Sharif."

"Maybe he isn't as old as you think," said von Honig. "Did you notice his teeth when he smiles? They're perfect in spite of his age and his origin. He's lucky he didn't live in ancient times. He'd likely be suffering tooth wear, pulpal exposure, and caries. He certainly is a well-preserved specimen."

"Do you take every man's measure so closely?"

Von Honig nodded. "Every person. So, Margot, since I haven't been there yet, show me the way to the bar."

As they strolled down the upper deck, Margot stopped and turned to the railing to look out at the ocean. A half-moon wreathed in gauzy cloud silvered the swells and waves. "So, Conrad, you never did tell me why you're going to Australia."

Von Honig laughed. "Why do I feel as if I'm being interviewed?"

"Because I suppose in a way you are. Being a journalist is akin to being a policeman. You're never really off duty. That's true of people like yourself too, isn't it? Always watching for news of some new sighting?"

"Yes, it's true," said von Honig. "But I'm not independently wealthy. My research takes financial backing before I can begin."

"But like journalism, you can pursue whatever interests you and someone else picks up the tab, isn't that right? So long as you bring back results to put in print."

"I never really thought of it that way."

"I'm sorry," said Margot. "I don't want to sound like that dreadful Wiegand. I suppose people like him go with the territory."

"They *are* the territory. So let's go have that drink."

The bar was as elegantly fitted as the main salon, but the lights were soft and a pianist tinkled through a medley of big band standards, then switched to some light pop, none of which von Honig recognized. They settled into a corner booth. Margot ordered a Manhattan and von Honig a Tanqueray and tonic. The drinks arrived, and after some small talk, they lapsed into silence for a while, as the pianist shifted gears again.

"'Round Midnight,'" von Honig said. "Thelonius Monk's best."

"I always liked John Coltrane better. I'm curious, Conrad, why did you earn four bachelor's degrees - psychology, anthropology, sociology, and theology - instead of a Ph.D. in one field?"

"A doctoral candidate devotes himself to a very narrow topic in a very narrow field of study. I wanted a broader scope, and I've found that my diverse education allows me to draw from many spheres in my work."

Margot pondered this for a moment. "That's a fair answer."

"You've me quizzed about myself, Margot, so now it's my turn. Why are you going to Cape Town?"

"I'm on assignment to do a photo interview. Ever hear of Nelson Mandela?"

"South African. The anti-apartheid activist."

"You keep up with current events. He's been jailed for a long time. My editors got me permission to do an interview and photo shoot in the Robben's Island prison."

"I'm surprised you'd be allowed. Mandela's become something of a *cause célèbre* on the world stage. I would think that the South African government would want to keep him out of the spotlight."

"The tides change. I'm taking advantage of it while it lasts."

"I've seen your photographs and read your articles. Very impressive."

Margot raised her head and locked eyes with von Honig. After a brief silence, she said, "I was waiting for you to say, 'for a woman.'"

"I don't think that way. Good work is good work."

"I appreciate that. I'm no strident women's libber. I just want a fair game for everyone."

"Like Nelson Mandela."

"And like you as well." She looked at her watch then reached for her clutch. "This has been very interesting. I hate to beg off, but I'll be shooting exteriors of the ship at first light."

"Another magazine feature?"

"No, a commission from the cruise line. A girl has to take work where she finds it."

"I'll walk you to your cabin, if you like."

"Another time, maybe." Margot rose from the table. "Thanks for the drink, Conrad. Next time, I'll buy."

Von Honig signed the bar tab and headed toward his room. As he entered the corridor, he saw a figure that seemed in a hurry just rounding the corner at the other end of the passageway. He thought nothing of it until he entered his stateroom. When he opened the door, he found the desk lamp lit, and he was sure he had turned it off before he left.

He reached in and switched on the overhead light. The room looked as he'd left it, but something seemed out of place. He closed the door behind him and carefully moved from one pile of papers or stack of books to the next. His seemingly slovenly habits allowed him to locate items by piling them in chronological order, the most recent at the top, and recalling the order in which they were used.

Beside the escritoire, his heavily annotated copy of Fraser's *The Golden Bough* sat atop a precarious pile. He'd consulted it the day before, and other books should have been on top of it. *The person I saw rushing around the corner,* he thought. *He must have just left the room before I got here. If I hadn't dallied with Margot* – then the thought struck him. Was the journalist playing him for a story? Distracting him while a henchman searched his room for clues to his quest?

He decided that he would look into that possibility tomorrow. He'd be spending the rest of the night going over every book and note in the room to make sure nothing was missing.

Hours later, von Honig determined that nothing had been taken. Whoever had come into the room was no common burglar. A pair of his cufflinks lay untouched on his dresser, as did his heavy Rolex chronometer on the nightstand, a watch five times more valuable than the dressy Gruen he wore with the tuxedo. A handful of coins and a few bills lay scattered on the dresser as well. Whoever came into that cabin came to steal information.

Von Honig dug into his trunk and pulled out a leather case a little larger than a brick. It contained a Norelco cassette recorder, one of the first models, well made and reliable. He'd carried it with him for years and found it indispensible for dictating notes in the field. The next time he left his cabin, he would know if not who, then when someone entered.

~ ~ ~

The next morning after breakfast, Chambers, the first mate, took von Honig on the promised tour of the *Aphrodite*. The ship was magnificent, a true floating city – and no expense spared making her a work of art as well.

They found Margot Bane on the promenade deck shooting pictures of a young couple lounging in the bright sun in canvas deck chairs. She looked up from her camera as von Honig and Chambers approached. "I'll wait 'til you're past, unless you want to be in the shot."

"I think I'll stick around and watch the artist at work." He turned to Chambers. "Thank you for the tour. I was very impressed."

"My pleasure, Mr. von Honig." Chambers gave a little salute and went on his way.

"That's a very old Graflex," von Honig said, as Margot bent over her camera. Today, the photographer wore tennis shorts and a white jersey blouse that flattered her athletic build.

"Yes," she said out of the corner of her mouth. "The lenses on the newer cameras just aren't the same quality. I think craftsmanship suffers from mass production."

"No argument there." He stood a while, watching while she lined up a shot. She ignored him as she concentrated on her work. "Well, I'll leave you to it," he said after a few minutes. "I'd better get back to my stateroom before someone comes in and rearranges my papers."

Margot looked up from her camera, her expression puzzled. "What?"

Von Honig chuckled. "A run-in with the chief steward. Tell you the story later." He left Margot to her shoot and returned to his cabin. He found the recorder as he'd left it, the forty-five-minute cassette nearly run to its end. He punched the STOP and REWIND buttons and watched as the tiny reels spun. Margot not only seemed to know nothing about the break-in, but she showed no real interest in him at all. If the burglar was working with her, she gave no sign of it.

The reels stopped. Von Honig pressed PLAY and settled back in his chair to listen. For fifteen minutes, he heard only the hiss of the recorder. *Snick*. The lock opening. The sharp knock of the deadbolt. A cautious step.

Von Honig traced the sounds across the stateroom with his eyes. Two steps, a rustle of paper as a shoe brushed a pile of notes. The sound of pages turning, a book being riffled, then another. The desk chair dragged across the carpet and the creak as someone sat in it. Single sheets of paper lifted and turned. Another faint sound. It took a moment for von Honig to recognize it as the click of a camera. The intruder was photographing his notes.

The reels spun. A knock. The furtive noises ceased abruptly. A muffled voice. "Steward, sir. Here for your trays." Another knock, then the sound of a key in the stateroom door. The rattle of the knob. "Very well, sir," the steward said, annoyance in his voice. "I'll return later." A moment of silence, and the clicking camera resumed. The sounds continued for at least another ten minutes, and then von Honig heard the deadbolt and the sound of the closing door. Silence for a time, then the sound of his own arrival.

The mysterious visitor had returned. A quick inventory of the papers on his desk told von Honig that nothing was missing. Someone was copying his notes and spying on his research. The next question to be answered was who, and the next one after that was why.

~ ~ ~

Von Honig decided that the best way to deal with the intruder was to lay a trap, and his best ally would be Margot Bane. If she helped him catch the mysterious visitor, she wasn't on the same team. If she balked at involvement, she moved up a notch in suspicion.

He found her at lunch sitting alone at a table in the cafe. "May I join you?"

Margot looked up and smiled. "Please do. Try the conch salad. It's much better than I expected."

The waiter took his order, and von Honig waited until his salad arrived and the waiter departed before saying, "I wonder whether you could help me with a little problem."

Von Honig was well-versed in reading people for "tells," mannerisms and facial tics that betrayed what a person was really thinking. As he recounted the story of the break-ins, Margot's expressions varied from curiosity to anger to concern, but her reactions gave no indication of involvement. "Why would someone want to copy your notes?"

"The most obvious answer is someone who wants to beat me to press, an unscrupulous author or publisher. Books on UFOs and other paranormal topics have been regular sellers for years, but books on my theories are newcomers. Imitators pop up frequently, as my publisher has pointed out. Maybe someone thinks he can shortcut my research and push out a bestseller ahead of me."

"I see. A kind of literary industrial espionage." She speared a bite of her salad and chewed it reflectively.

"Shouldn't you report it to the captain?"

Von Honig shook his head. "The standard procedures would kick in – searches, questioning – and the intruder wouldn't show his face again."

"How could I help you?"

"You're a photographer. I want you to take a picture."

The plan was simple. Margot set up a camera and flash on a tripod at an angle that would catch the cabin doorway as it opened. A simple cord tied to the doorknob would trigger the apparatus, taking a picture of whoever opened the door.

"If he comes tonight," she said, "we'll get him."

"Or her."

Margot grinned. "Or her."

In honor of the final night of the cruise, the *Aphrodite* held its customary formal dance, and Margot Bane, wearing a stunning red gown, made her entrance on the arm of the tuxedoed Conrad von Honig. The orchestra played "Take the A-Train" as they entered the ballroom then segued into a medley of bossa nova melodies.

Von Honig held out his hand. "Shall we dance?"

"On a bright cloud of music, shall we fly?"

He smiled at the allusion. "I wouldn't have pegged you as a fan of Broadway musicals."

"I'm not. I played Eliza Doolittle in the student production my senior year at Chatham."

"We need to be seen so that the mysterious stranger knows I'm away and occupied."

Margot and von Honig each surprised the other by how well they danced. Holding her in his arms and looking into her eyes, von Honig felt the mutual attraction, but in the back of his mind, another line from *My Fair Lady* needled him: "Let a woman in your life and you're plunging in a knife."

They danced until almost midnight, when they decided that their quarry had had sufficient time to spring the trap. Admiring eyes followed the couple as they left, correctly intuiting their destination, but totally misreading their intent.

At the stateroom, von Honig found the door locked.

"Maybe he never came back," Margot said.

"Or he's covering his tracks." Von Honig gently turned the knob and opened the door a few inches. He reached inside and disabled the trigger cord, but it wasn't necessary. When he opened the door and switched on the light, they saw that the camera was gone. A porthole over the bed yawned open.

"Damn it," Margot hissed. "That was a good Nikon."

"I'll replace it."

"If you can find one. That model's been out of production for years."

Von Honig started to laugh.

"What's so funny?"

"Just the thought of the mystery man and the look he must have had on his face when the flash went off. And stumbling around 'til his vision cleared. Look at the mess he made."

Piles of books had tumbled and papers were scattered around the floor as if they had been kicked. No attempt was made to set the room aright. "I wouldn't be surprised if he pissed himself."

Then Margot started to laugh. The two laughed until they wound down, looked at each other and started in again. When they finally stopped, Margot said, "God, I haven't had a laugh like that in —" Her eyes met von Honig's, and the two stepped into each other's arms. She kissed him, gently first, then hard and passionate. She pulled back and looked into his eyes.

"I like you, Conrad. I like you a lot. You're attractive and you have a lot to offer, but I don't like to start something I can't follow through. We both have things to do, but there will be time." She kissed the corner of his mouth, slipped from his embrace, opened the stateroom door, and she was gone.

~ ~ ~

The transfer from the *Aphrodite* to the *Danae* went smoothly enough, with von Honig personally watching the progress of his trunk from one ship to the other. He saw Margot when she came down the gangway. He was too far to call to her and couldn't catch her eye. She was met by a man and a woman, both professionally dressed, and disappeared into the welcoming crowd.

His stateroom, if you would call it that, on the *Danae* was Spartan, but he'd had worse. Metal bunk beds, a wooden table and two mismatched chairs. He'd paid double to have the cabin to himself so he could work uninterrupted, and he was glad he did. There was scarcely room to move in the place once his trunk was brought in.

There would be no meals delivered to the cabin either. He'd have to eat in the mess hall with the captain and crew. He didn't mind that so much as he did leaving the cabin unguarded, but the freighter had few passengers, and none he saw boarding that he recognized from the *Aphrodite*. Things seemed secure for the moment.

Von Honig had sent a coded cable from Cape Town to Noel alerting him of the spy. If someone was making a run at him, they might try something at the *Édition Avancée* offices as well. Publishing was a cutthroat business, and no tactic short of murder would surprise either of them.

And now he could study the photos Marcel had airmailed to Cape Town from Paris, photos that showed a fourth location of the mysterious symbol von Honig had come to think of as the Sea Mountains. Marcel's accompanying note was brief. The symbol was carved beneath a bas relief figure on the facade of the Inanna Temple. What Marcel's note added was that the symbol was carved nearly a meter below ground level, apparently not intended to be seen. The photographs were taken in 1954, and since that time, a blasting accident during excavation damaged the stone and inconveniently obliterated the symbol.

Von Honig slipped on the horn-rimmed glasses he wore for close work. The first of the photographs was one he'd seen many times before. Ingenious bas relief carvings – alternating pillars and standing figures carved into stones set one on the other like bricks, hands pressed together over their chests in a gestures of prayerful devotion. All favored the long, curling beards that to von Honig's eye resembled the segmented coils of a breathing device. Marcel had drawn an arrow in red marker at the feet of one of the figures, pointing to the base of the wall.

The second photo showed the excavated foundation, twenty-ton blocks of stone laid end to end in a precise row. Another arrow pointed to a spot on the stone's surface. The third photo and successive ones showed the symbol in close up. It was the same. The sine curves were parallel to the ground, a departure from the customary Sumerian cuneiform symbol for water, which tilted either to the right or left, indicating gravity's effect and direction of flow. The mountains, if that was indeed what the sigil represented, were the same; three peaks projecting above the surface.

Supper was pork and beans, a far cry from the *Aphrodite*'s cuisine, but tasty nonetheless, and served with good, strong coffee. Von Honig sat a table with Captain Swenson and a half-dozen crewmen who conversed animatedly in a Norwegian dialect.

"I apologize, Mr. von Honig," Swenson said in English. "It is rude of us to converse before you in an unfamiliar language."

"That's all right, Captain," von Honig said. "I'm fluent in German, and I was able to pick up a phrase here and there."

Swenson said something to the crew that von Honig didn't understand, the crewmen all nodded, and the whole table switched to German.

Von Honig smiled at the crew's adaptability, gave a two finger salute, and said, "*Danke*."

Later in his cabin, von Honig spread a map on the table. He had already marked the previous three locations of the Sea Mountain symbol with asterisks. He added one to Warka, the modern day name for the Iraqi district containing the Uruk ruins. He studied the map for a long time, turned it ninety degrees one way then the other, turned it upside down and diagonally. The relationship of the sites suggested no pattern.

He folded the map. Maybe a good night's sleep would make things clearer.

~ ~ ~

The ship ran into heavy weather the next day, and despite himself, von Honig suffered the pangs of sea sickness. Late in the day, the ship stopped pitching and rocking, and he ventured out of the cabin. As he made his way to the mess hall, the wireless operator tapped him on the shoulder. "Cable for you, sir."

The message was from Noel. OFFICES ENTERED STOP SIBERIA FILE STOLEN STOP MOVE WITH CARE STOP DE SAPIN. Noel had copies of everything he had brought back with him from Russia, stored for safekeeping. Von Honig had the only other copies of the enhanced Polaroid photo and his original notes in his trunk.

This ratchets things up a notch, he thought, and turned back to his cabin where he dug in the bottom of the trunk for the leather zip pouch that held a nine millimeter Beretta automatic. He checked the shells in the magazine, worked the slide and dry-fired the pistol, letting the hammer down easy with his thumb.

Von Honig had dealt with violent people more than once in his travels and didn't fear for his own safety, but he hated to see Noel and his staff put at risk. *First they spy, then they steal,* he thought. *Who are they, and what next?* He didn't feel any threat on the *Danae*, but from this point, he'd sleep with the pistol under his pillow. He tucked the Beretta in the waistband of his trousers, pulled his sweater over it, and started back toward the mess hall in the hope of eating something he could keep in his stomach.

~ ~ ~

When the *Danae* docked in Port Hedland, von Honig was the first off the ship so that he could watch the handful of passengers and see who met them at the dock. All five were men, and none had done or said anything to him during the four-day voyage to make him suspect them. The only one who had talked with him at any length about his books and theories was Captain Swenson, who was an omnivorous reader and had read all three of his books at least once, and *To Seek the Space Gods* twice. None of the crew or other passengers seemed particularly interested.

As he waited for his trunk to clear Customs, von Honig watched the five men haggle with the duty officers over their luggage. He was able to see into their bags, and in one case watched as an officer dumped the contents of the man's suitcase onto the table. There was an argument over an expensive clock, but no more. Nothing looked amiss. Two of the men had family meet them, and one was met by a pair of men in suits. The other two melted into the crowd.

A man in an Economy Bookings uniform approached him with a clipboard under one arm. "Mr. von Honig?"

"Yes."

"Car for you as ordered. Green Land Rover in the parking area other side of the wharf." The man held out the keys in the palm of one hand and the clipboard with the other. "If you'll just sign here."

The Land Rover was a boxy 109 with high ground clearance, close-set headlights, and the spare tire flat on the hood. Von Honig loaded his trunk into the back of the rental, and fifteen minutes later, he was behind the wheel and rolling away from civilization.

Driving to the farm would take most of two days. The further he got from Port Hedland, the narrower and worse the roads became. He stopped in Newman for supplies and soon left the last of the pavement. The final leg of the journey took him to the scrublands just east of Lake Carnegie. The drive would have been 1,300 kilometers, but von Honig was familiar with the territory and short-cut the route across the barren desert relying on the Rover to get him over the unpaved roads and trails to the interior.

Von Honig had traveled the southwestern United States and appreciated the beauty of its deserts, but he still felt they were a poor second to the red rock mesas and broad flat expanses of the Western Region covered with blue and green spinifex, the hummock grasses so vital to the aborigine population, and skeletal trees just greening up in the inverted season. The Rover kicked up a cloud of dust as he drove. *Easy enough to follow me,* von Honig thought, *but over this landscape, they'll have the Devil's own time at it.*

It was still cold enough at night that he slept in the Rover instead of on the ground outside, and in the morning poured water into the radiator and petrol into the tank before he went off the road onto a trail that was little better than a footpath. The further south he drove, the closer he came to Lake Carnegie, and the greener the land became. He left the trail for an unpaved road and began to see an occasional farm and herds of sheep and cattle. Late in the afternoon, he spotted the sign beside a familiar cross buck gate: Katzeff Farm.

He had wired ahead to Matthew Doone and his wife Helen that he was coming, and they would have the main house ready for him, although he doubted he'd spend much time there. He pulled the Rover in and got out to close the gate behind him. The last thing he wanted was to let the sheep escape and spend the waning daylight chasing them through the scrub.

As he drove up the lane, he saw the wide veranda that wrapped around two sides of the house, and above it, the low pitched cedar shake roof. As he got closer, he noticed a white Holden sedan parked beside Doone's battered stake-side truck. He parked on the other side of it and as he climbed out, he saw the caretaker coming around the corner of the equipment shed wiping greasy hands on the bib of his overalls.

"Ullo, Conrad. See you made it all right. That's a fine machine. Must'a cost you big bikkies, eh?" Like so many Aussies, Doone dropped his H's and pronounced his A's as I's.

"Only a rental, Matthew." Von Honig tipped his head at the Holden. "Did you buy a new one?"

"Nah. That'n belongs to yer friend. She come this morning. Said you was expectin' her."

At that moment, the screen door opened, and Margot Bane stepped onto the porch. No dress this time. She wore Levis tucked into knee high boots and a blue gingham blouse, tails knotted above her belt buckle. Her blonde hair was pulled back in a pony tail that swayed side to side as she came down the steps.

"I didn't think I'd see you again," von Honig said.

"Don't be silly. You owe me a camera."

~ ~ ~

"So how was your interview with Nelson Mandela?" Von Honig and Margot sat in wicker chairs on the veranda of the main house.

"Preempted by some bureaucrat who thought I should sleep with him for the privilege." She sipped her gin and bitters. "I hoped to negotiate the situation, but when he put his hand on my breast, I punched him in the mouth and knocked him flat on his back."

"I hope you didn't start an international incident."

"I think Mr. Kruger was too embarrassed to let anyone else know what happened. Anyway, I lost the interview. So, I had a few idle days and thought maybe I'd come see the Outback."

"And maybe find a story?"

Margot smiled. "Maybe." Her gaze swept past the yard and across the fields beyond the fence. "This is one of the last wild places left. It's like the Old West in the U.S."

"A blank space."

She frowned. "Blank space? I don't get it."

"Ever read Joseph Conrad?"

"Sure. *Lord Jim, Nostromo, Victory,* every English major does."

"And *Heart of Darkness?*"

"Yeah, that too. But it was a long time ago."

"I'll be right back." Von Honig set down his drink and went into the house. He came back leafing through a book. He turned the pages to a dog-eared corner and read:

"Now when I was a little chap I had a passion for maps. I would look for hours at South America, or Africa, or Australia, and lose myself in all the glories of exploration. At that time there were many blank spaces on the earth, and when I saw one that looked particularly inviting on a map (but they all look that) I would put my finger on it and say, 'When I grow up I will go there.'"

Margot nodded. "That sounds like your basic operating credo."

"You're right, I remember reading it as a teenager and how it resonated with me. Blank spaces. That's where you find the mysteries. As civilization closes in, they disappear one by one, and someday there will be no mystery left."

"That would put you out of a job, wouldn't it?"

"All the more reason to do it now."

Margot lit a cigarette and was quiet for a moment, then she said. "That's why you've come back here, isn't it?"

Von Honig hesitated then replied, "Yes."

"Do you need an experienced photographer?"

"I don't think *Édition Avancée* has the same kind of budget as Hearst Publications."

"I'll do it cheap."

"How cheap?"

"Room and board in this lovely house."

"Sorry, I can't make that deal. Where I'm going, you'd sleep on the ground and eat C-Rations."

"I've worked in jungles, deserts, war zones, and the Arctic Circle. In the last five years I've probably slept on the ground as much as I have in a bed."

"I must admit, your name on the book could boost sales, but I can't guarantee what Noel could pay you."

"It doesn't matter." Margot gave him a challenging look. "Maybe I just want to watch you work."

~ ~ ~

For supper, Helen fixed steak with snap peas and mashed potatoes.

"This is a really good steak," Margot said, chewing a bite. "From your own herd?"

"I don't herd kangaroos."

She stopped chewing. "You're kidding."

"No, kangaroo meat is a staple of the indigenous people. And for the rest of us, it's not exactly a delicacy, but like eating any wild game in the States."

Margot started chewing again. "Every day's an adventure."

After supper, von Honig poured each of them a snifter of brandy and they went back outside to sit on the veranda.

"So many stars," Margot said. "That's another thing about the wild places, no pollution to dim the night sky."

"Or city lights to blunt the stars' radiance."

"I know the northern constellations, but I don't know any of the southern ones except the Southern Cross."

"There are a few that are visible from both hemispheres. Come on." Von Honig led her into the yard. "Right there over the silo is Orion." He turned and pointed. "There's Andromeda over the paddock, but she'll have to wait 'til summer for Perseus to come rescue her."

He pointed across the yard. There, over the tree is Lupus, the wolf. He's upside down at the moment, but as the Earth turns, he'll come right around. Poor devil's being speared by Centaurus, a name you don't need translated. Two-hundred-eighty-one stars in Centaurus, and most people see only a handful."

"So you've spent a lot of time studying the night sky."

"Learned that from Uncle Benjamin. He watched the sky every night. I shouldn't tell you why, but I will. One night, a year after he settled here, he saw what he thought was a shooting star over that way." Von Honig pointed northeast. "Then another joined it, then another. He said that they 'danced around one another' then flew off in different directions."

"He saw UFOs."

"That's what he believed, and although no one took him seriously, he swore for the rest of his life that his story was true."

"And you, did you believe him?"

"When I was a teenager, I wanted so to believe. And now that I'm an educated adult, I do."

"And did he ever see them again?"

"He said the lights appeared often for a short time, then he never saw them again."

"But only he saw them."

"Right. When I lived here, I spent many nights outside watching, but I never saw a thing. Whatever the lights were, they went away and never returned."

"And that started you on the quest of a lifetime."

Von Honig nodded. "And I'll keep looking 'til I find proof or die, whichever comes first." He was silent for a moment, as if making a decision. "Tomorrow we'll head out onto the desert."

"Is that why you rented the Land Rover?"

"No. We won't be using it on this trip." He took her by the elbow and steered her toward the equipment shed. "I want to show you something."

Inside the shed, away from the tractor and its attachments, a canvas tarp covered a nondescript shape. "Meet the Scout." Von Honig yanked the tarp away like a magician uncovering a bowl of goldfish.

"Oh, my."

Under the tarp was a red Indian motorcycle, complete with a sidecar. "How old is it?"

"It's a 1932, complete with a suicide clutch and a hand shifter." The fenders had been removed to accommodate fat, oversized tires. "It was Uncle Benjamin's."

Margot eyed the bike dubiously. "And you expect me to ride in that sidecar?"

"No, the sidecar is for equipment. You'll ride behind me on the saddle." He pointed to what looked like an oversized bicycle seat. "You can hold onto the handrails around the back of the seat, or you can just put your arms around my waist."

"I'll hold onto you. If I fall off, you're coming with me."

~ ~ ~

In the early morning, von Honig handed Margot a pair of goggles to keep the sand out, and they climbed into the saddle of the Indian. The plan was simple: cross the desert, turn around, and cross it again in a grid pattern. When Margot asked why von Honig didn't simply charter a plane, he said, "Airplanes fly over the area regularly. If there were something obvious, it would have been spotted long ago. We'll ride the grid for a few days and see what we may find up close. We'll ride north to Ayer's Rock, then shift west and head south gain. I'm starting across the center because I have an idea."

"What's that?"

"Except for Uruk, the other locations where the Water Mountain symbol has been found are in remote places, almost dead center in those 'blank spaces' on the map. I'm guessing that whoever left those symbols chose locations as far from people in every direction as possible, at least in early history, and possibly in more recent eras. The cult, order, or whatever the symbol represents may have begun in Uruk and either experienced a diaspora or fled persecution."

"If they were proselytizing, they would go where there were people to convert."

"Precisely. Persecution is a more likely reason, but there may have been others."

"Like what?"

"I don't know, but I hope to find out."

~ ~ ~

The Indian roared across the red sand zig-zagging through tall clumps of triodia, the tough grass favored by aborigines to weave for shelter, and desert bloodwood trees, their leathery leaves emerging in the Australian spring.

"Those trees can be a ready source of water," von Honig called over his shoulder. "In dry times, the local tribes extract it from the roots."

"Glad you know that," she called back with a laugh. "I feel much safer now."

A day's ride took them nearly to the center of the desert. They stopped for the night at a red rock mesa that rose ten meters or so from the desert floor. "While I pitch the tent, you gather some scrub for a fire. Your boots will protect your feet and legs, but be careful where you put your hands. This region doesn't have as much fauna as some deserts, but it has its share of scorpions, lizards, and spiders. Their bite may not kill you, but you'll wish it would."

"Thanks for the warning."

Von Honig pitched the tent and built a circle of rock for the fire. By the time Margot returned with an armload of wood, the sun was about to set, lighting a sky full of cirrostratus clouds a deep salmon pink that darkened into violet in the pockets.

"Wow," Margot said. "Now that's a sunset."

"The Dragon's breath," von Honig said.

Margot opened her knapsack and pulled out one of her cameras. "Stand right where you are. I want a silhouette against that sky."

The shutter clicked and the winder whizzed as Margot moved from position to position, catching von Honig from every possible angle against the brilliant colors.

"Can I move yet?"

"One more." Margot circled around in front of him and snapped a head on shot.

She paused, tilting her head for a better view. "That scar on your neck. I didn't notice it before."

"I usually wear a neckerchief. It's a souvenir from a fight with a Tunisian bandit."

"It goes well with that square jaw of yours. Pull your collar down a little. Let more of it show. It'll make you look more adventurous on the back cover of the book."

He laughed. "Wishful thinking. We'll see what Noel says about that."

That night, they sat by the waning campfire as the stars came out again. "We'd better turn in. It'll be a lot of riding tomorrow, and probably rougher than today."

"I'm not as saddle sore as I thought I'd be," Margot said. "That Indian's more comfortable than I expected."

"Uncle Benjamin loved it. So do I. It's better than a horse out here, or even a camel, since the engine's air-cooled."

"Camels?"

"Yeah, every once in a while you'll see wild dromedaries, descendants of the ones some enterprising people brought here the last half of the nineteenth century. They were useful for a time, but many were turned loose into the wild and now there are herds of feral camels. Most of them are in Queensland and the Northern Territory, but a few found their way out here." He stood and stretched. "I could go on, but we'd both better get some sleep."

Von Honig secured the tent, "to keep out the scorpions and the thorny devils," he explained. "Zip your bag tight to be safe."

A little while later, von Honig heard Margot stir, then he heard the long zip of her sleeping bag. "Conrad?"

"Yes?"

"Remember when I said I didn't want to start something I couldn't follow through?"

"Yes."

She leaned over and kissed him gently on the mouth. He felt her warm breath in his ear as she whispered, "I think it's time to start now."

~ ~ ~

In the morning, Margot woke to find von Honig still sleeping. She dressed quietly and undid the lacing of the tent. She stepped outside into the chill morning air to find eight half-naked men with spears. Most wore only a loincloth. Some had pieces of bone through their noses or earlobes. They stared at her, revealing no emotion.

"Conrad!"

Von Honig crawled out of the tent and stood. He was a full head taller than the brown-skinned men, but their fierceness made up for the difference. He said something in a sort of pidgin dialect Margot didn't recognize, and suddenly, all raised their spears. Margot stood frozen in fear. "Oh, my God," she breathed.

Then von Honig and the aborigines broke out in laughter. "Meet Tjangala." The leader bobbed his head. "These men are of the Pintupi. I've known them since I was a teenager. I told them to raise their spears. Just wanted to see how you'd react."

Margot punched his arm. "Damn you, I almost fainted." The natives laughed again.

"But you didn't."

Tjangala said something and the others laughed. He replied, and the leader's face split into a smile that showed a huge mouthful of what looked like perfect teeth, and they all laughed again.

"What was that all about?"

"He asked me if you were my woman, and why I let you hit me. I told him you were nobody's woman but your own."

Tjangala spoke again. Von Honig nodded then turned to Margot. "He asked whether I brought any tobacco, and of course I did."

Von Honig squatted in a circle with the hunters and engaged in an animated dialog with them, punctuated with broad gestures and grimaces. Margot's camera clicked and whirred as she snapped picture after picture of them.

The conversation over, von Honig retrieved two pouches of tobacco from the sidecar, and the Pintupi men jogged away.

"What were they telling you?"

"I asked them where in the desert were the taboo places, as if to avoid them. If I'd told them I wanted to go there, they would have refused to tell me for my own protection. I showed them the Water Mountain symbol, and they told me it marked a place of great magic to the northeast. Tjangala said his people had seen what he called 'spirit lights' and heard 'great sounds,' so they never go near the place."

"But we will."

"You bet your life."

The gear stowed in the sidecar, von Honig pointed the Indian northeast and they rumbled across the sand. Maybe it was his imagination, but Margot seemed to hold just a little tighter than the day before.

Near day's end, von Honig slowed to a stop.

"What is it?"

He pulled up his goggles and reached into the sidecar for a pair of binoculars. He studied the landscape ahead for a full minute before he handed them to Margot.

"What am I looking at?"

"The hummocks of spinifex. Most are about the same height, except for that group ahead; they're taller. They're growing out of mounds; very low, very subtle mounds. Remember, I found the symbol in a cave. I wonder what's under those hummocks." He shut off the motor. "We'll walk from here."

Von Honig and Margot carefully moved from the cover of one spinifex clump to the next until they reached the first of the mounds. It was less than a meter high, and von Honig had to walk around it three times before he saw the opening hidden in the rough grass. He put on gloves and carefully parted the blades, careful of the sharp tips. The opening was less than a span in diameter and capped with a domed cover that let in air but kept out the sand. He put his ear to it and heard a low-pitched hum; not the throb of machinery but a steady drone. He looked all around the cap with the thought of removing it and shining a light down the shaft, but it seemed to be a single piece.

"Margot, come here and bring your camera." When she didn't answer, von Honig turned to see her flanked by two men in long dun-colored robes. She stared, open-mouthed, as if to scream, but she was frozen in place.

"Let go of her," von Honig snarled.

The two men simply shook their heads, unspeaking.

"Alright, have it your way," von Honig said, drawing the Beretta and aiming it at the captor to Margot's left. He fired, but the shot went wide, hitting the robed man in his shoulder and spinning him away.

Before von Honig could pull the trigger again, the other man pointed a small gray box at him. The man moved his thumb, and a jagged blue arc like the spark from a van de Graff generator shot from the box and enveloped von Honig. Though completely aware and conscious, he could not move, not even his eyes.

A third man stepped into his line of vision. "Mr. von Honig," he said, "you have become such a problem for us. What shall we do with you?"

The figure drew back his hood, and von Honig found himself staring into the face of Pakhomios. He nodded to his companion, who thumbed the box again, and von Honig sank to the ground unconscious.

~ ~ ~

"Conrad. Conrad." Margot's voice sounded very distant, although she whispered into his ear. "Wake up, damn you. Don't you die on me now."

Von Honig's eyes fluttered open. He found himself in a dim chamber with rough-hewn stone walls and crude furniture, a table and chairs. A pottery jug and cups sat on the table beside a simple oil wick lamp. He and Margot were on the floor of the otherwise empty room, bound hand and foot. He shook the cobwebs from his head. "How long have I been out?"

"No more than an hour. I thought they'd killed you when you shot that man."

"What did they say? Did they tell you what they want with us?"

"They said nothing. They just took us through some sort of tunnel and brought us here. We seem to be pretty far underground, but I can't say how deep." Her face showed concern. "Are you sure you're all right?"

He nodded. I've been shocked unconscious before, but this is different. It feels as if I've had a good night's sleep."

The door of the room opened, and Pakhomios and two others entered, one a man and one a woman. Both had long dark curling hair, olive skin, and Mesopotamian features, as if they'd stepped from a bas relief carving. They shared the self-possessed, mature bearing of the Egyptian.

"Pakhomios," von Honig said, "What's going on here?"

"Nothing that hasn't happened since before recorded history. You have found us. I realized when I read your notes on the *Aphrodite* that it was inevitable that you would. Now we must leave."

"Us? Who are 'us'?"

"It will do no harm to tell you, since the knowledge will do you no good. I admire your curiosity and your zeal. You are a clever man, von Honig, but I fear this time you have been too clever."

Pakhomios reached into his robe and drew out a medallion on a chain. It was the Water Mountain symbol. He raised it to his lips and kissed it reverently.

"That symbol, what does it mean, Pakhomios?"

"At dinner on the ship, you referred to Utnapishtim, so you know the story of the Great Flood and Utnapishtim's role in it."

"Utna–" Margot began and faltered.

"Utnapishtim," von Honig said. "He's the Noah counterpart in Sumerian myth. He built a great ship and saved humanity at the command of the deity Enki." Von Honig cursed. "How could I miss the significance of the symbol? Mountains covered by water. The Great Flood."

"Your theories are closer to the truth than you have thought," Pakhomios said. "Enki did indeed come from the heavens. He came to this world from the shoulder of Uru-An-Na, Orion, you call the constellation.

"Some of the gods wanted to destroy humanity, but Enki believed that all life is sacred and so he tasked Utnapishtim with saving men from the Great Flood. But the task did not end there. Enki was wise enough to understand that given a free rein, men would likely destroy themselves someday, so he gave Utnapishtim life everlasting to see that humans did not die out."

"You're saying that Utnapishtim is still alive after thousands of years?"

"He lives. He is our father."

Von Honig took a moment to digest that revelation. "Then you are immortals as well?"

"We are. You remember Endama." He gestured to the man at his left. You shot him in the arm. His bleeding was severe. It was perhaps a mortal wound, no?"

Endama opened his robe and von Honig saw the puckered flesh of a nearly healed bullet hole along his shoulder.

"You can restore life and health? That knowledge could end the suffering of all humanity."

"And upset a very delicate balance," Pakhoimos said. "If everyone lived forever, humans would soon overrun the Earth, and you can imagine a race of immortals suffering the constant torment of hunger after the last ear of corn is eaten, the last fish. They would sink into eternal madness and depravity, a much crueler fate than death. We are like the seed grain kept back for the next season to ensure that the human race will survive no matter what may befall it."

"So you hide in the most remote places on Earth where you're least likely to be found. But those places are becoming few and far between, aren't they?"

Pakhomios nodded assent. "Yes, as the world's population grows, it shrinks and slowly the world of men closes in on us like a noose."

"Then why hide? Why not reveal yourselves?"

"Above all things, man longs for life more than gold or power or worship. If we became known, we would have no peace unless we destroyed the race that we were charged to perpetuate, and to us, all life is sacred."

"Then if all life is sacred to you, that means you can't kill us. What are you going to do? Keep us prisoner forever?"

"That will not be necessary. When we leave this place for another, which we now must do again, you too will leave. You will take back no proof to satisfy science and the skeptical. Only a story, and no one will believe what you say, save a handful of your devoted followers."

"But if I found you once, I'll find you again," von Honig said, challenge burning fiercely in his eyes.

"That is possible, perhaps even likely, but we will deal with that if and when the time comes. We have hidden ourselves for thousands of years. I suspect we will continue to successfully do so." Pakhomios nodded to his companions who turned and swept out of the room. Pakhomios paused at the threshold. "If only you could be trusted, Mr. von Honig. The wonders we could show you."

"Wait! Wait!" von Honig called after Pakhomios, but he was gone.

"Conrad, what will we do? If they leave us tied up here, we'll starve to death or die of thirst."

"Not if I can help it. Wait a few minutes 'til we're sure they're gone."

When he had heard no sound from the corridor for several minutes, von Honig said, "I'm going to turn around so that you can get your hands on the heel of my right boot." He rolled on his side and jackknifed his body so that Margot could reach his feet. "Both hands, twist the heel clockwise."

The heel came off in Margot's hand. Under it was a hollow containing a few matches, a needle and thread, some pills in a foil packet, and a small folding knife. "Can you get the knife open?"

Margot worked at it behind her back. "Yes. I've got it."

"Okay, pass it to me."

Von Honig pulled his knees to his chest to bring his hands under his boots and in front of him, but his captors had bound him too well. "You'll have to take the knife back and cut my hands free. Be careful. That blade's as sharp as a razor. Try to not hit an artery."

Von Honig felt Margot sawing at the rope. Then he felt something else, a rumble that vibrated the stone floor of the chamber. Sand and bits of stone began to fall from the walls and ceiling. "Hurry. This place is going to cave in any second."

The ropes parted. Von Honig took the knife and slashed the ropes at his feet. Margot shouted something, but von Honig couldn't hear her. A roaring sound filled the chamber, and he realized there was no time to cut Margot's bonds. He dragged her across the room and huddled with her in the doorway as the ceiling cracked and sand poured in like a waterfall. The lamp went out, but the room suddenly filled with blinding white light. They squeezed their eyes shut, but the light seemed to burn through their lids and sear their retinas.

Then silence and darkness, as if someone had suddenly shut down a movie projector.

Von Honig spat out a mouthful of sand. "Margot, are you all right?"

"Yes, I think. Cut me loose so I can take inventory."

After five minutes of scooping sand away, von Honig uncovered Margot. He cut away her ropes, and she struggled to her feet in the waist high sand. "How do we find our way out of here?"

"Look up." Von Honig pointed to where the ceiling had been. Through a wide gap, they could see the sky overhead. "Pakhomios didn't leave us to die. They must have designed these chambers for escape in case an earthquake or some other catastrophe caved them in. All we have to do is climb out."

"I couldn't imagine being immortal and being buried under a hundred tons of sand and stone."

Von Honig looked upward and in the starry sky saw the shoulder of Uru-An-Na and knew in his heart that up there, light years away, Enki was watching.

~ ~ ~

It was nearly dawn when they finally managed to scale the sloping sand, clawing their way to the surface, three steps upward and two sliding back down. They lay exhausted on the ground as the sun rose, painting the sky a vivid red.

"Red sky at morning," Margot said.

"It doesn't rain here often, but when it does, it's a beaut. We'd better get to the Scout and get moving before we get bogged down."

The Indian sat where they left it. The sidecar with their equipment looked untouched, but then Margot gave a disgusted cry. She pointed to a nearby rock where her camera was smashed. Strips of film hung from the spinifex like drying laundry.

"They ruined it all."

"Don't feel too bad." Von Honig dumped his knapsack on the sand. "My notebooks are gone too."

"But you've still got it all up here." Margot tapped her forehead with her index finger.

Neither spoke for a moment then Margot said, "You're going after them, aren't you?"

Von Honig nodded. "I know where to start looking."

"Blank spaces."

"And this time I know *what* I'm looking for. Besides, I owe Noel a book."

Margot squared her shoulders. "I'm coming with you."

"Haven't you had enough?"

"Hell, no. Now those bastards owe me *two* cameras."

THE QUEST CONTINUES

Conrad von Honig's globetrotting saga includes an additional story recently discovered in a classified dossier! For a free copy of this seventh tale written by Thomas Fortenberry, contact flinchbooks@yahoo.com. Find the truth…or die trying!

CONTRIBUTORS

Fred Adams, Jr.
Fred Adams, Jr., is a former Penn State English instructor who has written 15 novels and as many novellas and short stories in the new pulp genre since retirement. He is a life-long resident of western Pennsylvania, and also a life-long fan of horror, fantasy and science fiction. His creations include such characters as C.O. Jones, Ike Mars, The Smith Brothers, and the Hitwolf team. "Utnapushtim's Children" is his first story to be published by Flinch Books.

Terry Alexander
Terry Alexander and his wife Phyllis live on a small farm near Porum, Oklahoma. They have three children, thirteen grandchildren and three great-grandchildren. Terry is a member of Tahlequah Writers, The Oklahoma Writers Federation, and Ozark Creative Writers. His stories have appeared in several anthologies published by Airship 27, Pro Se Publications, May December Press, Hazardous Books, Moonstone Books and Flinch Books.

Jim Beard
Jim Beard is co-founder and content editor of Flinch Books. He became a published writer when he sold a story to DC Comics in 2002. Since then, he's written official Star Wars and Ghostbusters comic stories and contributed articles and essays to several volumes of comic book history. His prose work includes the novel SPIDER-MAN: ENEMIES CLOSER; co-editing and contributing to PLANET OF THE APES: TALES FROM THE FORBIDDEN ZONE; a story for X-FILES: SECRET AGENDAS; GOTHAM CITY 14 MILES, a book of essays on the 1966 Batman TV series; SGT. JANUS, SPIRIT-BREAKER, a collection of pulp ghost stories featuring an Edwardian occult detective; MONSTER EARTH, a shared-world giant monster anthology; and CAPTAIN ACTION: RIDDLE OF THE GLOWING MEN, the first pulp prose novel based on the classic 1960s action figure. Jim also currently provides regular content for Marvel.com, the official Marvel Comics website.

John C. Bruening

John C. Bruening is an editor and co-founder of Flinch Books. He has been a professional writer since the mid-1980s, initially as a journalist and later as a marketing and corporate communications specialist. His nonfiction writing has won awards from the Society of Professional Journalists (Ohio Chapter) in 2000 and 2010. His debut novel, THE MIDNIGHT GUARDIAN: HOUR OF DARKNESS, was published by Flinch in 2016, and his short story, "The Warrior and the Stone," appeared in the 2017 Flinch anthology, RESTLESS: AN ANTHOLOGY OF MUMMY HORROR. His second novel in the Midnight Guardian series is scheduled for publication in 2018. He lives in a suburb of Cleveland, Ohio, with his wife and two children.

Mark Maddox

Mark Maddox is a Rondo Hatton and Pulp Factory Award winning artist. He has provided illustrations for a variety of magazines: DOCTOR WHO, SCREEM, HORRORHOUND, LITTLE SHOPPE OF HORRORS, VIDEO WATCHDOG, INFINITY, MAD SCIENTIST, UNDYING MONSTERS, DIABOLIQUE, and BOOKMARKS. Mark has also contributed to several Moonstone Comics titles, including: KOLCHAK: THE NIGHT STALKER FILES, THE HEAP, THE RED MENACE, FLINT and more. In addition, he has lent his talents to such companies as Warner Brothers, EMCE Toys, Monsterverse, Hemlock Books, Publicis Worldwide, The Stark Raving Group, Cornerstone Publishing, Alchemy Werks, New Legend Productions, Flying Labs Software, White Rocket Books, Breygent Card Company, and Black Coat Press. For more info about Mark and his work, visit www.maddoxplanet.com.

Brian K. Morris

Brian K. Morris is a full-time freelance writer, independent publisher, blogger, and former mortician's assistant. He writes a regular blog, "Novel Writing Made Less Impossible," at www.freelance-words.com and does a twice-weekly Facebook Live show, NEVERMIND THE FURTHERMORE (yes, it's all caps), mostly to shamelessly promote his personal appearances, as well as his numerous novels and contributions to various anthologies (and he's proud as heck to be a part of this one).

His latest books are THE ORIGINAL SKYMAN BATTLES THE MASTER OF STEAM as well as THE HAUNTING SCRIPTS OF BACHELORS GROVE. His next projects will be a sequel to his Vulcana novel as well as a biography of Disney animator Philo Barnhart. He lives in Central Indiana with his wife, no children, no pets, and too many comic books. You can find his work at www.amazon.com/author/briankmorris

Desmond Reddick
Desmond Reddick is a writer, teacher and podcaster living on Vancouver Island, BC, where he gorges himself on superhero comics, horror movies, weird fiction and heavy metal. His first novel, MOTHER OF ABOMINATIONS, mixes occult ritual, military intrigue and kaiju action. He has hosted the weekly Dread Media horror podcast for the past ten years. He's currently working on a second novel, and occasionally even writes about himself in the third person.

Frank Schildiner
Frank Schildiner is a martial arts instructor at Amorosi's Mixed Martial Arts in New Jersey. He is the author of three novels: THE QUEST OF FRANKENSTEIN, THE TRIUMPH OF FRANKENSTEIN and NAPOLEON'S VAMPIRE HUNTERS. He is a regular contributor to the fictional series TALES OF THE SHADOWMEN, and his short stories have been published in numerous anthologies: THE NEW ADVENTURES OF THUNDER JIM WADE; SECRET AGENT X, Volumes 3, 4, 5; and THE AVENGER: THE JUSTICE FILES. He resides in New Jersey with his wife Gail, who is his top supporter, and two cats who are indifferent on the subject.

ALSO AVAILABLE FROM

FLINCH! BOOKS

***RESTLESS:
AN ANTHOLOGY OF MUMMY
HORROR***
Six stories chronicling the ancient dead
from around the globe who reemerge from
the tomb to mete out a dark vengeance and
balance the eternal scales.

"If you love old-fashioned horror…dim the
lights and sit down for an evening of reading
pleasure."
–Ron Fortier, Pulp Fiction Reviews

***THE MIDNIGHT GUARDIAN:
HOUR OF DARKNESS***
Aided by technology decades ahead of
its time, a masked hero emerges on the
streets of Union City in the 1930s to stop a
sociopathic crime lord's rampage of terror.

"Get this book. New Pulp doesn't get any
better than this."
–William Patrick Maynard, Black Gate

Available on
AMAZON.COM
and
BARNESANDNOBLE.COM

ALSO AVAILABLE FROM

FLINCH! BOOKS

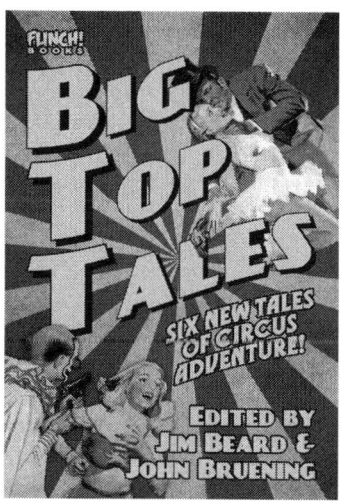

**BIG TOP TALES:
SIX NEW TALES OF CIRCUS
ADVENTURE**
Follow the Henderson & Ross Royal Circus
on a coast-to-coast journey of mystery,
mayhem and murder during its 1956
summer season.

"…a stellar collection…Highly
recommended."
–Ron Fortier, Pulp Fiction Reviews

**SOMETHING STRANGE IS GOING ON:
NEW TALES FROM THE FLETCHER
HANKS UNIVERSE**
Ten new stories spotlighting characters
originally conceived by one of the most
offbeat creators from the Golden Age of
comics.

"…a tribute to the man's twisted, warped
genius."
–The British Fantasy Society

Available on
AMAZON.COM
and
BARNESANDNOBLE.COM

87624828R00130

Made in the USA
Lexington, KY
27 April 2018